Dex danced and darted, his blade flicking in and out while Stennet stomped and shouted and wildly slashed thin air in places where he'd apparently expected Dex to stand and wait and be dismembered.

He very deliberately nicked the lobe of Stennet's left ear. Then put a matching mark on the right.

He sliced neat chevrons onto both Stennet's biceps, and opened a gash, a rather deeper one than he'd intended, on the point of the man's chin.

Dex nicked and snicked and spanked the bigger, older man until Stennet's shirt was wet with his own gore and he was gasping for breath.

"Yield, sir, or I'll finish you."

"I . . . yield," Stennet gasped.

"So be it." Dex stepped back.

He heard a gasp of shock from the crowd, and spun around.

Stennet had a pistol in hand, a small and lethal little two-shoot derringer that he must have had in his pocket. He was already aiming it. . . .

DON'T MISS THESE
ALL-ACTION WESTERN SERIES
FROM THE BERKLEY PUBLISHING GROUP

THE GUNSMITH by J. R. Roberts
Clint Adams was a legend among lawmen, outlaws, and ladies. They called him . . . the Gunsmith.

LONGARM by Tabor Evans
The popular long-running series about U.S. Deputy Marshal Long—his life, his loves, his fight for justice.

SLOCUM by Jake Logan
Today's longest-running action Western. John Slocum rides a deadly trail of hot blood and cold steel.

BUSHWHACKERS by B. J. Lanagan
An action-packed series by the creators of Longarm! The rousing adventures of the most brutal gang of cutthroats ever assembled—Quantrill's Raiders.

DIAMONDBACK

THE NOVEL

◆ ◆ ◆

Guy Brewer

JOVE BOOKS, NEW YORK

DIAMONDBACK

A Jove Book / published by arrangement with
the author

PRINTING HISTORY
Jove edition / September 1999

All rights reserved.
Copyright © 1999 by Penguin Putnam Inc.
This book may not be reproduced in whole or in part,
by mimeograph or any other means, without permission.
For information address: The Berkley Publishing Group,
a division of Penguin Putnam Inc.,
375 Hudson Street, New York, New York 10014.

The Penguin Putnam Inc. World Wide Web site address is
http://www.penguinputnam.com

ISBN: 0-515-12568-7

A JOVE BOOK®
Jove Books are published by The Berkley Publishing Group,
a division of Penguin Putnam Inc.,
375 Hudson Street, New York, New York 10014.
JOVE and the "J" design
are trademarks belonging to Penguin Putnam Inc.

PRINTED IN THE UNITED STATES OF AMERICA

10 9 8 7 6 5 4 3 2 1

DIAMONDBACK

♦ 1 ♦

"Dex? Honey? I . . . oh . . . oh . . . *oh*!" Lucy Anne squealed and began to wiggle. Dexter grabbed hold with both hands and tried, not too hard, to keep her still.

"Right there, honey. That's it. Now, faster, Dex. Oh, God. Faster. I . . ." She squealed again. Louder. Dexter didn't mind. He bore down harder, and after a few more moments Lucy Anne's squealing rose almost to a shriek as she came trembling and quivering to a halt.

Her face and throat and chest were flushed a rather fetching shade of red. She was also almighty wet in certain other, more tender portions of her anatomy.

Dexter Yancey lifted his head to give her a grin and a wink, made a broad show of wiping his chin, and then, laughing, planted a light kiss upon the girl's navel.

"Dex honey, I swear I do love you ever so much."

"I love you too, Lucy Anne." Which was something of an exaggeration. But then Dexter had been taught all his life to be polite to ladies. Above all else a gentleman was expected to be polite. So how could he do any less.

"Sweetheart, I do so want to feel you inside me. You know?"

"I know, Lucy Anne."

"If we were to be married, Dex honey, we could do it that way." Oh, butter wouldn't melt in the girl's mouth when she said that, he was sure. "You know my daddy would be happy for me to marry a Yancey, Dex honey. You know he would."

"I know that, Lucy Anne." Lordy, it was true enough for a fact. Old Merriman Thibidoux would sure to pieces be happy to see his little girl married off to one of the Yancey boys.

Not that Merriman cared a fig about the Yanceys, but the man sure as fire admired the mile and a half of Mississippi River frontage that formed the eastern boundary of the Yanceys' Blackgum Bend. Lucy Anne's daddy had a plantation at least as large as Blackgum Bend, but had no river access. All its production had to be carried to market by wagon, while the Yanceys enjoyed the convenience of a private landing with water deep enough to accommodate the biggest steamers on the river.

Dexter didn't doubt for a moment that Lucy Anne's daddy would be pleased to see his little girl married off to a Yancey, and that was a fact.

"Sweetheart? Honey? If we're going to get married anyway, it wouldn't really hurt for you to take me proper, now would it? If you want me, that is." She simpered. Dexter really hated it when a girl simpered. He was careful to keep his smile in place, however.

"I don't think we should do that, Lucy Anne. In case, well, if something should happen. You know? I wouldn't never want to shame you, Lucy Anne. You know that. And you got to be a virgin pure when you come to your marriage bed. You know that too."

Lucy Anne sighed. At least that was an improvement over the simpering. "All right, Dex honey. I know you're right. It's just that I want you so awful bad, sweetheart."

"I want you too, Lucy Anne." And that, at least, was the natural truth. His balls felt so full he was fair sure they would soon bust if they weren't unloaded.

He mentioned the fact to Lucy Anne, and her eyes became wide. He didn't think the girl was funning him either. Lordy, he guessed she believed he was about to come to harm. That he would literally, physically burst if the pressure wasn't soon released.

Of course there were worse things a pretty girl could believe. Dexter decided not to educate Lucy Anne as to the niceties of hyperbole.

Instead he crept up beside her, planted a gentle kiss on her very full lips, and lightly touched the back of her pretty head.

Lucy Anne understood that just fine. She smiled and kissed him back, then teasingly let her hair and nipples drag lightly over his belly as she made her way south toward the flagpole that stood tall, bouncing lightly with each heartbeat, from its roots in Dexter's middle.

The girl smiled at him again, then parted her lips and dipped her head to him.

Dexter closed his eyes and lay back in quiet contentment as Lucy Anne labored to save him from the grievous injury of potentially exploding testes.

Dex listened as the rattle and crunch of Lucy Anne's carriage faded down the path. Then he sprang to his feet. It always pleased Lucy Anne to believe that she was capable of wearing him down to a nubbin. The truth was that he felt just fine now. Vigorous and full of life. Drained in certain other aspects, of course. But definitely full of life.

He pulled a tarpaulin down from the shelf where he'd stored it, shook it out, and laid it over the crude cot and mattress where so many of his fondest memories resided, then looked around to make sure nothing was out of place.

Not that anyone else was apt to come here. The cabin—shack was more like it—sat at the river's edge and had not been used for years. Once it had served as a base of operations for nigras assigned the choice task of running catfish trot lines to gather food for their fellow slaves.

Use of the cabin had been a privilege and a mark of favor for the select few. Or so Dex was told.

With the collapse of slavery, however, the plantation owners no longer had to provide all of life's necessities for the relative handful of former slaves who remained on as employees, and Dexter's father, Charles Yancey, stopped sending men to the riverside cabin. He had no intention, he explained, of paying a wage while the lazy nigras went fishing. Any who wanted to eat catfish could henceforth do the fishing on their own time. And as the shack was far from the Quarters, the place fell into disuse.

Except, that is, for Dex's visits.

Feeling quite content with the world now, Dexter checked the state of his hair in the piece of broken mirror he'd brought to the cabin long ago. He used the heel of his hand to smooth down a rumpled spot, then turned away, genuinely unconscious of his own features.

In his late twenties, Dexter Lee Yancey was an uncommonly handsome young man. He was tall for a Yancey, standing just an inch or so—why quibble about a quarter inch—shy of six feet. He had dark blond hair, and was clean shaven save for sideburn whiskers that flourished down to the shelf of a finely chiseled jaw. He had brown eyes and a lean build, and did not at all mind the fact that most women seemed to find him quite fetchingly handsome.

He dressed in no particular hurry, pulling on a tailored silk shirt, tight-fitted gray trousers, black stovepipe boots, a swallow-tail coat in a darker shade of gray, and an ivory-colored planter's hat with its low, flat crown and slightly rolled brim.

Dex inspected himself to make sure he was properly tucked and buttoned, then picked up his riding gloves and walking stick and ambled out into the pleasant warmth of a Louisiana afternoon.

Life, he reflected as he tightened the cinch of a leggy black gelding, was remarkably good.

• 2 •

Dex's horse rounded the last bend in the path at the smooth and fluid running walk that the breed was known for, and broke out of the thicket into bright sunshine. The leafy green canopy of the forest gave way to dark earth and row upon neat row of tiny emerald shoots that eventually would grow into the ugly, spindly, dusty gray plants that the Yanceys and all their neighbors found to be so incredibly beautiful: cotton.

The path Dexter followed ran along the south edge of this particular field, skirted the somewhat smaller horse pasture, and ended at the household barn and carriage shed behind the big house.

Several smaller houses suitable for overseers or other white employees lay on the near side of the Yancey's two-story, white-columned main house, while the produce barns and Quarters—they hadn't actually been slave quarters for more than a dozen years now, but the name remained—were out of sight a quarter mile or so beyond the house, separated from the main buildings by the household gardens and a pecan grove. Other barns and working buildings were scattered willy-nilly to the south and west of the house. The layout of the plantation was unorganized, unplanned . . . and thoroughly, comfortably familiar to Dex as he came in sight of home.

A thin column of smoke, so pale it was barely visible against the cloudless sky, lifted from the chimneys of the kitchen, separated from the house by a sheltered breezeway so as to keep the heat of the cooking fires out of the house. The sight of the smoke brought a smile to Dex's lips and a burst of saliva into his mouth as he thought about what might be in the pots and ovens and pans inside that old kitchen. Pecan pie was what he was hoping for, the rich pale nuts from their own trees, molasses from their own cane grown down along the river, and a golden brown crust made with wheat from—who knew? or cared?—Blackgum Bend was not, after all, entirely self-sufficient. What mattered was the flavor. And that Dex could anticipate just fine, thank you.

He was looking at the white-painted kitchen—Dex's father believed that slovenly maintenance of a man's own home bespoke a slovenly attitude within the man himself—when movement beyond the structure caught his eye.

Rising in his stirrups for a better look, he realized there were people gathered in the yard that lay between the house and the horse barn.

Quite a lot of people, he thought.

Nigras. All of them? It appeared so. But the nigras shouldn't be there at the house. Not at this time of day. They should all be out chopping weeds. Keeping the fields free of weed intrusion was a never-ending necessity, and especially important now while the plants were young and easily choked.

If the nigras were here at the house . . .

Something was wrong. Something had to be very badly wrong.

Dex felt a tight, acid churning in his belly.

He sat back onto his saddle and jabbed the black with his heels, lifting the gelding into a canter and then, as a sense of dread filled him, gouging it into a hard run instead.

Something was very wrong at Blackgum Bend.

◆ 3 ◆

He swept into the yard at a run, scattering the blacks who were gathered close around the back door. Dex jumped from his horse and tossed the reins to the nearest hand. "Take care of him, Hally."

"Yessuh, Boss." The response was directed toward Dex's receding back as the tall young man was already halfway up the steps leading into the back of the house.

Dexter hurried inside to find the ground floor empty save for two of the young, light-skinned house maids. Both of them were huddled in a corner of the indoor kitchen—preparation and serving room would have been a more accurate name as little actual cooking was done there—whispering softly. They gave Dex a worried look when he came inside.

"What's wrong?" he demanded.

Neither girl spoke, but the taller of the two, a girl in her late teens, rolled her eyes upward toward the heavens. Dex opened his mouth to speak again, then realized she probably meant not Heaven but the second floor of the old house. He strode quickly on into the foyer and dashed upstairs, taking the curving steps three at a time. He was breathing hard, from worry much more than from the small amount of exertion, by the time he reached the landing above.

A Yancey was in peril. He was sure of that. The major question now was whether it was his father or his brother who had come to harm.

The thud of Dex's boot heels on the hardwood floorboards brought a response from the left, from the direction of Charles Yancey's rooms. Dexter's twin brother Lewis heard and came to the door frowning.

"What's wrong?"

"It's Poppa," Lewis told him. "One of the niggers hit him with a hoe. In the head. Cut him pretty bad."

"What?"

Lewis put a hand on Dexter's chest to keep his brother from barging into their father's bedroom. "Don't go in," Lewis said. "Not yet. I . . . I don't want to say all this in there. Not where he might hear. Understand?"

Dex swallowed, his stomach churning and a constriction in his throat. He was afraid that he did understand. All too well. "Tell me, Lewis. Please."

Lewis took Dex by the elbow and pulled him partway down the hall toward their bedrooms, well away from their father's door.

"Dr. Bentley is in there with him. He—"

"How long ago did this happen, Lewis? Why didn't somebody fetch me and—"

"Will you let me tell this? Please?"

Dex shot an anxious glance down the hallway toward the blank surface of their father's bedroom door. But he held his silence this time, and merely nodded for Lewis to go on at his own pace and in his own way.

"It happened this morning. Poppa was out checking on the nigras in the field over by Mamsen's Creek."

Dexter nodded. He knew the one Lewis meant.

"They were to be chopping weeds there today, and Poppa wanted to make sure they weren't getting lazy an' laying about, being so far from the house and everything. He would have sent Jonas, I suppose, except he'd gone to the Corners looking to buy some salt to replace the bags that got wet. You know?''

Dex nodded again. Jonas was their chief overseer. He was responsible for keeping the hands hard at their tasks. He was also, Dexter recalled, responsible for maintaining the equipment and the outbuildings, and was therefore responsible for the leaky roof that had let some of their stocks of salt and cornmeal become spoiled recently. It was Jonas and not the boys' father who should have been in that field this morning.

''I don't have the whole story yet, of course, but Poppa was saying something to that skinny nigger with the two-tone face, the one got burnt or something?''

Dexter knew the man Lewis meant. He was called Spot as a rather cruel reminder of an accident he'd had when a child. Scars from a spill of boiling water had left part of his face a pale and shiny red.

''The other nigras say Spot came up with his hoe and chopped Poppa in the face with it. Caught him in the throat and ear. He was bleeding something terrible, of course. Spot took off into the woods running. The other hands, some of them ran off too. A couple of them grabbed Poppa up and carried him back up here, though by the time they got him here he was awful weak.

''Aunt Lottie had them carry him upstairs and made a cobweb poultice. Dr. Bentley says that's the only reason Poppa is still alive. It got the most of the bleeding to quit. Aunt Lottie watched over him, and I grabbed a horse and went in to the Corners for the doctor. No, don't go butting in on me, I can see you're wanting to say something and I already know what it is. I told Binny to find you and get you back here quick. Lordy, I didn't know would Poppa still be alive when either one of us got back to the house, and I sure didn't want to wait around looking for you before I went to find the doctor.''

''You did just right, Lewis,'' Dex assured his brother, not wanting just then to berate him for sending an ignorant field hand like Binny to find him when there were any number of household helpers who might have known the likely places to look for him.

"Dr. Bentley came quick as he could. He said . . . he said Poppa is weak. He's lost an awful lot of blood. Maybe too much to recover from. But at least he's got a chance thanks to Aunt Lottie."

Dexter grunted. Aunt Lottie was their cook. Had been for the past five years or so, and had served the family as the cook's helper for virtually all of her life until then.

Aunt Lottie was all right. And if Poppa Yancey survived his injuries, the family would owe her Poppa's life.

"What about Spot?" Dex asked.

"I sent some of the nigras after him, and I sent word to Sheriff Ryan when I was at the Corners fetching the doctor. By now there's sure to be a manhunt on for him."

"Uh-huh. What about James?"

"I sent your pet nigger after that son of a bitch Spot, Dexter. Figure he'd know where a nigger would hide if anybody could. Is that all right with you, brother?" There was a hard edge of challenge in Lewis's voice. Dexter chose to ignore it. This was not the time for the two of them to get into a squabble.

"I want to go in and see Poppa now," Dex said instead.

"Later. The doctor said he shouldn't be disturbed just now. He said he'll let us know when we can go in again."

"I want to see him, dammit, I—"

"Later," Lewis snapped. "The doctor *said*."

Dex sent a miserable, baleful look down the hallway. But the closed door gave him no measure of relief for his concerns.

"Later," Lewis said again, more softly this time. He took Dex by the elbow and guided his brother on toward the study—their playroom in their youth—that lay between their bedrooms at the opposite end of the hallway. "Dr. Bentley will let us know when we can go in and see Poppa, Dex. Come on now. We don't want to tire or upset him. Do we?"

Dex looked unhappily back in the direction of his father's bedroom, but allowed himself to be pulled away from the sickbed. After all, the doctor was with him now and the doctor would know best what needed to be done.

◆ 4 ◆

Dexter turned at the sound of the door being opened, but it was only Lewis. Again. His brother's system must have been affected by the nervous strain of waiting to hear from the doctor, Lewis had left the room to relieve himself three times now. And still no word about their father's condition.

"What?" Lewis demanded. "Why are you looking at me like that?"

"I was just . . . I was hoping it was the doctor. Did you look in on Poppa?"

Lewis shook his head. "I tried to go in and ask, but Dr. Bentley shooed me away. He held a finger to his lips and went like this." Lewis made a sweeping motion by way of demonstration.

"How did Poppa . . . ?"

"Asleep. At least, I hope he's only sleeping. He isn't awake yet, I'm sure of that."

Dexter turned back to the window he'd been staring out for the past several hours. He had no idea what was going on out in the yard. Hadn't paid any real attention to the scene before him in all that time.

It would soon be dark, he knew that. From the playroom window he could not see the crowd of field hands who'd been gathered at the back of the house when he came in, but he was sure they would still be there, patiently waiting to hear how the old boss—most of them still spoke of Poppa Yancey as the old massa—was. Whether their old owner would survive. Whether he'd been permanently cut down by one of their own.

It occurred to Dex that he honestly did not know just how the majority of the hands would regard this incident. Would they think of it as a tragedy? Or as a righteous retribution?

It startled Dex to realize it was a question to which he had no easy answer. Startled and distressed him too.

Dexter was comfortable in the knowledge of his own place in the feelings of the nigras. But it only now occurred to him that he did not have the same sure sense when it came to his father or, for that matter, to Lewis either. It was a question Dexter had never discussed with any of the nigras before, of course, and never would. To do so would have been unthinkable. It would have crossed the very clearly defined line that divided the two races as deeply as an unbridgeable chasm might have done. A high-born white Louisiana boy could in no way discuss such a thing, not even with a free nigra.

Well, they were all free now, Dex reminded himself. Even so, some were more free than others. Some always had been. Others, in a way, never would be, no matter the relatively recent laws to that effect.

Dexter frowned. Such gloomy thoughts.

But then this was a gloomy day.

Unseen in front of him, the tall, upswept limbs of the Blackgum Bend pecan grove began to fade as twilight settled onto the plantation.

Unknown at the other end of the hallway—how very distant that seemed to him now—was the fate of Dexter's beloved poppa.

He wished Bentley would tell them something. Any news would be . . . no, that was wrong, he corrected himself. Not just any news would be welcome. It was a very specific outcome that Dexter so fervently wished for now. He leaned against the playroom wall and closed his eyes. He hadn't ventured an actual prayer since he was . . . how old? Not very. It had been an awfully long time. No matter. He prayed now, awkwardly and in silence, but he prayed for his injured father's life.

• 5 •

The playroom door opened. Again Dex responded with a hollow sense of cold dread in his belly, but it was only the housemaid Netty, who beckoned to Lewis. The girl went onto tiptoes to whisper something into Lewis's ear. Lewis nodded, whispered something back to her, and turned to speak to his brother.

"I'll be right back," he said. "Stay here, Dexter. If the doctor comes, send Netty to fetch me, all right?"

"Sure. Whatever." Dex turned back to the window. It was fully dark outside now. Lamplight in the room caught and reflected off the cleaned and polished glass windowpanes. The window acted like a mirror, and Dexter observed without particularly intending to as Lewis bent low as if to whisper again to Netty. Instead he grinned—the expression seemed out of place to Dexter, considering—and nuzzled the side of her neck, then nipped gently at her earlobe before straightening and slipping quietly out of the room.

Netty remained behind, tidying the pictures on the wall, tugging at the tatted doilies the lamps were placed on, trying to find excuses to stay. Waiting for Lewis to return? Not that Dex cared. Dexter and Lewis were brothers; they were twins; they were not close. And one neither asked nor needed the other's permission to do as he pleased. That would apply to Netty as much as to anything else.

And the girl was pretty, Dex readily conceded. She was slim and petite, a fairly dark mulatto in color with perfect skin, large eyes, and overlarge breasts that were far out of proportion with the rest of her. In a few years she would be sagging and homely, but right now she had the taut flesh and eager vitality of youth to recommend her. And if she did not object to Lewis's advances, Dex certainly was not going to intrude.

All of Lewis's girls were small, Dex noted, not at all for the first time. But then Lewis himself was short, as was their father.

The Yancey brothers were twins, but no one who saw them would ever have guessed that fact, for they were fraternal twins rather than the much more common identical sort.

Where Dexter was tall and athletically lean, blond and eternally laughing, Lewis was a good three inches shorter and stocky of build like their poppa. Lewis had black hair and dark eyes. His disposition too was the opposite of his twin's, Lewis being silent and dour, often morose and brooding. Dex years earlier had given up any efforts to understand Lewis or to share his own thoughts and feelings with his very slightly younger brother.

Twenty minutes. That was the difference between them in age. Dexter was twenty minutes the older, although by an odd quirk of the clock the twins' birthdays were different. Dexter, the firstborn, came into the world a few minutes before midnight. When he was a boy, Dex remembered their father chuckling when he told the oft-repeated family yarn, commenting that the clock began to chime the end of one day and the commencement of another just as the doctor's assistant was severing Dexter's umbilical cord. Lewis, therefore, was born the following calendar day.

Dex and Poppa Yancey had found amusement in that, but Lewis never seemed to. Starting on—Dexter had to think back trying to remember—on their ninth birthdays? or had it been their tenth? Sometime around then, though, Lewis had insisted that the twins' birthdays be celebrated separately, Dexter's on the third day of the month and Lewis's on the fourth.

Dexter hadn't actually minded the change. After all, it gave them each two parties to enjoy instead of just one.

Ever since then they—

The door latch turned and the hinges creaked just a little.

Dexter spun around.

Dr. Bentley was standing there. Lewis stood a pace behind him.

Both wore the solemn expressions of bereavement.

◆ 6 ◆

The succeeding days were a blur for Dex. Mercifully so.
They were filled with sorrow, disbelief, rage, and confu-
sion. Charles Yancey's friends heard and they came. Pol-
iticians, planters, and cronies came from as far away as
New Orleans and Vicksburg to pay their respects to one
of their own. A delegation of priests came up from Baton
Rouge, and another from Natchez. Three women who
were decidedly *not* ladies arrived weeping from God-
knows-where, grieved vocally, and left without introducing themselves.

Dex's impressions of that period were a jumble of
whispers in the parlor, whiskey on the porch, and a stomach made queasy from too-frequent assaults by greasy
fried chicken, pastry crusts heavy with lard, and cloying
oversweet yams baked in honey.

When Charles Yancey was laid reverently to rest in the
family cemetery overlooking the river and the last of the
mourners departed, Dex was left feeling empty and afraid.
Empty because the focal point of his entire existence had
been vacated. Afraid because now, as the elder son,
Blackgum Bend and all its holdings and all its people
were his responsibility.

All his life until this moment had been an exercise in the pursuit of fun and good times.

Now, years before any ordinary progression should have called for it, now Dex would have to . . . grow up. It was as simple as that. A carefree life of dalliance would have to be replaced now with maturity, industriousness, and close attention to the smallest of details.

And Dexter was quite frankly afraid that he would not be up to the task.

Through all his years he had spent more time on horseback than in study. Fit and naturally agile, quick of wit and hand, he could ride, shoot, and fence with the best of men. He could waltz, reel, or tumble with the best of women. And the worst.

But he cared nothing about tidy columns of figures in a ledger, knew less about the needs of the fields or the marketing of the plantation's produce. His father had always taken care of those piddling and mundane details. Lewis cared about such drivel, but Dexter certainly never had.

Now he would have to.

He would, he determined, lay as much of it off onto Lewis as possible. Dex suspected that was a decision that would be pleasing to both of them, to Lewis so his own importance would be recognized, and to Dex so his efforts would not be required.

It was, if Dex thought so himself, an ideal solution to a most unpleasant necessity, and he resolved to discuss it with Lewis at the first opportunity.

Which should be—he consulted the mantel clock in the playroom-turned-study—which should be sometime that afternoon. Dexter had been only vaguely aware of Lewis's presence during the past few days of hectic visitation and public mourning, but this morning a note had arrived to inform the Yancey brothers that the family lawyer would arrive in the early afternoon to settle the details of Charles Yancey's will. Lewis would be there for that, Dex was sure. Lewis was a stickler for detail, if not for gracious manner. Lewis would not be one to allow a *t* to go un-crossed or an *i* undotted.

Dexter glanced at the clock again, and decided he had time enough to go down to the quarters and see how things fared there. He had been very dimly aware of the presence of the nigras in the backyard throughout the mourning. Some, the household help mostly, had been allowed to slip in to view the old master's laying out. Most of the field hands, though, had been conspicuous more for their absence than their mourning.

And it occurred to Dex at this very late date that he had never once taken the time since his father's death to inquire about the nigra whose hoe had cut Charles Yancey's life short. He would have to find James and ask him about that. Among other things.

And come to think of it, dammit, where had James been these past days? Why hadn't his oldest friend and companion been at his elbow during Dex's time of pain and sorrow?

Dexter shook himself—literally shook himself like a dog emerging from water—as he tried to shake off the sense of disoriented detachment that had fallen over him ever since he'd first learned that he and Lewis were orphaned years before what could be considered a proper time. If there was such a thing as a proper time for loss of a parent.

He took the back stairs down into the kitchen and waved Aunt Lottie away. Aunt Lottie was one who believed that any sorrow could be done away with if treated with a sufficiency of food. Dexter's stomach roiled and rumbled in rebellion at the mere thought of another biscuit, one more slab of ham, one single added morsel of crispy chicken skin. He waved the tall, hatchet-jawed nigra back to her stool beside the huge cast-iron range and hurried outside.

James. He needed to find James. He needed his friend's help to regain some small semblance of normalcy, and he would need James's counsel even more when it came time for Dex to assume charge of the workings of Blackgum Bend. He would need that for all their sakes.

• 7 •

"You black, ugly bastard."

"Pasty-faced white sonuvabitch!"

Dex grabbed James and gave him a bear hug that held more relief than welcome in it. It was good to see James again. Good to see that at least some things remained normal. Dexter hugged his lifelong friend and then stepped briskly back away, half embarrassed by the show of emotion.

"Are you all right, Dex?"

"Yeah, sure, of course. I mean . . . I will be. That is . . . oh, Jesus, James, no, I'm not all right."

Without warning Dex felt heat and moisture well up behind his eyes. Tears began to flow, trickling down his cheeks, the salty fluid picking up sunlight and seeming to magnify the brightness so that his eyes burned.

Four days. Four days since his father had died, and Dex hadn't cried in all that time. Until now. Now the loss, the sense of isolation, the weight of responsibility all over-whelmed him and came pouring out in spite of his efforts to hold back the flow.

James put an arm around his shoulders and led Dex into the shade of an oak tree where there was an ornate cast-iron bench. He guided his friend to a sitting position and, glancing around to make sure no one was watching, sat down close by.

"It's all right, Dex. It's okay to let it out."

Dex shook his head. "It isn't all right, James. It won't never be all right again."

"It won't ever be the same again, Dex. Of course it won't. But it *will* be all right. Honestly." James pulled a starkly white, freshly ironed handkerchief from his pocket and offered it to Dex to dry his eyes with. Dexter did, then blew his nose loudly, refolded the hanky, and stuffed it into his own pocket so he could have it washed before he returned it.

James smiled. He knew perfectly good and well why Dex hadn't handed the soiled hanky back to him, but with a slight smile he said, "Uppity damned ol' white boy, think you own everything, even a poor black boy's snot rag."

Dex managed a small smile of his own. "Own everything around here, boy, including your sorry black ass."

James got a laugh out of that. Although there was a time when technically it had been quite true. When both were born—James was younger than Dex by less than a year—James had been a slave and the son of a slave and chattel property. When both were toddlers, Charles Yancey gave James to Dexter as a play-toy and gave Lewis a boy they called Jason. Lewis hadn't liked being around Jason, and eventually the child was sent back to live in the Quarters. He eventually became skilled in harness mending and when he was old enough, chose to leave Blackgum Bend as a freeman. Dexter doubted that Lewis so much as knew that. Certainly Lewis would not have cared if he did know.

With Dex and James, though, it had been a very different matter. Dex had always felt closer to James than he ever did to his natural brother, Lewis. Dex and James had been inseparable. Whenever Dex and Lewis were tutored, James was always present, sitting quietly in a corner of the room and seeming to pay no mind to the important business of the privileged white boys. When later Dex and Lewis were sent off for advanced schooling, James went along as Dexter's personal servant. And always, in every class, James would be hunkered silently in a corner, or if nothing else, stationed at an open window, beneath a doorway transom, somewhere close by and ready to meet Dexter's slightest need or whim.

What no one but Dex seemed to notice was that through all that, James was receiving the exact same education as the Yancey brothers.

What no one else dared understand was that James had also learned to shoot every bit as well as Dex—which was infinitely better than Lewis—and to ride, wrestle, box, and fence. But then, Dex reasoned with a smile from time to time, he had to practice with someone, didn't he? And Lewis was woefully inadequate when it came to matters of sport. So who better than James, with whom he was so very well matched.

Indeed the two were matched quite well, mentally and physically. Dexter even thought they looked a trifle alike, save for certain small details like the shade of their flesh.

James was approximately the same height as Dex and had a similar lean and athletic build. He was a mellow mulatto in color, suggesting that his father had been a white man. James's mother had been the Yancey family cook until poor health forced her retirement, and she was as black as a lump of coal, so Dex knew for certain sure there was no white blood on her side of James's heritage. James had thin lips and a finely chiseled nose to reinforce the mix of blood.

None of which, however, mattered in the slightest to Dexter. To him the fact was simple enough to require neither explanation nor apology. James was his friend. Always had been, always would be. And that was the end of that.

Of course both of them, as boys and as men still, knew that their friendship would not be tolerated by others black or white. When they were alone they were friends. When in the company of others James "kept his place." The two of them had been maintaining this facade for so long that neither of them ever had to consciously think about it. It was simply the way things were, and they acted accordingly.

Now, in Dex's time of grief, James was there to comfort and divert him.

"You're gonna be fine, Dex. You will be."

"I know. But God, James, I'm scared. There's so much that I don't know." He paused for a moment and took a deep breath. There really was much to be done now.

And it was time for him to begin doing it.

"Lewis said he sent you after Spot, James. It was Spot that killed Poppa, wasn't it?"

James nodded, and Dex noticed that his friend's expression was grim. "Edward," he said.

"What?"

"The name his mama gave him was Edward. Everybody called him Spot, but he was really Edward."

"I didn't know that."

James shrugged.

"He is the one, though?"

Again James nodded. "He did it. He . . . it doesn't matter why."

"Poppa could be hard on the people. I know that."

"He was hard on Edward that day, Dex. Don't get me wrong. Edward was wrong to do what he did. He was wrong as wrong could be. But he didn't . . . he deserved better than what he got."

Dex raised an eyebrow, but remained silent. James would tell him.

"I took a couple of the people, men I knew I could trust, and we followed after Edward. He wasn't very smart, you know, and he hadn't planned any of this. It just . . . your poppa leaned on him hard that day, and Edward lost control of himself and chopped at the old man with his hoe. I think Edward was more surprised and scared than anybody when he saw how bad he'd hurt your poppa. So he took to running. Into the brakes. He didn't know where to go. I expect he thought if he could, like, get down to the swamps and the bayous he could hide, maybe get away. He didn't have a plan. No food or knife or fire starter, nothing like that. He just did what he done and then ran away.''

"You caught him," Dex said.

"Oh, we caught him, all right. We just followed along beside the river and through the brakes, and we caught up with him. Should have brought him back that same way, but I guess I just wasn't thinking." James's voice had turned bitter. "It's my fault. I had Edward's hands tied and a piece of string around his neck to lead him by. It wasn't but a little string, you understand. It couldn't hurt him or anything."

That point seemed important to James for some reason. Dex nodded to show that he understood that James had meant no harm to Spot.

"I thought it'd be quicker and easier to come home by the road instead of coming back through the brakes the way we'd gone down."

"Uh-huh."

"Sheriff Ryan and a bunch of men were riding up and down the roads, Dex. They were searching for Edward, I suppose. I don't know how they expected to find him out in plain sight like that. They didn't have any dogs and they weren't looking in the brush. Just racing up and down the roads. And drinking, of course. They were all of them pretty drunk." James shook his head. "I should've known better than to come back on the public road, out in the open like that."

"What happened, James?"

"I couldn't stop them, Dex. I suppose . . . it wouldn't have mattered anyway. But the people would've felt an awful lot better if Edward had got a regular trial and proper hanging. You know?"

"Spo—Edward. He's dead?"

"Oh, yeah. He died bad, Dex. Screaming. They didn't just hang him or shoot him. I guess I could've forgave them that. But they were drunk, and he'd gone and hit a white man. They didn't know then that your poppa was dead, mind you. None of us did. I didn't know until just this morning. Anyway, Sheriff Ryan and them, they decided to teach Edward a lesson he wouldn't forget. Well, he won't forget it. Neither will I or the men who were with me.''

''They killed him?'' It wasn't really a question.

''It took him a long time to die, but . . . yeah, Dex. They killed him.''

''Don't tell me about it, James. You don't ever have to tell me about it.''

James looked Dex in the eye and said, ''I'm sorry about your poppa, Dex. I hope you know that.''

''I do, James.''

''But I wish Edward had been allowed to die quick. They would have hanged him. All us niggers knows that. Hanging would have been fair after what he did. But not . . . not like what happened to Edward. Not like what Sheriff Ryan and those men did to him down there.''

Dex nodded. And tried to comfort his friend. It seemed that both of them needed that just now.

· 8 ·

"You. Boy!"

"Yessuh?"

"Get out. I don't want you in here," Lewis snapped.

"Yessuh," James repeated, bobbing his head and starting to back away.

Dexter bristled at his brother's tone of voice. "He's supposed to be here, Lewis. James is mentioned in Poppa's will. Isn't he, Mr. Whitley?"

"He is," the lawyer confirmed from his position at the desk that had belonged to Charles Yancey. The reading of the will was to take place in the pecan-paneled study that the elder Yancey had so enjoyed. To him the dark, masculine study had been the heart of the house with its comfortable chairs, filled bookshelves, and cheery fireplace. Dex had difficulty looking at it now and knowing that his father would never again swivel his creaking old chair around to deliver a lecture or make a small—and usually quite bad—joke with his son.

"The freeman James, son of the former slave and household cook Maybelle, is indeed mentioned in your father's will, Lewis. Not only is he entitled to be here, his presence is required." Whitley tilted his chin down and peered at Lewis over the wire rim of his half glasses. "Dr. Bentley, on the other hand . . ." The lawyer sent a questioning look first toward the doctor who had attended Charles Yancey in his last hours, and then toward Lewis, beside whom the doctor was seated.

"Dr. Bentley is here at my invitation. He will remain," Lewis said firmly. "And the nigger can leave."

"I already informed you, Lewis, that—"

"You will call me Mr. Yancey from now on if you please, Mr. Whitley."

"I see." Whitley sniffed, somewhat louder than might have been strictly necessary, and said, "As you prefer. *Mister* Yancey." Whitley was approximately the same age as Charles Yancey had been. He did not look at all amused by Lewis's newfound airs.

Whitley turned his attention to Dexter and to James. "If you two would be seated, we can get this over with."

The lawyer turned the loudly complaining desk chair around, picked up a thick and very official-looking envelope, and carefully inspected the wax seal that had been placed over the envelope flap. "I have already inspected the seal, gentlemen. Would any of you care to do so before I retrieve the document?"

"Not me," Dex said. He looked around at James, who was standing silent in a corner as if trying to pretend he was elsewhere.

"It doesn't matter if the seal is broken or not," Lewis declared, standing. He reached inside his coat and produced a sheet of paper. "The will you prepared for Poppa is no longer valid, Mr. Whitley. Poppa swore to and signed a new will just before he died. That's why the good doctor is here. He was one of the witnesses to Poppa's signature."

"There were two witnesses or more?" Whitley asked. "That is required by law, you know."

"There were two," Lewis said.

"Dr. Bentley is one, you say. And the other?"

"The nigress known as Lottie. She is a free person of

legal age. She was present when Poppa signed the new will."

"And she appended her own signature as witness?" Whitley asked.

"She made her mark. She will affirm it in a court of law if she has to."

"I see." Whitley looked at Dexter. "Were you aware of any of this, Dex? Or should I call you Mr. Yancey also?"

"You've called me Dex, or worse, my whole life, Mr. Whitley. I expect you still can. But . . . no, sir. This is the first I've heard about Poppa changing his will."

"Your document is no good, Mr. Whitley. This one supersedes it."

"So you say. May I see the, um, alleged testament?"

"Alleged nothing. It will stand up. Dr. Bentley and Lottie will testify to what they saw. So will the nigress Annetta."

"Annetta?" Dex asked.

"Netty."

"Oh."

"She likes Annetta better. Says it sounds nicer than Netty."

"Whatever."

"She'd testify that Poppa wanted to change his will. She was there when he spoke about that."

"Netty was in Poppa's room with the doctor? So was Aunt Lottie? I take it you were there too?"

Lewis nodded. "I was."

"Then why wasn't I allowed in to see him, dammit?" Dex roared, rising from his chair and clenching his fists. "Why wasn't I allowed to see Poppa when he was dying?"

"That is a very good question indeed, Dexter," the doctor put in, his voice harsh. "Your father begged to see you. He knew he was dying. He asked for you all through the afternoon, but no, you couldn't be bothered. You were off gambling or drinking, laying about with soiled women or whatever it is you do with yourself when you should be occupied with decent pursuits. Your father begged for you to come to him, Dexter Yancey, and it broke his heart to learn that you could not be bothered."

"Not be bothered? I was right down the hall worrying and praying and wanting in to see him for only a second, but you wouldn't let me in."

"I, sir? I will thank you to watch your tongue, young mister. I am the one who asked for you to be brought to your father's bedside. I am the one you responded to when you said you would come in the evening."

"In the evening? What the hell are you talking about? I never said anything like that."

"That was not my understanding at the time."

"And I never heard that you wanted me there. I was told Poppa couldn't have anybody in, that he was too weak and asleep."

"Your father was awake throughout his ordeal," Bentley said. "He was well aware that he would die. His last words called out to you, Dexter. His body was already destroyed, but when you would not come to him his heart broke also."

"But I didn't . . ." Dexter looked with a growing sense of horror at his very slightly younger brother.

It had been Lewis, after all, who'd told him he was not allowed into the room.

And Lewis himself had spent little time in their playroom/study that terrible afternoon. Lewis came into the room only briefly, then quickly departed again complaining of a loose kidney and bowel. Lewis had . . .

Oh, God! Dex realized. Lewis had lied to him, and worse, Lewis had lied to Poppa.

Poppa had died thinking Dex did not care enough to come to him.

Poppa had died not knowing how very much Dex loved him.

Poppa had died not knowing that . . .

Dex glared with dawning fury across the large room at his brother.

"Why?" he roared. "Why, damn you?"

Lewis looked stoically back at him, unflinching in the face of Dexter's anger. Lewis looked smug, Dex thought. Then, correcting himself, he amended that impression. It was not smugness that Lewis exhibited exactly. It was a look of haughty superiority.

The lawyer looked up from his perusal of the newly presented handwritten Last Will and Testament of Charles Yancey, recently deceased. "This is, um, quite a departure from the will Charles had me prepare," he said.

"But I believe you will find it is legal and proper," Lewis said. "I have witnesses, and it was written out in Dr. Bentley's hand to Poppa's dictation. I believe he will swear to that if so required."

Whitley looked at the doctor.

"That is correct, sir. Charles indeed directed my hand in the matter. The words are his, and I would testify as well that Charles was in full command of his mental faculties to the very end." Bentley looked away from the lawyer and shifted his attention to Dex. He looked troubled now. "You say you were physically present in the house, sir, and that you were given to understand that I forbade your entrance into your father's bedroom?"

"That's right."

"Then God help you, sir. And you," he added, turning his gaze on Lewis, "for I believe a great wrong has been done to a fine gentleman and friend. And now there is no way for the wrong to be rectified." To Dex he added, "You have my sympathies, sir, and my apologies as well."

It was only beginning to occur to Dex what Bentley meant by that.

It was beginning to be clear to him what the new will must surely provide.

• 9 •

"Mr. Yancey."

Dex had to look around first. But he was indeed the gentleman the good doctor wanted. He had to be since Lewis was still inside the house, and the doctor was in the driveway preparing to climb into his carriage.

Still, it felt very odd to Dex to be called Mister now. Mr. Yancey had always been his father. He felt a pang of loss and memory, then put it aside and responded with the courtesy he'd always been taught. He left the shaded comfort of the broad porch fronting the Blackgum Bend main house and went down to join Bentley beside his rig. "Is there something I can do for you, sir? You look . . . forgive me for saying this, but you look troubled."

"I just . . . were you truly at home that day? Were you really down the hall waiting to see your father?"

"Yes, I was."

The aging doctor sighed and looked away. "I am so very sorry," he whispered.

"About?"

"Your father. Had I known . . . more to the point, sir, had *he* known. Your absence troubled him greatly as his hour approached. He wanted to see you so desperately.

And then your brother told him. . . ." Bentley bit his lower lip and shook his head as if in anger. "I witnessed the making of the new will, sir. I signed it as witness. I cannot testify in any way but the truth, Mr. Yancey. But my heart would be lighter now if I could take back those moments. What I did was wrong. I am sorry, sir. Terribly, horribly sorry."

Dex smiled easily. It was not at all difficult for him. "Doctor, please don't worry yourself about it. In a way, I'm almost glad it turned out the way it has. The actual ownership doesn't mean nearly so much to me as it does to my brother." He chuckled softly. "Means a lot to him, I'd say. But what Lewis never did understand, sir, is that I would have thought the whole thing a burden. In fact, I intended to share control with Lewis anyway. I suspect he will do a much better job of managing the plantation than I ever could have, and that is the important thing, isn't it. Our home, our people, everything our father built here will continue. The name on the courthouse documents isn't truly very important, now is it?" Dexter's smile lingered.

"Your attitude is remarkable for someone whose inheritance has just been . . ." Bentley seemed unwilling to finish the sentence.

Dex laughed. "You needn't worry, sir. I have no intention of repeating this conversation."

"Yes, well, um . . ."

"I mean that, Doctor. It isn't really that important to me. Except for knowing that my father died thinking I'd abandoned him. That knowledge is painful. But as for the rest . . ." He shrugged, then held out his hand for the doctor to shake.

"But I feel responsible," Bentley insisted.

"Don't." Dex laughed again. "Poor Lewis. He's going to get the shock of a lifetime when he discovers that I don't care about what he did."

"Mmm, you have a point there. I doubt he will believe it, though."

"This may amaze you, Doctor, but it doesn't concern

me overmuch what my brother does or does not think.''

"I'm beginning to understand that, Mr. Yancey.''

"Please, Doctor. You've called me Dexter about as long as I can remember. There's no reason for you to speak formally now.'' The smile returned. "Particularly since I'm no more the landed gentleman today than I was before.''

"I admire your attitude, Dexter. And please understand that if there is anything I can ever do on your behalf, I, well, I simply feel that I've acted badly in this matter. It would please me if I were allowed to make amends.''

"No need for that, sir, but I thank you for the offer.''

The two gentlemen shook hands, and Dex helped the doctor into his carriage, then latched the carriage door carefully closed. "All right now, boy, drive on.''

"Yessuh.'' The driver took up his reins, and the carriage rolled forward, iron tires crunching loudly on the gravel of the circular driveway at the front of the mansion.

· 10 ·

Dexter saw with no small degree of surprise that Lucy Anne Thibidoux's carriage was already parked—hidden really—behind the screening presence of a clump of tall Jerusalem artichokes that had been allowed to grow up unkempt and now rarely harvested beside the old fishing shack. Dex dismounted and tied his gelding close by, near enough that the two horses would not begin whickering and calling to one another, but not so close that they could get into a tussle.

He patted the black horse on the rump and whistled softly, two notes, the first high and the second lower in pitch, to tell Lucy Anne that it was indeed he who'd arrived at their rendezvous. He mounted the steps onto the rickety front porch in two long strides and rapped lightly on the door.

"Come."

"I intend to," he said as he pushed the door open and entered the darkly shadowed interior.

Lucy Anne was ready for him. My, oh, my, he reckoned that she was. She was already naked, lying sprawled out on the bed with her legs wide apart and a welcoming smile on her pretty lips.

"Your note didn't say exactly what it was you wanted to see me about," Dex teased. "Did it ever occur to you that I might not come alone?"

"Never. Didn't occur to you either, I daresay." Her smile became coquettish. "Besides, you know I could not have made the invitation any the clearer. After all, a lady is not supposed to know words like those."

"Words like what?" He began disrobing while they talked.

"You know."

"No, tell me."

"I would blush, sir, to utter them aloud."

"Well, I think it would be unfair of me to ask anything of you beyond what you are comfortable speaking about," he countered. "If the mere words are too indelicate for you, then surely the acts would be scandalous in the extreme." He stepped out of his smallclothes and perched beside her on the edge of the bed. His hand fell as if by accident onto the slope of her right breast. It was soft and a trifle doughy, but with a nipple that was pink and quite fetchingly pretty.

"Scandalize me," Lucy Anne whispered.

"Tell me what you want."

"You know what I want."

"Tell me," he insisted.

"Fuck me," Lucy Anne told him.

Dexter blinked, taken quite aback. "I thought we talked about that already."

"Don't be such a 'fraidy-cat, Dex honey. You know it's what we both want. And now that you are the master of Blackgum Bend, there is no reason we can't be married."

"Oh, you knew about the reading today, did you?"

"Don't be silly. Every planter along the river knew. There are no secrets in Louisiana. You know that."

"I suppose everyone also knew the contents?"

Lucy Anne shrugged and lifted her chest, pushing the fullness of her breast tight against Dexter's palm. "Touch me, sweetheart. Yes. Like that. Squeeze. Not too hard. Yes, perfect.''

"You didn't answer me. Did everyone know what would be in the will, Lucy Anne?''

"I suppose so. More or less. After all, it isn't like it was a secret. You are the elder. You become the new master. Everything else is only detail. Now lower, Dex honey. Yes. Touch me there. Oh, god, I've been wanting this day for as long as I can remember. I've always loved you, Dexter honey. Did you know that? Even when we were wee small, I loved you. Well, I was wee little. You were already most grown. So handsome. I worshipped you.'' She giggled. "I still do. And I've wanted to fuck you for ever so long, honey. Now we can. Now there's no reason why we can't do it, sweetie.''

"I thought we agreed you should be a virgin on your wedding night.''

"Fine. We can drive into town this afternoon and marry. But fuck me first, Dex. Please.''

He ran his fingertips over and through the warm and startlingly wet lips of her pussy.

"You have to post banns before you can marry, Lucy Anne.''

"We could have a second ceremony later. After the banns. Father Condon would marry us today. You know he would. After all, dear, the Yanceys are the finest family on the river. You know he would do it for you. For us.''

Lucy Anne was gilding the lily with her statement. But of course she was right in that the good father would indeed perform a ceremony if Dexter insisted. The good father would allow himself few qualms when it came to pleasing the gentry. Everyone knew that including, or especially, those who were not considered gentlefolk.

"I don't think it would be a good idea, Lucy Anne. Your father would be very angry.''

"Papa would get over it. Oh. Do that again. Yes, right there. Harder, sweetheart. Inside now. Please. Damn you, why won't you do what I want?''

"We've talked about this a hundred times, Lucy Anne. Not until we are married."

"Oh, pooh. What possible difference could a few hours make?"

"It isn't the timing, Lucy Anne, but the fact that not everything is quite the way you think it is."

"I know that I adore you, Dexter. I know that I want you ever so badly. What else could matter?"

"Well, I don't know what you'll think about it, but I'm pretty sure your father would be upset."

"But he has always wanted me to marry a Yancey, sweetheart. You know that. It isn't like he's made any secret of the fact. Can you still reach me if I turn and do this, dear?" She adjusted her position so she could lick and nibble Dex's erection. His hand tightened, and a finger quite inadvertently slipped inside Lucy Anne's overheated body. Yeah, he could still reach her just fine, thank you.

"Your father isn't going to like the fact that I am not the master of Blackgum Bend, darling."

"What did you say, dear?" She stopped what whe'd been doing—Dex wished she hadn't; it was feeling almighty good—and peered up at him from her position on his lap. Her lips were wet. But frowning.

"I said I'll not be master of Blackgum Bend, Lucy Anne. Lewis is."

"Lewis!" She shrieked, and suddenly distracted from their more pleasurable activities, sat bolt upright. "What the hell d'you mean Lewis?"

"What, are the words too big for you? I said Lewis is the new owner of the plantation. Not me."

"But I thought . . ."

Dex explained. "It doesn't matter, Lucy Anne. We don't have to change a thing. We can go right on just like—"

"Go right on, *hell*," she bawled, pushing him away and jumping off the bed. "This is terrible. This changes everything."

"Oh, really?" The sarcasm in his voice was lost on Lucy Anne. "Just what does it change, *sweetheart*? *Dear*? *Turtledove*? Tell me. Just what does that fact change?"

"It changes . . . everything, Dexter. Everything, that's all." Lucy Anne looked as though she was about to cry.

Dex considered it a rather good thing that he hadn't wanted to marry the girl. But dammit, he did wish she'd finished what they'd started before she'd decided to have this fit of . . . whatever sort of fit it was. Dammit.

"Are you telling me you don't want to fuck now?"

"Dexter. Honey. Sweetheart. You know I want to. But dear, I can't. I simply can't. Don't you understand that, Dex honey?"

"I, uh, I think I've been the one trying to tell you that we shouldn't, Lucy Anne."

"God, Dexter, I can't . . . I have to think about this. You know?"

"I know that I'm still awful horny, Lucy Anne, and I know you and me can have a power of fun without me putting it inside that tasty little pussy of yours. Now whyn't you come back to bed and—"

"Dexter! Really. Be serious now. I have to . . . honey, I hate to do this to you. Honestly I do. But I have to run. I have to go now. You'll forgive me, won't you, dear? Of course you will. You're wonderful, and I do love you, Dexter, just ever so much."

She gave him a smile—the same sort that a bayou alligator might give to a turtle a moment before having the turtle for lunch—and rose onto tiptoes to plant a rather chaste kiss on the side of his jaw.

Dexter reached for Lucy Anne's tit, but he was too late. The girl had already turned to gather her clothing into her arms and was heading for the door.

"I'll be damned," Dexter mused as he dropped back onto the side of a bed that was still warm from Lucy Anne Thibidoux's recent presence, still smelled hauntingly of her scent.

The rough material of the blanket that had been the

scene of so many of their trysts felt harsh on the bare skin of his butt.

Dex sat there until he heard the sound of Lucy Anne's carriage being driven quite rapidly away. Then he stood and began slowly to dress.

◆ 11 ◆

God, he loved it. Walking into the Crystal Palace was like returning to his second home. He should have thought about coming here days ago. First Lewis's betrayal, then Lucy Anne. Dex was glad finally to be "home" where he could relax and just be himself.

He handed his cape and walking stick to the liveried black man who had been the cloakroom attendant at the Palace since . . . probably since Dexter was still in dresses . . . almost certainly since the days when the man would have been considered part of the property and not an employee. Dex tugged off his gloves, dropped them into his hat, and gave them to the ebony attendant also. "Yessuh, Mistuh Yancey; very good, suh." The man bowed and backed away with his eyes downcast.

Dex turned to the huge room that lay before him. He breathed deep of the aroma of the place and rejoiced to the sounds and the scenes that greeted him.

The Crystal Palace was a gaming establishment and much more. The proprietor, M. Jarvais, entertained the most distinguished of guests, serving nothing but the choicest and most delectable of foods and wines and li-

queurs. His tables were as famous for their honesty as his
ladies were notorious for their beauty.

The room itself was beautiful too. Gas lamps hissed
from jewel-like sconces on the flocked and fancy walls
while overhead the ornate lead ceiling panels were lighted
by hundreds of candles blazing in the chandeliers. Every
wooden surface gleamed with wax and every visible por-
tion of brass or glass or silver was polished to a mirror
shine.

All around Dex were gentlemen in swallow coats and
silk cravats. A few early diners—it was scarcely nine
o'clock—supped on quail and roasted oysters. The card
tables were abuzz with the conversations of gentlemen at
their leisure. At the far back corner of the large room a
girl with a thin voice—but a powerful chest from which
to throw it—tried vainly to overcome the noisy gaiety.
Dex could hear the faint tinkling of her piano accompa-
niment, but had no idea what song she was trying to sing.

Not that it mattered. The evening was complete simply
with the joy and the welcome afforded the patrons of the
Palace.

"Would you care for a table, suh?"

Dex shook his head. "Not yet."

He made his way through the crowd to the bar, nodding
to acquaintances here and there as he passed among them.
This was his element, and he felt alive and vibrant and
without care here in this magnificent room.

He felt good tonight. Lucky. He might well take a seat
at one of the games, although in general gambling was
not his sport.

But later. He could think about all that later. As for
now . . .

The barman, his name was Henri, noted Dexter's arrival
and quickly brought a snifter and Dex's personal bottle
of Napoleon. "Would you care for anything else, sir? A
plate of fruit and cheese? Or we have some oysters on the
half shell."

"Oysters, I think."

"Very sensible, sir," Henri said, rolling his eyes suggestively and glancing toward the staircase leading to a second story.

Dex laughed. He held the snifter in the palm of his hand to warm the dollop of brandy, paused to breathe in the aroma, and sipped. The fiery liquid flowed across his tongue and stoked a fist-sized ball of heat in his belly. The heat lay there momentarily, then spread into and through his tissues. The first taste was so welcome he had another, and the second was even better.

"There you are, sir." Henri placed an etched crystal platter—no metallic serving pieces for the oysters, ever—on the bar and backed away.

Dex reached for a slim bottle of peppery vinegar sauce and tapped some onto each oyster with care, then raised the first wet shell to his lips and tipped its contents into his mouth. The oyster was plump and fresh and delicious. And wonder of wonders, free of sand or grit as well. Perfect.

Dexter finished the dozen oysters, had another brandy, then left the bar and wandered back toward the footlighted stage where the blond girl with the tiny voice and the magnificent tits was still trying to make herself heard over the rumble of the crowd.

"Is she any good?" he asked of a gentleman standing nearby.

"Who knows?" The fellow smiled. "But then again, who cares?"

"She's pretty."

"Aren't they all?"

"Have you spoken for her?" Dex inquired. He would not want to offend.

"Not I, sir. Too much for my purse."

Dex nodded and left the fellow, moving a little closer. The girl was pretty enough, no doubt about it. She had dimpled cheeks, shapely calves—her costume was cut high enough that he could see that quite plainly each time she swayed or turned with the music—and an impossibly narrow waist.

Not a bad little piece, he concluded after a bit of judicious examination. And having reached this tidbit of wisdom, he looked around until he caught the stage manager's eye, then crooked a finger.

· 12 ·

Ah, very nice. When seen up close like this she proved to be quite young. For once the carbide footlamps had offered no lie. She was young and dimpled and really very pretty indeed.

Dex handed her a tulip glass of champagne, and raised his own to her in a silent toast of genuine appreciation.

"Thank you, sir."

"My pleasure. What may I call you, dear?"

"My name is Dolly," she said, flashing her dimples.

Her name quite certainly was not Dolly, Dexter knew quite good and well, but no matter. This charade was all part and parcel of the little game they played.

"And you, sir?"

He hesitated. Normally he gave his true name. And why not? Nearly all the employees here knew him full well, had known him for years. But this evening . . . "Lewis," he said with a grin.

"Have I leave to call you by your first name then, Lewis?" The girl peered at him above the rim of the champagne glass, taking only a wee sip now and then.

"You should feel free to do as you please, my dear."

"In that case, handsome sir, may I make myself comfortable?"

He smiled, and Dolly set her glass of champagne delicately aside and began very slowly to disrobe.

Dexter knew a bravura performance when he saw one. He perched on the edge of the wide, soft bed in the second-story Rose Room—his favorite among them all with its soft coloring and subtle placement of lamps—and watched with true admiration as Dolly postured and preened before him, all the while pretending to act as if she were quite alone and unobserved.

Once she was naked, she smiled and performed a slow pirouette so that he could enjoy the view from all angles.

Dolly was one of those very rare girls—always quite young—who actually looked more attractive without clothing.

He had no idea how old she was. And knew better than to ask; her response would not be trustworthy regardless, and to invite the lie was to invite disappointment. Young, though. He was certain of that. Large as her breasts were, they were yet firm enough that they barely sagged.

In a few years they would hang shapeless and doughy below her waist. But now? They were magnificent.

Dexter rarely was impressed by a girl's tits anyway. Generally his tastes ran to something small and tidy.

But for Miss Dolly he was willing to make an exception.

The aureolae of her nipples were as large as demitasse saucers, but the nipples themselves were dainty enough. And light pink in color. Dex liked that. Dark, gross nipples did not please him. Dolly's did.

Her waist, amazingly enough, had been held in by no artificial constraints. No whalebone and laces as he'd fully expected, only a chemise and gown to cover her body. He couldn't help but comment on the fact.

"Do you like it?" she asked, holding her tummy in and turning back and forth so he could see the deep, hourglass inset of her waistline.

"Very much," was his honest answer.

"I had my lowest ribs removed. Can you see?" She moved closer, took his hands, and placed them on her flesh.

Her skin was cool and very soft to the touch.

If there were scars remaining from the surgery, Dex could not see them. Then Dolly moved even closer, leaning forward with a soft chuckle to capture his face between her breasts, and he could see nothing at all. But then vision was not the sense he was most interested in at that particular moment.

The girl smelled of perfume and powder. But lightly so, the scent not being so strong or so sweet as to cloy.

The texture of her skin was a marvel of satin matte perfection.

He began to lick and suckle what she presented to him. Dolly clasped his head in both hands and began to moan softly. Dex rather wished she wouldn't do that. Bedroom pretenses annoyed him. And she was, after all, a whore. She was here for the money, he for the pampering.

"What would you like me to do, Lewis?" she whispered. "I will do anything you want. Anything."

He smiled, and pulled her down onto the bed beside him. That was, of course, the whole idea, wasn't it. It was the reason they were both here.

"Everything," he whispered back, his lips playing now over hers.

Dolly laughed and ground her hips against him. "Here. Let me help you out of your clothes, Lewis, dear."

She tossed his things aside and pressed him flat on his back, straddling him with one shapely thigh on either side of his waist. Her breasts dangled over him like a pair of ripe melons. He took one in each hand and squeezed. Dolly tipped her head back and let her eyes droop shut.

She had—quite without him noticing—shifted position very, very slightly. Just enough to capture his erection within her body. He felt himself slide inside, and Dolly's eyes popped wide open.

"Goodness," she said. "I didn't expect anything like this."

"Mmm?"

"It's so big."

It was a comment he'd heard often enough before, but he never knew whether to believe it or not. After all, it wasn't as if he had any real basis for comparison himself. And any tart worth the fucking would flatter a man, especially when it came to his own manhood.

"Do you mind, Lewis dear?"

"Mind what?"

"I'm enjoying this. I always do when I'm on top. Would you mind if I get you off this way the first time? Then we can take our time and play some more after. But don't worry. I promise I can make it nice and hard again."

That was not of concern, but he was too polite to say so. And after all, what did he know about the things she might find to be common.

"Is that all right with you, Lewis dear?"

"Perfectly," he said. And it was. That was one of the lovely aspects to spending time with a willing girl like Miss Dolly. One didn't have to concern oneself with where to put things or what pleasures to avoid. "Nice" girls had to remain virgins, and that could be really quite annoying. With Dolly . . . well, as she'd already told him herself, she was willing to do anything he would enjoy, anything at all.

And given an entire night in which to think up playfully inventive variations, Dex suspected the two of them could take the idea of "anything" and expand the possibilities to a wonderful extent.

He certainly was willing to give that a try, Dex reflected as dear, dimpled Dolly began to slide more and more vigorously up and down the length of his impaling shaft.

· 13 ·

The captain of the *Queen of Hearts* blew his whistle as soon as they came around Tysdell Point a half mile below the Blackgum Bend landing. Three long blasts of the steam whistle rolled sharp and piercing across the rich, black earth of the delta, vibrated through the emerald forest and over the rows upon neat and orderly rows of calf-tall cotton.

Home. It was always good to come back. As much as he enjoyed the pleasures of the cities, this was and always would be Dex's home.

This time, though . . . this was the first time he was returning to a house without his father in it. The thought brought a pang of sorrow into his chest, and for a moment created such a lump in his throat that he was afraid he might do something to embarrass himself.

He held the grieving back, however, to be examined at some more convenient time, and tried to concentrate on watching the deckhands, their dark skin glistening with sweat, as they prepared the dock lines and made ready the port gangway.

The *Queen* veered slowly out of the main channel and drifted majestically, almost magically under the deft hand of the helmsman, toward the Yancey family's private landing.

Dex heard the clanging of signal bells from the pilot-house, and a moment later the sleek stern-wheeler began to back water, the paddles slapping hard onto the river surface with explosive splashes and a great boil of froth.

The *Queen* slid into place only feet from the dock, and four of the deck crew leaped the short distance from the rail onto the solid planking of the landing. Hawsers were made fast with quick wraps around the bollards, but the spring lines remained aboard. The steamer would be stopping only long enough to discharge Dex and his luggage.

Dex's trunk and two smaller Gladstones appeared on deck as if by sleight of hand, and were quickly transferred to land. The gangplank was lowered, but not secured. Dex made the obligatory courtesy call on the captain to express his thanks, then dropped lightly down the ladderway and across the swaying gangplank.

Almost as soon as Dex's feet touched the wood of the landing, the *Queen's* deckhands were retracting the gangway and taking in the hawsers.

Dex waved to the captain standing high above, and received a salute in return. The *Queen* moved sluggishly away from the dock, gathered steerage way, and began once more to churn her way upriver toward an eventual turnaround at Cincinnati.

Dex by then was already thinking about other things, though. He left the dock, standing on his own soil again, and looked away toward the roof of the house, visible beyond a screen of brush to the north and west. The landing had been built for ease of access from the fields, not the house, and that seemed to Dexter to be very much as it should be.

He heard the rattle of a wagon before he could see it, then observed a haze of rising dust on the far side of the brush. Good. Someone at the house had heard the signal and was coming to fetch him. He wouldn't have to walk home through this heat after all.

· 14 ·

It was a farm wagon that came for him, not the surrey, and the driver was a stable hand called Marquis, the sort of fancy name that had been his father's idea of a joke on the same order as naming a sow Queenie.

There were a pair of young boys riding on the tailgate. They jumped down and carried Dex's trunk and other baggage to the wagon. Marquis acted as if he didn't know if he should get down to help Dex onto the driving box, or if he should stay where he was to handle the horses. He sat in fearful indecision until Dex was in the wagon and there was no longer any need for a decision.

"What's wrong with you, Marquis? You look like you've got a fever or something. You feeling poorly, boy?"

"Naw, suh, I fine." Marquis bit his underlip and concentrated on driving the team. The two youngsters in back were silent also.

Something was bothering them. Dex was sure of that. He was equally sure that he could not wring the truth out of them without creating resentment, and then it would likely turn out to be nothing more important than dissatisfaction with the latest distribution of rations. Which

nowadays were paid for out of wages tallied, and therefore
had become a source of discontent. That sort of thing had
never happened when the laborers were chattel, but was
commonplace now.

Marquis drove Dexter to the front of the big house, let
him off, and drove around back so the luggage could be
taken inside.

Once indoors, Dex could see Lewis bent over some
papers at the desk where their father had spent so many
hours. Dex knew good and well Lewis would have heard
the steam whistle, the rattle of the wagon, and now his
own footsteps on the hardwood floor. If Lewis chose to
ignore his return, well, that was up to Lewis. Dex called
out a cheery hello in spite of it, and went into the back
of the house to see what Aunt Lottie had by way of a
snack. She generally had pastries on hand. Pralines thick
with golden nuggets of pecans, if one was lucky.

There were no pralines today, but there were cinnamon
and pecan sweet rolls. That was almost as good.

Dex helped himself to a sticky bun and bit into it.

"Don't you be ruinin' your supper, young man. I won't
have it."

"You know nothing could take my appetite, Auntie.
Not so long as you're doing the cooking."

"One more then. But that's all. You hear me, white
boy? Just one more."

Dex took two, winked at the woman, and feigned great
fear when she grabbed for a rolling pin to wave at him.
He popped the last morsel of his second sweet bun into
his mouth and licked his fingertips. "Where's James,
Aunt Lottie? I was expecting to see him at the landing
like usual."

The cook turned to tend a fire that Dex could see
needed no tending.

"Aunt Lottie?"

She didn't answer.

"Aunt Lottie." His voice was firmer now, sharper.
"Where is James, Aunt Lottie?"

"That boy don't work here no more, Mistuh Dexter. That boy been fired."

Dexter gaped, for a moment too speechless to ask any further questions.

"I don't know nothin' 'bout it neither, Mistuh Dexter. Nothin'. You hear me? Nothin'." She let the iron door to the firebox slam closed, grabbed up her skirts, and hurried outside toward the summer kitchen.

Dex found himself standing alone in the house with a sticky, unwanted pecan roll in his hand and empty puzzlement in his thoughts.

·15·

Lewis continued to pore over the papers. Dex would have been willing to bet everything he had—little though that seemed to be—that the back of Lewis's neck was crawling. Lewis knew he was there, dammit. Lewis surely could *feel* him standing there. But Lewis gave no indication that he knew Dexter was in the same parish, much less inside the same room with him.

"Let me know when you're ready to talk," Dex said, his voice controlled and calm. He knew the best way to set Lewis off was to display anger. In a situation like this it would be anger that Lewis wanted. Denying him that gave Dex a measure of control over the situation. Lewis wouldn't like that, of course, but so what.

Dex walked over to the sideboard where the best brandies and whiskeys were kept, and poured himself a tot of the colorless liquor their father had always favored above all others. The white whiskey was, of course, quite perfectly illegal. It was distilled by an old man who was said to have been ancient when Charles Yancey was born.

Dexter suspected that was an exaggeration, but he knew for a fact that the man had originally been bought by his and Lewis's grandfather Evan Yancey. Dex had seen the bill of sale on the old fellow. And the manumission document that Charles Yancey had prepared long before the general emancipation. The former slave still made whiskey the old-fashioned way, with multiple runs and not a grain of sugar permitted anywhere near the fermenting pots. His product was famous, if circumspectly so, for a hundred miles upriver or down. Justly so too. The whiskey the old man made had the clarity of springwater, the flavor of divine nectar, and went down so smooth and mellow that drinking it was said to be akin to swallowing a warm cloud.

Dex poured a generous measure from the cut-glass decanter kept beside those of the "better" liquors and liqueurs, then carried his glass to a wing-back leather chair and settled into it to wait for Lewis to acknowledge his presence.

He hadn't long to wait.

"Back from your carousing, I see," Lewis said as he swung his chair around to face his very slightly older brother. His voice was testy and his expression pugnacious.

Lewis wanted a fight. Dexter could see that, and was determined not to give him one. He faked a smile and said, "Yes, and it was great. You should have come with me."

Lewis sniffed. "When have you ever invited me?"

"I used to."

"You haven't taken me on your trips for years."

"I used to ask. You never wanted to come."

"No, and I wouldn't have this time either. You're a wastrel, Dexter. A dilettante."

Dexter grinned, quite genuinely this time. "That's true, Lewis, but even you will have to admit that I'm a damned *good* wastrel and dilettante."

"Is that all you came in here for? To waste my time with idle boasting about nothing at all?"

Dex became serious again. "You know very good and well what I came to talk to you about."

"All right. Fine. I'd knew you'd bring it up. It's about that pet nigger of yours."

Dex nodded. "I want to find out what happened to James, that's true enough."

"He quit."

"I heard he was fired."

"He quit, I say. Are you going to take some nigger's word over mine?"

"You know better than that, Lewis. Why did James quit? Surely he would wait for me to get back before he'd just walk out."

"The black-assed son of a bitch quit, that's all."

Dex took a sip of whiskey and, his expression calm, waited. He knew Lewis. His brother would want to show off his new authority. Lewis wouldn't let it go at this.

"I gave him a chore to do and it was beneath his high-yellow dignity, if you can imagine that, a nigger thinking he's too good for honest work."

"What'd you want James to do, Lewis?"

"The black bastard hasn't done a lick of useful work around here since he was last needed for your play-pet. You know that? And he's been drawing cash pay. Did you know that, Dexter? I didn't. Poppa paid that black son of a bitch forty dollars a month, cash money. For nothing. Can you believe it? Forty dollars. Cash. Well, I won't. You can count on that, let me tell you. Poppa was too easy on the niggers. Forty dollars!" Lewis's agitation had him on the edge of his chair.

"When I saw that in the books I called him in here. Told him right off his days of laying in the sunshine at Yancey expense were over with. Done. If he wanted work he could have it, same as any other nigger. Fifteen dollars a month, less the cost for food and housing. Same pay and the same work too. Field work. That's his proper place anyhow, you know. Picking cotton. About damn time your nigger learns what it feels like to do stoop labor. About damn time he feels what a sore back is like and raw hands."

Dex knew it was a mistake even while he was saying

it, but he just couldn't stop himself. With a smirk and a shake of his head he said, "And how is it that you'd know anything about that, Lewis? You haven't picked any more cotton than I have, and I know for damn sure you could put all the cotton I've ever picked into your ear and still be able to hear just fine."

"It's just that sort of smart-aleck attitude that your pet James had, Dexter."

"He wouldn't pick cotton, eh?"

"The nigger son of a bitch sassed me, damn him. I should've had him strung up and whipped. He stood right here in this room and he said he wouldn't . . . never mind exactly what it was he said. Bastard sassed me, and that's the truth. Then he walked out of here. I haven't seen him since. Don't want to either. I wouldn't hire him now if he came crawling back on his belly and begged me for a job. I wouldn't let that black bastard clean out my thunder mug."

"It isn't legal to whip nigras anymore, Lewis. I don't supposed anybody got around to telling you that."

"Bullshit. You've never heard of a white man being charged for anything like that and you never will. I don't give a crap what some priss-ass Yankees pass for laws up north there. Niggers aren't human. Not completely, they aren't."

Dex took another swallow of his whiskey. He wasn't about to get into an argument with Lewis on that subject. It wasn't worth the bother. Lewis—and for that matter a good three fourths of the whites in the parish—believed what they believed and would carry those convictions with them to their graves. "I wasn't asking about nigras in general, Lewis. I just wanted to know about James."

"He won't ever see another penny of Yancey money, Dexter. Not as long as I'm alive, he won't. And don't you think you can hire him back. You can't. I'm in charge now. Don't you ever forget that."

Dex shrugged. "I know you won't understand this, Lewis, and prob'ly won't believe it either, but I really don't mind. The truth is that you will do a much better job of running the plantation than I would have. Heck, if I'd gotten control I would have asked you to handle most of it for me anyhow."

"You put on a bold face, don't you?" Lewis challenged.

"No, I mean it. I'd already thought about that before the, um, the reading of the new will."

Lewis gave him a look of contempt. "Do you want to know something funny, Dexter? I almost do believe that. But then you've always been a fool, haven't you."

Dex shrugged again and drained off the last of the mellow whiskey. "Fire whoever you like, Lewis. That is up to you." He grinned. "But keep old Cornfed in the budget. I'd sure as hell hate to have to do without his whiskey." He returned his empty glass to the tray on the sideboard and left the room, very careful to show Lewis none of the anger he was feeling. Or the odd sense of loss.

· 16 ·

Normally Dex would have taken his horse cross-country to old Maybelle's house. It was a route he—and James—had taken probably a thousand times or more, often together, sometimes alone.

Now, though, today, Dex felt a certain sense of formality about the call. He rode all the way out to the road and turned down it.

Aunt Maybelle had been the Yancey family cook from the time of Dexter's birth and then some. When he and Lewis were boys, it was Aunt Maybelle who gave them treats from the kitchen, swats on the backside when they erred, and hugs or sympathy whenever those were needed. Apart from being James's mother, Aunt Maybelle had been as close as Dex ever knew to having a mother of his own.

Lewis had never been particularly close to the old woman, and had resented her attempts at discipline, rejected her hugs. But Dexter loved her as completely as if she genuinely was his mother, and could not begin to fathom Lewis's contrariness.

Lewis, for reasons that he'd never bothered to explain to his brother, had seemed happy when age and dropsy forced Aunt Maybelle into retirement and Lottie replaced her.

Their father, Charles Yancey, on the other hand, seemed as sorrowful as Dexter to see Aunt Maybelle leave the kitchen. He gave her an honorable retirement, setting aside a small parcel of good land at the southwest corner of the Yancey holdings, building there a small but tidy home for her, and awarding her a pensioner's income. Each spring Charles also never failed to send a crew of workmen to Aunt Maybelle's to see to any repairs, prepare her garden plot, and accomplish whatever other labor she might need. Dex hoped Lewis would respect their father's wishes enough to continue that help. He knew Lewis would have no interest in helping Aunt Maybelle, but perhaps Dex could convince him to maintain the practice on behalf of Charles Yancey.

Not that Dex would bring it up soon. He knew better than that. Sometime later next winter perhaps, but certainly not now while Lewis was still hot on the subject of James.

A small smile creased Dex's face when he thought about James and Lewis. He wondered just exactly what it was that James had said to Dexter's baby brother. It must have been powerful, whatever it was.

Dex's black gelding cantered smoothly down the road, making quick work of the several miles. Dex brought the horse down to a jog when the lane leading to Aunt Maybelle's came into view, then slowed to a walk as he reined into it to allow the horse to cool off.

The garden was already taken care of for this year, he saw with satisfaction as he neared the house. Pea vines were already recognizable, and several rows of tiny bright green shoots showed that other varieties were emerging also. Aunt Maybelle would know what each would be. An expert gardener might well be able to identify the eventual produce by looking at the developing plants. Dexter had not the vaguest notion what any of it might be.

He knew, however, that Aunt Maybelle would turn

whatever it was into something mouthwateringly fine.

There was no sign of the old woman herself. The rocker that used to sit close to the ovens in the Yancey kitchen was empty. The battered old rocker held a thousand memories for Dex. He was glad Aunt Maybelle still had it.

He dismounted and tied his horse to the handle of the pump Charles Yancey had had installed in place of the usual, and difficult to operate, bucket-and-windlass method of drawing water. There had been a flurry of disapproving gossip when the elder Yancey did that. A good many complained because there were few white families in the parish who owned pumps. Some accused Charles Yancey of coddling his servant; others grumbled that a luxury like that would make Aunt Maybelle uppity. Charles Yancey never bothered to answer any of his neighbors' comments. He did, however, respond. He bought all the pumps on hand in town, and had more brought in on special order. Within two months every well on Yancey property was serviced by the latest and most modern hand pumps available.

Charles had liked that so much that he went a step further and ordered in some of the newfangled wind pumps to draw water for the livestock, and a premier model that now kept the household cistern full.

God, Dex thought as he tied his horse there, he was going to miss his father.

"Aunt Maybelle? Where are you, Auntie? If you have any gentlemen callers inside there, you'd best see that everybody is decent, because I'm fixing to come inside."

Dex ran lightly up the steps to Aunt Maybelle's porch and let himself into the cool, shadowy interior of her house.

· 17 ·

The old woman was seated in a cane-back chair with her feet and lower legs propped on a small cask that was padded with a thick pillow laid on top. Dex's heart nearly broke every time he looked at her. Aunt Maybelle had once been strong and vital. Now dropsy had turned her legs into grotesque caricatures of legs. From the knees down her legs had become huge sausage rolls of swollen, fluid-laden flesh that were painful to look at. Dex did not know if they hurt as bad as they looked. Aunt Maybelle never complained if they did.

She saw him come inside and struggled to rise, but he motioned her back into her chair and hurried to give her an embrace.

"You came to see me, honey."

"Don't I always?" He kissed the old woman's mahogany-colored cheek and hugged her again.

"James told me you was away."

He nodded. "Down the river. Having fun."

"Just so you be a good boy."

"Yes, ma'am." He was not precisely sure what was required in order for one to be a "good boy," and suspected he was better off not going into detail about it.

This way he could assure Aunt Maybelle that he was indeed the good boy she wanted him to be and not necessarily breach her faith in him.

"You want I should make you some biscuits, honey?"

"No, you set still. I'm not hungry." Dex knew better than to say anything that could be interpreted as a compliment for Lottie's cooking. Aunt Maybelle had *not* been ready to give up her authority over the kitchen—and the family—when Charles Yancey retired her from the hard work that was involved. Involved, Dex was willing to concede at this late date, in *both* areas of responsibility.

"You come to see about my other boy, didn't you, honey?" Other boy. For as long as Dex could remember, Aunt Maybelle had referred to both him and James as her boys. In fact, as far as he could determine, the old woman genuinely considered Dexter to be a son too.

"Yes, ma'am. I heard there was some trouble."

"No trouble. Just that white boy showing off, making sure ever'body know he the boss now."

Aunt Maybelle hadn't ever liked Lewis. Dex knew that. He doubted that his father ever suspected it, but Dex knew. "That white boy" was a common term when she spoke of Lewis. There were other terms she used too, but Dex wasn't supposed to know about those, and pretended not to have overheard them.

"Is James here, Auntie?"

"No, he working today, honey."

Dex raised an eyebrow.

"He working for Mistuh Thibidoux."

Dex's eyebrow remained up.

"He chopping cotton, honey."

"I ought to ride over there and take a look at that. Rag on him a little," Dex said.

"Don't you do that, honey. Please don't you do that. James, he be ashamed if you was to see him workin' like a common field han'."

Dex's amusement faded. "I only meant. . . ."

"I knows what you mean, honey. James, he would too by-an'-by. But not now. Give him time. You know? Later on, he get used to bein' what he is anyhow, later on you go past. Stop an' make him smile some. My boy James could use some smilin' right now, honey.''

No, there was no amusement in this. None at all. Dex bent and gave the old woman another kiss on her leathery cheek. ''What can I get for you, Auntie?''

''I'm fine, honey. Don't need nothing.''

''Are you all right for money?''

She nodded. Dex did not believe it. He dug into his pocket and pulled out what he had left over after his gaming and good times in New Orleans. He did not bother to count it. He knew it was not much. Not enough probably. But it was what he had. He tucked the coins into Aunt Maybelle's palm and wrapped both of his hands around hers to prevent her from trying to refuse the gift.

''Do me a favor, Auntie?''

''Tell me, boy. You remember any time your whole life long that I wouldn't do whatever you ask?''

Dex smiled and shook his head. Then he grinned. ''Sure, I do. You wouldn't let me climb up in that pecan tree. Remember that time?''

Aunt Maybelle laughed. ''I remember. Broke two limbs off that little tree and one on you.''

''And then it was you that took care of me after. Set and wrapped my arm and washed my tears off and held me on your lap till the hurting went away, didn't you?''

She seemed pleased that he remembered. As if he could ever forget.

''When James comes home this evening, tell him I'd like to see him, would you?'' Dex had another thought. ''If he isn't too tired. If he is, if he can't come over some evening this week, I'll be by on Sunday.''

''We be here after church. Be down by the creek in the morning, though. Don't you come by here early thinking to keep James from taking me to church. I won't have none of that, mind.''

''Yes, ma'am.''

''Better yet, you do come by early. That way you and

James both takes me to church.'' She grinned, pleased with herself for the idea.

"Maybe we can do just that, Auntie. Maybe we can." It wasn't a promise. Exactly. But he knew how much it would please Aunt Maybelle if he did manage to wake up early on Sunday. Any Sunday. She did love to sing the fine old spirituals. She couldn't parade and stamp her feet any longer, but she dearly loved to raise her voice in songs of praise and glory.

"I tell him," she promised.

Dex squeezed the old woman's hands, then went back out into the heat of the day to retrieve his gelding and head back to Blackgum Bend.

James. Chopping cotton. Incredible!

· 18 ·

Dex sat in silence at the dinner table. It was not that he felt unsociable. It was just that his only dining companion was Lewis, and at the moment neither of them seemed to have much to say to the other. Dex took a draught of the delicate, slightly fruity wine that their father had so favored, then set his stemmed glass down beside the elegant china and ornately fashioned silver of the Yancey dinner service. Dex thought it faintly silly to lay such a fine table for just the two of them, but their father had always insisted on it, and now the tradition continued under Lewis's guiding hand.

Lewis hunched over his plate and shoveled another hugely overburdened fork full of candied yams into his face. So much for elegance, Dex thought, dabbing at his mouth with a linen napkin. It was a wonder Lewis was not fat as a harvest season hog considering his appetites. To say nothing of his table manners.

But then Lewis's appetites and Dexter's had always been very different, for as long as Dex could remember and probably beyond that.

"Wine, suh?"

Dex nodded absently and the serving girl, a budding

child of thirteen or so named Clara, poured, a look of intense concentration on her dark face and the tip of her tongue showing in one corner of her mouth as she labored to perform the task exactly as she'd been taught.

Clara was new to the dining room. Before, she'd been assigned to help Lottie in the kitchen while Lewis's favorite Netty handled the dining room service. Dex hadn't seen Netty since . . . since the day their father died, he supposed.

Feeling an impulse to say something, anything, that would break the silence and perhaps bridge some of the gap between him and Lewis, Dex had another sip of wine—it really did reflect the excellence of their father's tastes—and said, "Where's Netty, Lewis?"

From the far end of the table Lewis glared at him. "That's none of your damned business. And I'll thank you to remember that she prefers to be called Annetta."

Dex couldn't help himself. It was the wrong thing to do. He *knew* that. Even before he opened his mouth he knew he should remain silent. But he just couldn't help taking a little dig at his often puritanical baby brother. "Going to have Annetta start taking her meals with the white folk, are we, Lewie?" Lewis despised being called Lewie.

The glare down the table became all the darker. "I shall not dignify that with a response," Lewis declared.

Dex grinned at him. "You just did, though, didn't you."

If they had been a few years younger—not really all that many years actually—Lewis would have thrown something at him. Not a punch, though. Lewis had learned very early not to engage Dexter in any physical confrontation because Dexter invariably came out on top in those.

Food, though, crystal, anything close to hand and manageable might have come flying. Their father never saw any of those outbursts, of course. They were reserved for Dexter's eyes only. Well, his and the servants'. But then the nigras didn't count. They knew better than to tell tales on their betters.

It was mean and petty of him, he supposed, but Dex felt a tiny bit better now that he had Lewis's dander up. He helped himself to a dab of Lottie's tangy slaw. Apparently the cabbage, a cold-weather crop anyway, was already producing.

Dex was pondering a second small slice of ham when Lewis spoke again. "I'm making some changes," he announced.

No, Dex decided, the ham was good, but the one piece was enough. "You're in charge, Lewie. Do whatever you think is right." No ham then, but another biscuit. A small one. He selected one from the platter and broke it open. Dex was reaching for the butter dish when Lewis said, "I'm putting you on an allowance."

Dexter lost interest in the butter. "What did you say?"

"I said I'm putting you on an allowance, dammit. Papa let you run wild. You've been wasting our money, throwing it away hand over fist."

"I have not," Dex protested. "I've been enjoying it. There's a difference."

"You've spent it on whiskey and whores and wild times."

Dex's face split wide in a grin. "Exactly. But you can't say that I've been wasting it. I enjoyed every penny, I can assure you."

"That may have been good enough for Papa, Dexter, but it won't make any impression on me. From now on you get twenty dollars a month. That's it."

"Twenty dollars? Lewis, I spend that much on bay rum to splash on my cheeks. Why, we pay the hands almost that much!"

"That's another thing. I'm cutting the niggers' pay to twelve dollars. They aren't worth fifteen."

"Lewis, they barely clear anything now after we take back food and rent. If you cut them back three dollars, they won't have anything left."

"That's their problem. And let me ask you. *Dexie!* What happened to Lewie? Huh? It's Lewis now, isn't it?"

Dexie. Lewis hadn't called him that in years. He'd quit

a long time ago when he'd realized that it honestly didn't matter to Dex if he was called that or not, unlike Lewis and the hated nickname Lewie.

"Hell, Lewis, I expect next you'll want me to call you Mr. Yancey. Would you like that? Huh? Lewie?"

"You son of a bitch . . ."

Lewis had gone too far. Dex was out of his chair and charging down the table toward him. Lewis threw his hands up and leaned backward, almost toppling over. He managed to right himself, and looked so comical doing it that Dexter almost laughed out loud at him. It did have the effect of blunting Dexter's rush of anger, however.

"I didn't mean to say that. You know I didn't," Lewis protested.

"Damn you, Lewis . . ."

"I said I was sorry, didn't I?"

In fact he had not. But Dex did not split that hair. Still burning, albeit on a lower flame, Dex stood towering over his seated brother. "I don't agree with what you're doing, Lewis. You are going to hurt Blackgum Bend, and I hate that. But you are the one who was given control. I'm not disputing that. I just wish you'd learn to use it wisely. As for this so-called allowance bullshit, we'll talk about that some other time. I don't think either one of us is much in the mood for it right now."

Dex turned and stalked out of the dining room. He strode out onto the porch and snapped at the servant who was waiting there, "Bring up that red gelding for me."

"Yes, suh, boss."

A canter through the night air would be calming, Dex thought. So might a tussle with Lucy Anne. Perhaps he just might drop in for a visit with Merriman Thibidoux. It would be the neighborly thing to do. Dex marched back inside to get his hat and riding crop while the horse was being saddled.

◆ 19 ◆

"Dexter Yancey. So nice of you to drop by. How are you, son? I know you miss your father. It was a bitter loss for us all, Dexter. For you and your brother most of all." The old gentleman smiled. The supper hour was past, and Merriman Thibidoux wore freshly blacked shoes rather than the customary riding boots. He was rather elegantly attired in a velveteen jacket with satin lapels, high-waisted trousers that showed off a figure that was trim and fit for a man his age, a silk shirt, and a scarlet cravat. Merriman Thibidoux was everything that was fine about a gentleman planter. And a good bit of everything too that was less than fine. He was decorous, proper, courtly, courteous . . . and vain, argumentative, proud to the point of arrogance. "Would you join me in a brandy, Dexter?"

"I would, sir, thank you. And would you be kind enough, sir, to have one of your people inform Lucy Anne that I've called?"

"This way. Please." Thibidoux lightly touched Dex's elbow and guided him in the direction of the smoking room. "I would be glad to have you announced to my daughter, Dexter, but I fear Lucy Anne is indisposed this evening.''

"I see," Dex said. He stopped and bowed rather stiffly. "In that case, sir, at your convenience please convey to her my compliments and my wishes for her early recovery.''

"That will be my pleasure, Dexter, and I know she will cherish your good wishes.''

"She will always have those, sir. But of course you knew that.''

"I did indeed, Dexter. Now about that brandy . . .''

"I hope you will forgive me, Mr. Thibidoux, sir, but I only now remembered a previously made engagement. May I lay claim to your brandy on another occasion?''

"At your convenience, of course. You are welcome in this house any time, Dexter. You know that.''

"Yes, sir, I do, thank you.''

Dex bowed to Old Man Thibidoux, retrieved his hat and crop from the liveried servant posted in the foyer, and hurried out into the night.

Indisposed my ass, Dex thought rather bitterly as he reclaimed the leggy red horse and picked the animal up into a thundering run away from the Thibidoux mansion.

Indisposed. Bull. Disinherited. That was the word. And not Lucy Anne, but Dex. Dex, who now could not deliver to Merriman the river landing he so badly wanted. Lucy Anne was now and continually would be indisposed at least insofar as the disinherited elder Yancey was concerned.

Indisposed. Shit.

Dex raked the sides of the red, regretting the childish petulance immediately, and raced through the night unmindful of ruts or potholes that might trip the speeding animal.

He urged the horse faster and faster until the wind of their passage roared in his ears.

He could not outrun the insult and the indignity that he'd suffered back there at the hands of Lucy Anne's old prick of a father.

· 20 ·

"Man, you sure know how to take good care of a horse, don't you? You want to tell me what's on your mind that'd make you ride like a crazy man?"

"Not really." Dex tossed his reins to James, went over to the pump, and yanked the handle up and down several times to get the cold water gushing, then leaned down and stuck his head into the flow. He yelped and shivered but held it there, the icy liquid drenching his shirt and seeping into the waistband of his trousers. When the flow slowed to a trickle and finally stopped altogether, Dex stood and shook his head vigorously back and forth, sending droplets flying in all directions.

"Feel better?" James asked.

"I feel great." It was a lie, of course, and both of them knew that. But what would be the point of complaining.

Dex wiped his face and turned. James had the saddle off the sweaty red gelding, and was busy wiping the animal down with a scrap of burlap. "You don't have to do that," Dex said.

James grinned at him, his teeth white in the moonlight in front of Aunt Maybelle's house. "Why's that, because I'm not employed at Blackgum Bend anymore?"

"Yeah. Among other reasons. You want to tell me what happened between you and Lewis?"

"Not really," James said, parroting Dex's own comment moments earlier. He continued working on the horse, finishing with the back and starting in on the forequarters.

"Fair enough," Dexter said. The two friends had long ago reached a tacit understanding that there would at times be areas of privacy that either might desire and that the other would agree to respect. Wheedling and prying were outside the bounds of the friendship. "Did you get my message from your mama?"

" 'Course I did."

"If you went over to the house tonight, I'm sorry. I wasn't. . . ."

"Don't apologize. I didn't go."

"No?"

James shrugged, moved to the off side of the gelding, and resumed rubbing. "Too damn tired, Dex. Too damn purantee bone-weary to walk all the way over there and back tonight."

"I didn't think of that. I'm sorry."

"No need for you to say sorry. It's none of it your fault." James straightened, leaning backward from the waist and planting both hands into the small of his back.

"Hard work chopping cotton, is it?"

"Harder than I ever suspected, I tell you that."

"You don't have to do it, you know."

"Got to do something, Dex. Can't support two people on what we can grow in Mama's garden."

"You don't have to chop cotton."

"True. I expect I could go read law instead. Maybe apply to college. Go off and become a doctor."

"You could handle either one of those if you wanted to."

"Smart ain't enough, Dex. Don't go stupid white on me."

"I know." Dex began to grin. "I could ride home and fetch back a poke of flour."

Both began to laugh then. James knew perfectly well what Dex was thinking about. When they'd been children, six or possibly seven years old, they had decided that James really could pass for white if only they could think of a way to change the color of his skin. As an experiment they sneaked into the larder and made off with a sack of rare and very expensive white flour that had been purchased for the baking of a cake. Dex could no longer recall the occasion that demanded the luxury of such a cake. Whatever it was, it passed without the intended cake because long before that could happen the flour was used in an effort to turn James white.

The boys' disappointment with the results of their efforts quickly disappeared in the hilarity of James's appearance with his face and most of his body encased in dough—they'd thought to make the flour stick better to James's skin by first getting him thoroughly wet—a failure so delightful to contemplate that they used the remainder of the bag by plastering Dex with flour too.

Aunt Maybelle had taken a switch to both their backsides after that escapade. But she'd never told Charles Yancey what happened to the supply of precious wheat flour. Instead she'd merely said that the cake did not turn out and she would not shame Blackgum Bend by offering the Yancey guests a failure. She'd served some other sweet and delectable concoction in its place. But neither Dex nor James was apt to forget their one long-ago attempt to turn him white.

"Dammit, James, get serious for a minute here," Dex protested.

"Don't look at me. I'm not the one brought it up."

"You have choices, you know. That's all I'm saying."

"Do I? Do you think so, Dexter? Fine. In that case, name me three choices. Any three at all."

Dex opened his mouth. Nothing came out.

"All right then. How about two? Can you think of two other things a smart black boy can do for a living around here? Can you do that, Dexter? Just two. No? Then how about one. One other genuine possibility. Just one."

Dexter's shoulders slumped. "Got you a point there, don't you."

"Yeah. I expect I do." James finished rubbing down the horse and tied its reins to the pump. He tossed the hunk of burlap onto the porch and went over to sit on the edge of the porch floor. His movements were slow and weary.

"I can't get you back on the payroll," Dex apologized.

"We both know that."

"The worst thing about it is that you were in Poppa's will."

James looked up. "That lawyer did try and say something like that when Lewis was busy kicking me outa the house that day, didn't he."

Dex nodded. "Poppa told me about it one time. I never knew the details, but he mentioned to me once that he was leaving something to you and to your mama too."

"He really done that, you say?"

"Uh-huh. I expect he forgot about those other provisions when he was scratching out the new will. He didn't have Lawyer Whitley with him then."

James made a face. "Just Lewis."

Dex shrugged. "I don't mind."

"Maybe you don't, white boy, but I sure do. Do you know how damn far it is to walk all the way over to those fields, work the whole long day, and then walk back here to Mama? Shee-it." James smiled. "I ain't used to this abuse, white boy. I a house nigger, I is. I built fo' speed, not plowin'. I a lover, not a fighter."

"You're an idiot, not a poet." Dex gave James a playful shove, and got one in return.

"Yeah," James said. "I'm that too."

"We'll have to get you a horse."

"Sure. Whyn't you get me a carriage and footman too while you're at it. You really do want the night riders to come after me for being uppity, don't you."

"Fine. No horse. How about a nice slow mule. A little one. Nobody would get after you about a mule. And you could use it to plow the garden too. I think it's pretty safe to assume that Lewis won't be sending any of our people over to help your mama with the planting again any time soon.''

"A mule. Yeah, I could use a mule, all right. But I want a big mule. And fast. Gotta be one fast son of a bitch so I can make some money off those lazy layabout niggers down at Hope Flats.''

"You really do know how to push a fellow, don't you.''

"Hell, Dexter, if a man's gonna wish, he might as well wish big.''

"All right, dammit. A big mule then. And fast. Fastest damn mule in the parish.''

"I want the fastest damn mule in *Loo*-siana, if you please.''

"Uppity nigger.''

"Ignorant white boy.''

The two friends sat there grinning at each other.

God knows why—for sure he couldn't figure it out for himself as absolutely nothing had really changed—but Dex felt better about things than he had when he got there.

• 21 •

Dexter came downstairs later than usual. He took his seat at the dining table and shook a napkin loose, then tucked it into his collar.

"Your usual breakfast, suh?" Clara asked from the doorway leading into the kitchen. Dex nodded, and the girl brought coffee and a pecan-topped sweet roll to hold his interest and his appetite until ham, eggs, grits, and biscuits were made ready.

As he was finishing his meal Dex asked, "Has my brother been down yet?"

"Yessuh, Mastuh Yancey done been an' gone. Real early."

Dex grunted. It did not seem worth the bother to inquire as to where Lewis went. In truth he did not much care, and in any event was pleased to have a breakfast in peace and quiet. He sopped a last bite of soft, crumbling biscuit in a pool of honey and idly asked, "*Master* Yancey, is it now, Clara? What happened to 'mister' around here?"

"Mastuh Yancey say he want to be called mastuh from now on, Mastuh Dexter, suh."

Dex shook his head. "Nothing so grand as that for me, child. Mister will do me just fine."

"Yes, suh. Thank you, suh."

Dex looked at the girl, but decided against saying anything further. He could not help but wonder, though, if Clara had had a sudden onslaught of good manners since being moved into the dining room . . . or if she'd developed a sudden case of fear. He hoped for the former, but suspected the latter.

Lewis had already announced he was cutting back on wages for their people. If he went too far and really pissed off the hands and the servants, it would be all of Blackgum Bend and not only Lewis that suffered the consequences, damn him. And that event Dexter would find intolerable.

Still, that was something that was beyond Dexter's control, and was best left for worrying about at a more convenient moment. Right now he had other fish to fry, and topping that list was the task of trying to make sure that the things their father had wanted around here were taken care of in spite of Lewis and his petty niggardliness. Things like making sure that Aunt Maybelle and James were taken care of. Dexter knew damn good and well that Charles Yancey had had no intention of changing that part of his will in the deathbed declaration that Lewis arranged to his own benefit. And if Lewis would not honor the original intent, then Dexter would.

He would start, he thought, by making sure James had that mule they'd joked about last night. A mule would do much more than provide James with transportation to and from a poor job with Merriman Thibidoux. It would also be a surety against future needs because a man with a mule could always find work, for the mule if not for himself. Dex knew that, and believed that buying James his mule would not be quite the same as providing an annuity—as Charles Yancey had desired—but would certainly be the closest thing to it that Dex could manage for them.

He finished his breakfast, dropped his soiled napkin beside the plate, and ambled into the study that used to serve as their father's office. It did not displease Dex at the moment to remember that Lewis happened to be out of the house.

Yawning, his belly full and a good night's sleep behind him, Dex felt fairly at peace when he bent down and pulled open the middle right-hand drawer of their father's ancient rolltop desk.

His eyes grew wide and his body stiffened in sudden anger at what he saw there. Or more accurately, at what he did not see.

◆ 22 ◆

The black horse was not lathered exactly, for the run had not been all that long, but the animal certainly had worked up a good sweat in that short distance. Dexter chided himself for the way he'd taken to using horseflesh lately. But dammit all . . .

He reined the black down to a canter, then to a slow jog as he came out of the low-lying brush of a fallow field and into the greening and orderly field where they'd said Lewis would be found.

Dex brought the horse to a complete halt and stood in his stirrups, puzzled at first because despite the late-morning hour, there was no one working in the field. Surely it was too late for the mid-morning break, and much too early for dinner. There ought to be fifteen or twenty hands inching along between the rows, hoes in hand, chopping the life-sapping weeds away from the young cotton plants.

Instead the field was empty save for the plants themselves and the shadow of a fast-moving cloud high overhead.

Dex looked a second time. And a third. Finally he relaxed and let himself back down onto the saddle. They were gathered in the shade of some oak trees on the far side of the field. Dex nudged the black forward again and cantered around the edges of the field rather than cut across through the crop rows.

He found the hands there, all right. Also the gang foreman Walter, a former slave whose family had belonged to the Yanceys for several generations back. And also Lewis Yancey, the self-proclaimed new Master of Blackgum Bend.

Not a single soul among them looked very happy at the moment.

Dex suspected he could guess why that might be so.

He brought the gelding down to a walk so as to raise no dust as he entered the cool shelter offered by the oaks.

"We don' mean no disrespec', Mistuh Yancey, suh, but we don' have to take no shit off'n no man. Not no mo' we don't, nossuh." It was Walter who was talking, and Dex knew that to be a very bad sign indeed. If any of the common hands complained, well, that was nothing to fret about. Field hands always complained. Hard work was their lot and complaint was their right and always had been, even before slavery came to its end. But when the foreman complained, well that was a far more serious matter indeed.

Dex reined the black to a halt and remained there, not sure he wanted to ride into the thick of this until he knew what the problem was. Knew for certain sure, that is. He suspected. And hoped that he was wrong.

With Lewis, though, well, with Lewis in charge, it seemed very unlikely to Dexter that he was misjudging his brother's actions or the likely responses that would come from the hands.

Dex would certainly like to be proven wrong about that. But he didn't really expect that he would be.

◆ 23 ◆

"What are you doing here, dammit?" Lewis snapped when he saw Dex join them.

"I came to discuss something with you. In private."

"Whatever it is, it can wait."

"I'm sure it can," Dex said in his most agreeable tone of voice. It would serve none of them any purpose for Lewis to get his back up now. "I, uh, I'll wait over there." He nodded toward the far end of the oak grove, then without waiting for Lewis's answer, jogged well out of hearing before he stopped again.

Lewis, Walter, and the hands spent long minutes arguing. Dex did not have to hear to know there was rancor in the air. Body posture and the sharp, abrupt bobbing of heads whenever anyone spoke was enough to convey that message just as clearly as the words could have done. No one was happy over there.

Dex dismounted and tied the reins of the gelding to a shrub, idled about, stepped behind a tree to take a leak, then wandered out into the field to inspect the progress of the plants that were growing there. They were thriving, well advanced for this time of year, and certainly looked healthy. He hoped they would stay that way. They needed constant attention and care, though, if they were to do so.

Eventually Dex saw Lewis say something to Walter, then yank the muzzle of his horse around and come thundering over to where Dexter waited.

"Something wrong?"

"Dumb sons of bitches," Lewis complained. "But don't worry. I'll show them."

"Right."

"What is it you want, Dexter?"

"The money box," Dex said. "It's gone."

The article both boys referred to as the money box was a tin container enameled in what had once been a rather gaudy shade of green, now chipped and worn by the passage of years and many hands. For as long as Dex could remember, the box had resided in the right-side middle drawer of the big desk in the study.

For as long as Dex could remember, any time either of the Yancey boys needed cash they could go there and help themselves. When they were children, the box always held at least five dollars in loose silver. When they were twelve, the amount was increased to twenty dollars in gold. At sixteen they began finding a minimum of a hundred there, and at twenty-one the amount was two hundred. If they wanted more than that they could ask their father. And for the most part receive whatever they needed or wished for. Anything up to the limits of the money box need not be discussed.

It occurred to Dex now that he had never once in all those years seen his father open that drawer or check the box. Yet no matter how often one or the other of the boys made "withdrawals," the coins in the money box were always replenished before the next contingency arose. Dex was not even certain that it was his father who performed the chore of keeping up with that. It could well have been one of the servants.

Now things seemed to have changed.

"I told you yesterday, Dexter. You have an allowance now. No more money box. Not ever again."

Dex felt a pang of . . . financial worry? The feeling was

unfamiliar to him, and he was not even sure that that was what it was. But to be without the money box now seemed perilous and more than a little frightening to him.

"I hadn't thought . . ."

"No money box, *Dexie*." Lewis lifted his chin and gave his brother a bold stare down the length of his nose. The posture would have been impossible if Dex hadn't dismounted, but now Dex was standing on the ground while Lewis was still astride.

"Damn it, Lewis, I need some money."

"Of course you do. And you shall have it. Twenty a month."

"That is ridiculous."

Lewis merely shrugged. And looked quite smug.

"I can't get along on twenty a month. You know that."

"Have you thought about getting a job, Dexie? Something suitable for a gentleman, of course. You might have a talk with Lawyer Whitley. He might welcome a clerk. You could read law under him and in a few years, if you do well and study hard, you might be able to open your own practice. Tell you what, Dexie. If you become a lawyer, I shall buy you your first shingle. Would you like that?"

"What I'd like is for you to drop dead, you asshole."

Lewis's eyes widened, and as if involuntarily, he began to back his horse away from his brother. "Damn you, Dexter, I'm going to ride in to the Crossing right now and see Whitley. I need a will drawn up. One that will make certain you never inherit even if I do die young. D'you hear me? It wouldn't do you any good to kill me even if you could think up a way to do it and not get caught."

"I wasn't . . ." Dex shook his head. Something like that wouldn't have occurred to him if he had the next five years to work on it. But it had leaped immediately to Lewis's mind. God, Dexter thought, it must be awful to be so tormented as to think your own brother would kill you for a few lousy dollars.

There was no point in trying to explain any of that to

Lewis, though. He could be informed, but he would never believe.

"This isn't getting us anywhere," Dex said in what he hoped was a calm and reasonable tone. "Let's get back to the money box."

"I already told you. There is no money box. Not anymore. There won't be ever again."

"And you have it all, is that it?"

Lewis snorted and bobbed his head. "Now you're getting it, Dexie. I have it all."

"It doesn't bother you even a little bit to think that you cheated me out of it?"

"Of course not. Why, there's even precedent for it in the Bible. Two of those old guys. One of them cheated the other out of his inheritance for a bowl of stew. Wasn't that it?"

"Maybe I should start calling you Jake," Dex suggested.

Lewis frowned. "I thought the guy was named Esau."

"Yeah, well, never mind about that. I need some money."

"You get twenty a month. No more."

"Fine. Where's my damn twenty?"

"I'll be back at the house for lunch. You can have it then."

Lewis seemed in much better spirits when he wheeled his horse and dashed away, cutting straight through the cotton field as he did so. Whatever discomfort he had suffered when talking with the hands and their foreman was soothed by seeing Dexter squirm.

Disgusted, Dex swung onto the saddle of the black gelding and turned back toward where the nigras continued to mill about beneath the stout, protecting limbs of the oak trees.

• 24 •

"Mastuh Dexter, sir." Walter snatched his hat off and clutched it in both hands in front of his belly, half bowing as he did so.

Dex gave the gray-haired black man a look of incredulity as he stepped down off the horse. "Dammit, Walter, I can remember a time when you called me a dirty-faced, snot-nosed uppity little white boy. An' at the time I deserved it too. You've called me that and likely worse, and most of my life you've called me plain Dexter or lately Mr. Dexter, which I will accept as a sign of respect. But you've never ever before right now called me Master, and I wish you wouldn't do it again neither. I'm nobody's master, not yours or anybody else. All right?"

"Yes, sir. That be fine." Walter grinned. "Mr. Dex."

"Good. That's better. Now what is the problem here?"

"Mastuh Lewis . . ."

"He only thinks he is," Dex declared.

"Yes, sir." The grin became a little wider. "Mr. Lewis, he say he gonna cut the wages of all these han's, Mr. Dex. Cut down to twel' dollar a month an' raise they rent too."

"We won' make nuthin, Mr. Dex," one of the nigras put in.

"It bad eno' tryin' to make out already. He cut us back, we work all damn mont' an' wind up in de hole. Owe de man more'n we paid. We be slaves again, Mr. Dex. That ain' right, sir. It ain' "

"We only make it that way do we give up eating, Mr. Dex."

"They're right, Mr. Dex," Walter said. "They ain't a man among us can make out if Mr. Lewis cut our wage back an' raise our rent too. We talking 'bout it now. If he do those things, sir, we got to quit. Go look some other place for a job. Take our people an' go down the river. N'Orlean'. Baton Rouge. Someplace like them. There got to be work someplace, Mr. Dex. Someplace where a man can feed his family. That's all these boys want. Work to do an' food for the table. We don't ask no more than that."

"We'll leave. Walk off and leave," one of the hands put in darkly. "Every one of us. You tell your brother that for us, eh? Let him try and make a crop without hands to chop and pick and bale. Let him try that. He'll see. Too late, that white man he'll see."

Dex sighed. "You say he intends to raise your rent too?"

"That's right, Mr. Dex. That what he says," Walter confirmed.

"Look, don't do anything right now. I can't make you any promises. I would if I could, but it isn't up to me. But I'll talk to my brother about this. Tonight. I'll ask him to back off from this. It isn't fair to you, and it's . . ." Dex had been about to say it was stupid of Lewis. Which it was. But that was not the sort of thing he could say to a bunch of nigras. He just couldn't do that. "It isn't in the best interests of Blackgum Bend," was the way he decided to put it.

That was also quite literally true, he saw, and the way he should approach Lewis about these stupid pronounce-

ments. Whatever was bad for Blackgum Bend was equally
bad for Lewis himself. Surely even Lewis could understand that simple concept.

"You'll talk to him tonight?"

"I will," Dex said. "I promise."

"We won't do nothing until then," Walter promised in
return. The foreman looked around at his crew and waited,
silently demanding their agreement, until one by one the
hands nodded. They too would wait. Nothing would be
done until Mr. Dexter had a chance to speak with Master
Lewis about the future.

Inwardly, though, Dex was groaning. His record of success with Lewis had never been particularly admirable.
And it was even worse of late.

Still, he'd made the promise and it would have to be
kept. He would have to speak with Lewis about this in-
sanity. He would have to do it tonight.

By morning Walter and the field crew—for that matter,
by then probably all the foremen and crews—would expect a response.

And in the meantime Dex had other things he needed
to see to. Like collecting his damn twenty-dollar allowance.

Twenty dollars! Impossible. He knew exactly how the
field hands felt about being cut off from their livelihood.
Well, almost exactly. Sort of.

He got back onto the horse and turned back toward the
home place. Lewis had said Dex could have his allowance at the noon meal. There was no sense doing anything that might aggravate him further.

Not until the twenty dollars was in hand anyway.

• 25 •

Dex did not like Stuart Oswald. Did not like him, did not like his son, Gerald, and liked even less their cousin Leonidas. Hadn't liked any of the bunch of them his whole life long.

Well, except for Georgeane, that is. Georgeane Oswald had been Dex's first "best girl." Also his first piece of ass. At the time—Dex had been fourteen, Georgeane a little younger—those two honors had seemed one and the same. It was only later that Dexter learned to fully comprehend that one could be separate from the other. He had come to rejoice in that difference ever since.

But he still had a soft spot in his heart reserved only for Georgeane.

He was thinking about her as he rode up the lane to the Oswald mansion. Stuart Oswald's house was no larger, and considerably less attractive, than the shack Dex's father had provided for Aunt Maybelle. The Oswald clan were regarded by their betters as poor white trash. And with considerable reason.

Back in the good old days the Oswalds were dealers in two-legged livestock slaves. And far from the best-quality working hands at that. If a planter owned a nigra who was deformed, retarded, stubborn, or simply mean, it was Stuart Oswald who would be invited to purchase the unwanted property. Cheap.

The other side of that coin was that if a planter found himself in need of extra hands for the harvest or to fill out the contracted numbers of a coffle bound for auction, if he needed a wet nurse or a wench to breed more potential field hands, it was Oswald who would always have something available to plug the gaps. Not quite so cheap.

After the disappointments of the recent past, the Oswalds continued in the business of buying and selling livestock, the principal difference being that now their wares had four legs instead of two. Oswald could always be relied upon if one wanted a cob, a cow, a litter of pigs . . . or a mule. The quality of his offerings, as before, was strictly up to the buyer to determine. To hear Stuart Oswald tell it, every animal on his shabby place was the best and fittest there had ever been. He guaranteed that to be his own personal opinion. Other guarantees, of course, did not apply. No member of the Oswald crowd would so much as guarantee a horse to have four legs. The buyer would just have to count them for himself if he wanted to be sure about it.

Dex jogged up the lane, and came to a halt in the trashstrewn yard between the Oswalds' weathered and sagging house and the well. He stepped down without waiting for an invitation. People like the Oswalds were not entitled to that sort of consideration from a planter's son.

"Hallo," Dex called as he looked around for a place to tie the black. He decided against the rails of the pigsty. They looked so flimsy he doubted they would hold if more than three dragonflies landed on them at one time, and he did not particularly fancy the idea of spending his afternoon chasing down Oswald's escaped porkers.

The well was the sturdiest structure in sight—better than the house actually—so Dex tied the horse to one of the uprights supporting the windlass and pulley.

"Dexter? Is that you? My God."

Dex turned to face the house. My God indeed, he repeated silently. "Georgeane?"

For a moment there he wasn't sure. He had not seen Georgeane in ... what? ... two years? Something like that. She'd always been a skinny redhead with big tits and a bigger smile. All freckles and laughter. Now she looked like she'd aged ten years since the last time Dex spoke with her. And now she had a naked infant propped on her hip in one elbow and a large wooden spoon in her other hand. Neither the kid nor Georgeane looked very clean.

The girl—Georgeane, that is; he had neither knowledge nor interest in the gender of the baby—had gained weight. Her body had become rounded and doughy, and the tits that once were large now had become huge. Handy, though. She could hold the kid at her waist and let it suck. Dex barely recognized her.

"It's good to see you, Georgeane. You look wonderful."

"Do I?" She giggled. "So do you, Dexter. Did you come to see me, honey?"

"Actually it's your papa I came to see today."

Georgeane made a face.

"I thought of coming to him first because I knew you'd be here," Dexter lied with a bright, flashing smile. The comment brought an even bigger smile onto Georgeane's rather puffy face. In a couple more years, Dex was thinking, poor Georgeane would look like one of her papa's sows.

"Is that true, Dexter?"

"Have I ever lied to you, Georgeane?"

She giggled again.

Surest thing in the world I have, Dex was thinking. But only every time you and me have talked.

"You really thought about me, Dexter?"

"All day long," he assured her. Or since he'd turned into the Oswald lane. Whichever of those fit.

"Papa is out back of the barn."

"Thanks."

"Dexter."

"Yes?"

"When you and Papa are done doin' business? I want to talk to you. In private. You know?"

His smile never slipped.

"I'm gonna go in an' put Leanne down for her nap," she added. "Then I'll sneak out an' meet you. You remember where."

Dex nodded. He knew where, all right. He wouldn't ever forget the place where he and Georgeane used to meet. Oh, she had been something then. Wild and pretty and fun. He could feel himself getting hard now just thinking about those times and the way Georgeane had been. Then.

"You'll meet me there, Dexter?"

"I will, Georgeane. Promise."

"Soon as you're done talking to Papa." Georgeane gave him another huge smile, then turned and disappeared back into the rickety shack where all the Oswalds somehow lived.

Dex turned and started off toward the barn, which was of course larger than the house, but also in considerably better repair.

· 26 ·

"Whoa, you stupid son of a bitch, whoa!" Gerald Oswald jerked hard on the longe line, yanking around the head of the young horse he was training. If that was what he was trying to do. Dex wasn't entirely sure.

Gerald charged hand-over-hand up the line until he was close enough, then took a cut at the horse's head with the short whip he was carrying. The horse, already sweaty and trembling, tried to bolt, but was snatched around to face Gerald again and received a slash of the whip across its face.

The horse was learning something, all right.

"Git him ag'in, son. Git him another. Learn the sumbish," Stuart Oswald advised from outside the small training pen.

Gerald obeyed his papa and slashed the young horse another one with his whip.

Dex kept his mouth closed. He had to grit his teeth to manage that, but he offered no comment. It was this exact sort of thing that made him despise Stuart, Gerald, and practically every other Oswald. They all handled livestock this way.

Always had, including when the livestock was human.

Dexter had damn small use for anyone like that.

He walked out of the shade of the barn, and Gerald spotted him first. Gerald grinned cheerily and waved. "Hidcy, Dexter. How you today?"

"Fine, thank you, Gerald, how you?"

"Keepin' busy. You know." Gerald seemed genuinely delighted to see his old friend Dexter Yancey. Had been ever since Dexter and Georgeane were such an item of community gossip. Gerald had assumed at the time that this relationship created something of a bond between himself and Dexter too, and had continued to believe it through all these years.

Stuart Oswald came waddling over and extended a hand to Dexter. It occurred to Dex that if poor Georgeane took after her father as she aged, she would go beyond looking like a sow. Dex had no idea what Georgeane's and Gerald's mother had been like. She'd died before Dexter ever became aware of the Oswalds. But then considering that the woman had agreed to marry Stuart Oswald, he doubted that he'd missed anything by not knowing her.

"Nice to see you, Mr. Oswald."

"Good t' see you too, son."

Never mind that Dexter was a Yancey and Stuart Oswald was trash. Oswald was the elder and was entitled to be called "mister," while Dex as a gentleman without land of his own occupied the lesser position in face-to-face conversation.

"What brings you by, son?" Oswald asked. Over in the training pen Gerald had resumed working with the young, heavy-bodied horse. A yearling, Dex guessed, give or take.

"Oh, I'm kinda thinking to add a mule to our place," Dex mused idly while he pretended to watch Gerald and the young roan nearby.

"Anything special?"

"Naw, not really. I just want something to put a boy on. For running messages and like that."

"Saddle mule, you mean?"

"Yeah, maybe. If I see something I like. It was just a thought, though. Maybe I won't bother with it."

Oswald pulled at one of his chins, turned his head to spit, reached inside his overalls, and contentedly scratched his crotch for a while before he answered. "I have something you might like. Mighty fine animal, though. Special. I been thinking about taking him down to N'Orleans. You know?"

Dex shrugged. "Long way, N'Orleans."

"Ah, the river, she don' care." Stuart Oswald roared in appreciation of his own finely honed wit.

Dex laughed too. "That's true, Mr. Oswald. That damn old river doesn't care about very much, does it."

"You want to take a look at this mule o' mine before I carry him down the river, son?"

"Sure, Mr. Oswald. I'm here. I might just as well look, hadn't I?"

"I got to warn you, son. You see this mule, you gonna want him. He's special."

"Any mule special enough to sell all the way down to N'Orleans, Mr. Oswald, I'd want to see anyhow even if I wasn't thinking about getting another mule for my nigra to ride."

Oswald cackled and led the way inside his barn.

· 27 ·

Dex couldn't believe that he'd done what he just did.

No one, but *no* one, paid that much for a mule.

On the other hand—never mind that it was Stuart Oswald who was selling it—never in his life had Dex seen a mule the likes of this one.

The animal was tall and proud and damn near dignified. And if you had to say something like that about a mule, well, it was one special mule indeed.

The animal stood a good sixteen hands tall, was a dark cream in color, and had points as white as cotton. Its feet would have fit into teacups, and its muzzle was purest velvet. Of course it *was* a mule. In addition to those features and its undeniably aristocratic demeanor, the creature had ears long enough to dust treetops with, a tail that looked like something a cat would bury, and a bray as loud and rasping as a nest of gators in mating season.

Still, this was the damnedest mule Dex ever did see, and he hadn't more than laid eyes on the animal before he knew he wanted it for James. James had said he wanted a fast mule? He might've been half joking at the time, but he damn sure had him one now.

Old Man Oswald saddled the mule for Dexter and let

him try it out on the public road. Which Dex had wanted to do. Out of sight of Oswald. Whee-ow, but that yellow mule had more sheer speed than enough. It wasn't so quick to jump off the line, but once it got its legs stretched, Dex doubted there was anything in the parish— hell, maybe not anything in the state—that could keep up with it.

He'd wanted it when he laid eyes on it. He purely knew he had to have it once he got it into a belly-down run.

The only problem after that was paying for it. After all, he had exactly twenty dollars in his pocket and no inclination whatsoever to go into debt to Stuart Oswald.

Twenty dollars wouldn't be close to enough to buy this animal, he knew. Oh, an ordinary mule would go for eight or ten, a good one for fifteen, sixteen dollars. But if Dex offered twenty, all he'd accomplish would be to piss Oswald off. He knew better than that.

The upshot of the whole thing was that he'd gotten some hunks of old burlap from Oswald to pack between his own good blanket and the bars of Dexter's handsomely crafted planter's saddle—the saddle was horsewide and wouldn't properly fit the much narrower frame of a mule without the extra padding—and now he was mounted on the yellow mule while his own fine gelding had taken up residence in the Oswald barn.

Dexter'd hated to do that. The black deserved better. But dammit, he'd wanted that mule.

Besides, he mused now, the swap had taught him something. Lewis might indeed put him on an allowance when it came to cash in hand. But the master of Blackgum Bend hadn't said anything about not honoring Dex's ability to trade and barter.

And hell, there were lots of things on a plantation the size of Blackgum Bend that Lewis wouldn't ever notice if they happened to go missing.

In a way Stuart Oswald had solved more than just one problem for Dex today.

Dexter smiled a bit about that as he rode the mule out of the Oswald lane and down the road a hundred yards, and then swung back into the woods that bordered the Oswalds' unkempt fields.

It wasn't that he did not want to be seen in public riding a mule—well, it wasn't entirely that anyway—but he'd made a promise. The time had come to keep it, so he took a deep breath, steeled himself for what was fixing to come, and headed for the little glade where once very long ago he'd lost his virginity to a then-twelve-year-old girl who'd given her own away a long time before she'd ever invited Dexter Lee Yancey to sniff around her honey pot.

◆ 28 ◆

God, she was . . . ugly. Poor Georgeane. She'd been such a sweet thing when she was young. Supple and laughing and eager to participate in any form of sex that either or both of them could think of.

Not that this willingness on her part covered all that much territory when they'd been kids. Variety back then consisted more of changing locale and position than anything really interesting. He and Georgeane had clawed at each other like a pair of minks for . . . three years? Closer to four? He doubted in all that time they'd either one of them thought to stick it anywhere except her pussy. Well, except that one time when they'd sat side by side on the grass during a Confederate Veterans Day picnic. It had come dark, and they sat right out in the open with a blanket thrown over themselves against the cool of the evening, and Georgeane giggled and reached inside Dex's britches and brought him off with her hand. He'd come a pint in his drawers, and felt all sticky afterward. Hadn't minded too much, of course, not at the time. Still, he didn't consider now that a hand job disallowed his claim that the only thing they'd thought to use in the past was her pussy.

He took a look at Georgeane now, and wondered if there was any way he could get out of humping her this afternoon.

The damn girl was already sprawled out in the lush, sweet-smelling grass of "their" glade, naked as a boiled egg but not nearly so tempting.

Back at the house she'd looked plump and blowsy. Naked, she looked just plain fat. Her tits weren't just big, they were positively unpleasant to look at. They flopped on either side of a chest and belly that looked like unbaked bread dough, the nipples dark and wrinkled and the rings around them the size of small saucers. Worse, Georgeane's skin was thin and almost transparent, so there was a spiderweb of blue veins crosshatching the meat of her dugs.

She had thick, suety thighs the shape and approximate size of tree trunks, and a waist that Dex wasn't sure he could have found if it wasn't for the belly button that gave it away.

About the only part of Georgeane Oswald that was still as he remembered was her pubic hair. That, at least, remained thick and curling and a bright and gleaming shade of red. Her head hair was washed out and sun-streaked, but her pussy hair was still that of the girl Dex remembered.

"I been waitin' for you, Dex honey."

"So I see." He got down off the tall mule and tied it to the limb of a small tree, then looked nervously around to make sure they weren't observed. By one clue and another those years past, he'd been fairly sure Gerald knew Dex was fucking his sister. Dex thought the old man knew too, although nothing was actually said.

It was one thing for youngsters to go at each other like that. Hell, a boy in his teens would happily fuck a snake if he could get somebody to hold its head for him, or a bonfire if someone threw a snake into it. Everybody knew that. But this was different. Dex wouldn't want anyone to find out he'd spent any time with a slattern like old Geor-geane had become.

Still, dammit, he didn't want to hurt her feelings. And it was rather clear what she had in mind, seeing as she was butt naked and already had her legs spread wide apart for him.

"You horny, Dex honey?"

"Ever know me to be anything else?" he asked. A thought came to him, a possible excuse to ride away with-out insulting the girl, and he added, "You married now, Georgeane?"

"No, why? Oh. Leanne, huh?"

Dex nodded.

"Nah, honey. She's Gerald's kid."

"She isn't yours, Georgeane?"

She laughed. "Sure. She's mine too. Me and Gerald. That bother you, honey?"

"No, o' course not. None of my business, I expect."

"You know I always loved you best, Dexter."

"I know you have, Georgeane."

"You come over here now, honey, an' let me he'p you outa those clothes. I been burning an' itching down here"—she showed him where—"ever since I seen you in the yard back there."

It occurred to Dex to hope with some degree of fer-vency that it was only desire that was burning and itching, and not a dose of the clap or crabs or some such. He didn't need any of that, thank you.

Still and all . . .

"Come over here, Dexter honey. Let me show you what all I learned since you and me was together."

Dex took a deep breath. And stepped forward. He tipped his head back—better not to spend too much time looking at Georgeane if he was going to get through this and still be able to convince himself to get an erection—and felt her fingers working deftly at the buttons of his fly.

He felt the cool of the air reach his flesh as Georgeane

pulled him out of his drawers. Then the warm, wet sensation of hot flesh engulfing him clean down to the root.

It turned out Dex didn't have a problem getting hard after all. Georgeane, bless her heart, had learned an awful lot these past few years.

♦ 29 ♦

James held the lantern high while Dex sorted through the dusty, musty junk piled on the shed floor.

"Over there," James said.

"Where?"

"There. Where I'm pointing."

"You're standing behind me, you idiot. How am I supposed to see where you're pointing."

"Under that red thing."

"Oh, yeah. Now I see." The red thing was an old horse blanket, worn out long ago but never discarded on the theory that a use might be found for it. Someday. Barely visible under one edge of the blanket was something that looked like the bottom curve of a steel stirrup. They were sorting through the junk in the shed behind the barn in search of a saddle James could use on the mule. Dex would simply have given him one of the good ones in the tack room, except the bars of those were all much too wide for use on a mule. "Move the light . . . yeah, that's better."

Dex took hold of the stirrup and gave it a tug. Stirrup, leathers, cinch, and saddle all came out from beneath the blanket with a clatter of dislodged objects and a great flurry of dust.

"It's perfect," Dex declared. "You can have it." He held the saddle triumphantly aloft, and James began to laugh. The thing they'd uncovered was a ladies' sidesaddle, its leather cracked and rat-chewed, hanks of padding streaming from the underside of the seat. "Don't want this one? Damn, you're awful hard to please."

He went back to poking through the mess. Another five minutes of searching disclosed a separate heap of ancient military saddles stacked rather tidily in a back corner and covered with a scrap of tarp.

"I remember these," Dex said, "Poppa bought a whole bunch of them after the war. Cheap. They belonged to the Fifth Louisiana Cav, I think. Captain LeBrun's troop."

"That will make me feel better, knowing I'm riding some grayback cavalryman's saddle," James said.

"You're getting uppity again, aren't you. If it makes you feel any better, these saddles were still in the warehouse. They never got delivered to LeBrun and his boys."

"Is that true?"

Dex grinned. "Damn if I'd know, but it sounds good."

James laughed. And took the saddle from his friend. "It does look like it'd fit. And it's in good shape. Dirty and dry, but that's nothing a little soap and oil won't take care of."

"You want it?"

"Since it looks like a choice between fixing up this old army saddle or getting boils on my ass from riding bareback, yeah, I've given this careful consideration and am prepared to tell you that I accept your generous offer. I'll take the saddle. Now, d'you have any blankets in there too?"

"We'll get a blanket out of the tack room. You wouldn't want anything we could find in here."

They went outside into the cleaner, clearer night air. The dust inside the shed made Dex's nose tickle and wrinkle. He cleared each nostril with a loud blow, then laughed when James had to dance sideways in a hurry to avoid the spray.

"I've decided what to call that mule," James volunteered as they walked toward the barn.

"Mmm?"

"Saladin."

Dex pondered the choice for a moment, then nodded. "I like it."

"Saladin whipped all you white boys, you know."

"Your mule did that? Oh, you mean *that* Saladin. Need I remind you that your Arabian Saladin never met up with me. I'd've taken him."

"Huh. You can't even take me."

"You think you can back up that boast, black boy?"

"Damn right. Name your time and place."

"Tomorrow. Right after you get off work. I expect you'll be softened up and ready for the kill about then."

James chuckled.

"Tell you what," Dex said. "I'll let you off easy this time and not whip your black ass. But you got to do me a favor."

"Sure. What?"

Dex stopped. They were between the shed and the barn, far enough from either that no one lurking around the odd corner was apt to overhear anything. Even so, Dex scanned the yard in all directions before he spoke, and then lowered his voice to do so.

"I talked with my brother tonight. About wages for the hands. I suppose you heard what he wants to do."

James nodded. "Forgive me for saying this, but your brother can be a real asshole sometimes."

"This is one of his moments," Dex agreed. "I tried to talk some sense into him. He insists on going ahead with it."

"The people won't put up with it, Dex. You don't want to know some of the things I been hearing about this."

"I'm trying to get him to change his mind, but I'm afraid of what could happen tomorrow. Walter and his

crew said they'd come around early to talk. They won't
like what they hear.''

"It won't be just Walter and his bunch, Dex. They're
all coming. There won't be one hand in the fields tomorrow morning. Nor tomorrow afternoon neither if Lewis
stands by his decision to cut wages. Every man of them
will walk away if he tries to do this.''

"Lewis thinks he won't lose very many people and that
he can easy enough replace any who do leave.''

"Lewis is wrong. There isn't a nigger in this parish
who hasn't already heard what's happening here at Blackgum. They're all afraid if Lewis does it here, the other
owners will do the same. Things are bad enough already
without that, Dexter. People hardly have enough to feed
their children as it is. Hell, I know kids ten, twelve years
old who've never owned a pair of shoes. What will it be
like for them if things get even worse?''

"I know, dammit, and I'm trying to do something about
it. But you know Lewis. If he thinks he's being challenged, he'll just get his back up and turn stubborn. Then
no one will be able to turn him around.''

James sighed. "You want me to put the word out,
right? Everybody go to the fields tomorrow like usual.''

"It's a lot to ask, I know. But yes. That's exactly what
I'm asking.''

James hesitated, staring off toward an unseen horizon.
Dex did not press, but waited patiently. Finally James
made a low, growling sound deep in his throat. Then said,
"I'll try. No promises, but I'll try.''

"I can't ask for any more than that,'' Dex told him.
"Now are you going to give me that blanket for a bribe
like you promised or not?''

"Damn, but I like a man who can be bought cheap.''

"I'll show you cheap, you uppity white boy. Give me
a day when I've got a little rest from chopping that damn
cotton and I'll wrestle your nose into the mud. Show you
a thing or two.''

"Any time, black boy. I'll whip your uppity ass any-time you say."

Dex grinned and punched James in the bicep, then led the way into the barn in search of a blanket suitable for a mule as fine as Saladin.

٠ 30 ٠

"I told you those black sons of bitches wouldn't give me any guff," Lewis said with considerable satisfaction as he took his seat at the head of the long table—in the place that had been their father's—and snapped open a crisply starched and carefully folded napkin.

"What are you talking about, Lewis?" Dex already knew what it was that Lewis referred to. He also knew it would cost nothing to let his brother gloat over this "victory" of his.

"The niggers. They're all out in the fields where they belong today. Not a one of them even showed up this morning like they said they would. They know who's boss here." Lewis nodded and reached for his wine glass. "They know."

"Looks like it." Dex also knew better than to say anything to Lewis about his own involvement in what still could become a very ugly problem for Blackgum Bend. And, for that matter, for all the other plantations up and down the river. The difficult matter of trying to arrive at an equitable system of wage and labor on large cotton plantations still involved trial and error. Worse, not every planter—indeed rather few—was overmuch concerned about the "equitable" part of that juggling act. Lewis Yancey for one seemed entirely uncaring about the needs of the plantation's people.

Lewis snapped his fingers and pointed to his plate, and little Clara hurried to fetch her new employer—master, as he preferred it—his dinner.

"I'll be going away for a few days," Lewis said around a mouthful of roasted chicken.

"Oh?"

"I deserve some time off."

"It's almost the end of the month, Lewis."

"Yes? So?"

"What about the hands. I don't have access to the cash box anymore. Who will pay off the hands come the first of next month?"

Lewis waved one hand in dismissal, and with the other plunged his fork into a heap of candied yams. "When I get back."

"Sure. Well . . . enjoy yourself."

Lewis laughed and winked at him. "Oh, I will do that, brother. Believe me, I will do that. I hear there's a new crop of whores at the Haitian's place down in Galveston. Jamaican sluts. I love to hear the way they talk. Not like field niggers. And they aren't so musky either. Don't have the stink on them that our homegrown niggers do."

Dex considered asking if Lewis would be taking Netty—no, Annetta it was now, he remembered—but decided against it. No sense in messing up Lewis's fine mood.

Lewis swallowed another deep draught of wine, then motioned Clara to him. He belched loudly and pulled the girl close, then reached beneath her skirt and began feeling of her. Lewis didn't notice, but the child began silently to cry, her shoulders quivering and bright tears sliding over her cheeks and dripping off her chin. Lewis was oblivious to the little girl's discomfort.

Dex was not. But dammit, he had to walk a narrow line with Lewis right now. He needed—all the people of Blackgum Bend needed—decisions from Lewis that were not the ones the younger Yancey brother was inclined to give.

He could do nothing to help Clara, Dex knew. Not right now he couldn't. But he did not have to sit there and observe her humiliation. He took a last small bite of chicken, pretended a sigh of contentment that he most certainly did not feel, and excused himself from the table.

''We'll talk again when you get back, Lewis,'' he said.

Lewis did not appear to have heard. Dex strode out of the dining room at a pace that he took care to control.

• 31 •

Sunday morning. There was something about Sunday mornings that Dex particularly enjoyed. Especially the ones on which he did not have a hangover. This Sunday morning he felt on top of the world.

He cantered down the lane to the New Hope Baptist Church, and felt at peace when he heard the sounds of many voices lifted in joyous song. From outside the white-painted walls the words were blurred and indistinct, but the strong African rhythms were clear. Dex had always enjoyed those. The spirituals were exotic and exciting, at the same time gay and most unlike the solemn and dreary Latin of the Yanceys' own rare appearances at Mass.

Dex reined the red gelding past the church, past the carefully tended cemetery behind it, and on through a patch of woods to the meadow the Negroes called Hope Flats. Or sometimes, like after a bad day, Flat Hopes.

Today Dex expected to be calling it Hope Flats for sure.

The flats were a narrow strip of lush grass surrounded by live oak and dogwood. The area must once have been a bog to produce soil so dark and rich. The ground would have been perfect for planting save for the fact that there was so little of it and it was so completely isolated.

Besides, Hope Flats had developed its own usefulness that far surpassed what little the land could have produced if plowed and planted. Almost three quarters of a mile long and perhaps thirty yards across, curving gently and very little, Hope Flats was an ideal track for the running of horses. It was the Sunday morning gathering place for blacks throughout the parish. The women and children went to church; their menfolk continued on to Hope Flats, where they could drink, gamble, and relax on their one day of rest from otherwise-unrelenting toil.

The Flats had been put to this purpose ever since the slaves gained their freedom. And if the truth be known, for several generations before that too. The white masters officially knew nothing about the goings-on at Hope Flats, but in truth they not only knew, they purposely remained blind to the weekly gatherings that were patently illegal prior to emancipation. Better, the wiser among them knew, that built-up pressure should be allowed to escape. Otherwise, one risked explosion.

That was then, though, and this was now, and Dexter had every expectation of increasing what little remained of the allowance Lewis had given him two weeks earlier.

Dex did not believe in cheating any man, white or otherwise. He believed in a fair wage for honest labor. He believed in live and let live. He also believed if he was able to win an honest wager, all the better for him and tough luck for the loser. White or otherwise. He would be quite willing to pocket just as much of a poor black man's hard-earned wage as the fellow cared to stake.

The red horse, no slouch for speed, although it was young and had not yet fully come to the muscle it would someday carry, broke out of the woods and into the Sunday morning sunlight.

Several dozen men were gathered around a rough-hewn bench where some enterprising soul had set up a small keg of spirits that he was selling for five cents a dipper.

Beyond them a number of horses and mules were tied, the wagons left back near the church where the lane petered out. Out on the edge of the grass, a young man was leading a leggy mare in small circles, while close by another was walking a tall bay stallion. Dex recognized the horse, and would have wagered a sizable amount on its owner being completely unaware of his prized stud's form of Sunday relaxation.

Grinning and eager, Dex guided his own horse through the crowd, tied it on the picket line established under the trees, and ambled back in the direction of the barrel and the Sunday celebrants.

· 32 ·

"Mornin', Mr. Dexter," a grinning black man said, snatching his hat off and bobbing his head.

"Mornin', Amos."

"You gonna run that red horse o' yours this mornin', suh?"

"Oh, I might be tempted. Got something in mind for me to match against?"

"Not me, nossuh, I got nothin' keep up with that red horse o' yours. How 'bout you run him again' old Lucifer there."

Dex laughed. "Sorry, Amos, but you caught me when I'm sober. I'd have to be powerful drunk to think my red could stay with Lucifer. Besides, it looks to me like Lucifer already has a match." He nodded toward the open flat where the fine-boned mare was being paraded.

Amos chuckled. "JimJoe, he offer to race Lucifer, but he the only one willin' to back that mare. Nobody else put money on that horse, so how you gonna have a match without nobody willin' to bet? JimJoe prob'ly got twenny cent in his pocket. How far you gonna spread that when ever'body else here today put his coins behind Lucifer, you tell me that much."

"Surely somebody would want the odds," Dex said.

"You willin', suh? Give you right good payback if that mare beat Lucifer."

"I told you, Amos. I'm sober this morning. I wouldn't put a dollar against Lucifer if you gave me fifty to one."

"I give you thirty, suh. Thirty shiny new dollar against one piddlin' coin o' yours. That's sure enough fair, ain't it?"

Dex only laughed and shook his head. "Not a chance, Amos. But I tell you what. You ask me again after I've had a couple dippers of Leon's gator piss." Grinning, Dex went over to the barrel and helped himself to the dipper. He was entitled to a full measure for his nickel, but experience taught him better than to attempt it. It took a few short measures first to numb a man's throat sufficiently that it would accept a long draught of the dreadful mix of alcohol and God knows what else.

He tasted of the stuff—the taste was something else that mercifully faded after a few repeat swallows—and made a face, shuddered, grinned, and dropped the dipper back into the barrel. "Chalk me up for one," he told the stoop-shouldered old man who had been manufacturing cheap rotgut for almost as long as old Cornfed had been distilling his own superb whiskey.

"You gonna run again' Lucifer, Mr. Dexter?"

Dex shook his head and walked out to have a look at the mare. Thirty to one wasn't even tempting. Not against Lucifer. But if he could interest JimJoe in running against the red horse, well, that might be all right.

Wind tore at his eyes. Tears streamed from them and were blown back into his ears, tickling and annoying there, the aggravation made all the worse by the ripping roar of noise as the same hot wind flowed and eddied past his ears.

The wind whipped his hair—his hat hadn't survived those first few surging jumps—and ruffled his sideburns. It peeled his lips back off his teeth to give the appearance of a grim rictus.

But in fact Dex was smiling.

God, he loved this.

The red horse strained for speed, muscles bunching and sliding beneath hot, gleaming skin. Dex laid his jaw close against the rise and fall of the horse's neck, and rejoiced in its speed and the feel of the powerful body. He had discarded his saddle to reduce the weight the horse was asked to carry—one of the rules imposed by custom was that a man had to ride his own horse—and so could feel the animal heat rise up to him as well as the thrust and flow of bone and sinew and muscle.

God, he loved it.

The red horse and the long-neck mare ran head to head, pounding down the Flats, banging shoulders twice as JimJoe tried to bump the red out of position or Dexter off its back, either outcome of which would have pleased him.

Dex laughed aloud, loving the exhilaration of it all, and used the ends of his reins to slash JimJoe's thigh in a gentle reminder—likely the young man would carry a welt into next Sunday's gathering because of the cut of the leather through his britches—that Dexter had been here before. It would take more than a bit of bump and slam to throw him off stride.

"Eeeeeee-ah!" Dex howled as the two horses swept nose to nose past the three judges who presided at the far west end of the Flats.

He sat upright and let the red slow to a trot before wheeling the horse back toward the bettors down at the starting line.

"Damn," he shouted, the joy in his voice not at all reflecting the discouragement implied by the word.

The judges had the white flag raised for the men down at the start to see. White was the right-hand line off the start. The mare was declared the winner, dammit.

JimJoe was grinning hugely. Dex rode to him and leaned over to clap him on the shoulder. "Good race, JimmyJoe. That was fun."

"Beat your ass, Mr. Dexter, me and Lizzybeth here."

"You damn sure did. But I'll get you next time. I guarantee it."

"You got to put money up and not just that guarantee if you want to go a next time," JimJoe said.

"I will too. But not today. Today belongs to you and your mare."

Dex waved a thank-you to the three old men who were the time-honored and trusted judges, then took the red back to the east end of the Flats at a slow, cooling walk.

He glanced to the right as he passed the picket line. Saladin was tied there now. That meant James had arrived. Good.

Dex slid off the red's slightly sweaty back and limped over to the barrel. He handed the horse's reins to a boy of ten or so who'd been allowed to come with his father for the excitement this morning. "Walk him out for me, would you, son? He's a slow old cob, but I expect he deserves to be treated decent."

The boy grinned and announced, "My daddy won twenty-five cents on your race, Mr. Dexter. You don't even owe me nothing for cooling your horse down."

Dex laughed and nodded. "Fair enough," he said. He turned to Leon at the popskull barrel. "Chalk me up for another," he said as he reached for the dipper.

· 33 ·

"How much money you got there, white boy?"

Dex emptied his pockets and counted. "Eleven dollars and twenty-two cents. What's it to you anyhow?"

James winked. "Never mind that. Give me fifty cents, will you?"

"Will a dollar do?"

"You're a real pain in the ass, you know that? Ask for one thing, you give me something else. But all right. Gimme the damn dollar."

Dex handed over a silver dollar, and James went over to the booze barrel. He bought a drink and tossed it down, then another.

"Leon. Take that dime I owe you out of his change, will you?"

Leon nodded and went back to selling his wares. Over the next hour or so James walked, then stumbled, and finally staggered his way to the barrel a dozen times or close to it. When he seemed so thoroughly oiled that it was miraculous to find him still upright, James climbed onto the bench and loudly bawled, "I wanna race m' new damn mule."

Dex thought the offer rather well received as horse

owners and bettors throughout the grove heard the challenge . . . and observed James's state of inebriation. They gathered round the bench like mice heading for the granary.

"I'll race you."

"Me and Babe can beat you, James."

"Try me, man, try me."

James swayed, came very close to losing his balance and toppling face-forward into the crowd, then managed to right himself. A broad, vacant, almost beatific smile split his dark face. "I wanna . . . I wanna run 'gin that Lucifer horse."

The crowd began to laugh, but the foresighted fellow who had appropriated the powerful stallion for the day was quick to accept. After all, he hadn't managed to find a match so far the whole day long. "How much you got to put up sayin' your stupid mule can beat ol' Lucifer? How 'bout that, James? You got money behind you?"

"I got . . . I got . . ." James wobbled, blinked rapidly, and for half a moment there looked like he was going to spew up his dinner, his drinks, and everything else in his stomach. The crowd in front of him parted quicker than a sleight-of-hand artist could have managed an illusion. "I got ten dollar t' bet," James declared.

"Cash money?"

"Cash money. Damn ri' cash money." James belched and clutched at his belly, and once more the crowd opted for safety before risk and scattered wide lest they find themselves anointed. "Cash," James mumbled again, a bit of drool escaping from the side of his mouth.

"What kind of odds are you giving on this match, Amos?" Dex shouted.

"Same as befo'. Thirty to one."

Dex grinned. "Is that for? Or against the mule?"

The crowd got quite a kick out of that one.

"Give me fifty cents on Lucifer," Dex hollered.

That set off a cacophony of shouting, milling men with coins and even a few paper bills in hand, everyone trying to get in on the bet before James's ten dollars ran out.

Free money. That seemed the consensus among the bettors. And bless James's heart for injecting some fun—and ten dollars—into the afternoon's Sunday recreation.

Eager hands helped James safely down from the bench—it would not have done to let the chump of the day fall and hurt himself and thereby negate the match—and half carried him out onto the grass.

Other helpers went to fetch the tall mule. They led Saladin out into the sunlight, where he received admiring looks from men who knew mules. Of course these same men knew there was no mule ever born who could run with the likes of Lucifer. But Saladin was a handsome creature just the same, and they liked what they saw in him.

Saladin's saddle, Dex noted, was clean and polished, the old and dry leather gleaming now from hours of rubbing with soap and oil, the leathers spanking new, and the cinch washed and now padded with a wrap of sheepskin.

"You want the saddle on him or offn?" JimJoe asked.

James blinked twice and seemed to be trying to concentrate on working out the meaning in the question. He opened his mouth once as if to speak, but gagged and closed it again. With a motion of his hand he indicated that he preferred that the saddle be removed, thank you.

That choice brought another explosion of grins onto the faces of the bettors, virtually all of whom were backing Lucifer. After all, it wouldn't matter a fig how fast Saladin was if his rider fell off. And once they got to the starting line the race was "official." Or as close to it as mattered.

Lucifer was led out and his rider—certain leeways were permitted as to the designation of ownership in these matters, the party bringing a mount to the event being judged owner and therefore rider, at least for the day—mounted.

Happy helpers were glad to take Saladin to the starting line, while others bodily lifted James off his feet and carried him to the mule. No one seemed sure that James could make the distance on his own. Once there, they lifted James higher and perched him atop the yellow mule.

"Make sure you put him on facing the front," someone in the crowd yelled. "You gotta be fair 'bout this."

"Are you ready?" Amos shouted. Tradition had appointed Amos as the official starter at these events in addition to his role as oddsmaker and keeper of all wagers.

"No," someone else responded. "Hold up der, Amos. The judges ain't ready yet."

Far down the Flats Dex could see a spring wagon still bouncing along toward the finish line. A few moments later the wagon pulled off to the side, and the judges waved.

"All right. Anytime now."

"Ready?" Amos repeated in a loud, authoritative voice.

He got a nod in return from Charlie Day, who was up on Lucifer.

"James?"

James hiccuped. He blinked. He grinned a little.

"I take that as a yes. All right now. You boys be ready. You be set." Amos paused for a moment.

"Go!"

• 34 •

"Y'know, Dexter, I don't think I've ever seen this much money in my whole life. Not all at once I haven't. Huh. Maybe not all put together I haven't."

"Don't get too excited. Half of that is mine," Dex told him with a grin.

They were sitting in the shade of a pecan grove on Alexander Dumont's property. Dex hadn't felt it politic to divide their spoils in front of the losers, particularly since Dex himself had been the first to back Lucifer and start the gold rush that followed.

Ten Yankee dollars at thirty to one. Less, of course, the half-dollar Dex lost to the stallion. What the hell. Call it three hundred in profit. The fifty-cent shill, like the drinks before it, were but the expense of doing business.

"Tell me about it," Dex urged. "I couldn't see what was happening from back at the start line." He laughed. "Except for seeing you and Saladin lost in the dust right to begin with."

James laughed. "That Lucifer, he's a horse, all right. Quick off the start too. When Amos gave us the go, Lucifer jumped so fast and so far I thought myself the race was lost. He was fifteen, twenty yards out front before I hardly knew what was happening.

"Then Saladin here"—James leaned forward and gave the yellow mule an affectionate pat on the neck—"he got his legs under him and began to run. I tell you, Dex, I never knew anything could go this fast. I mean, Lucifer was fast. But Saladin was flying. Belly down and go like hell. Even so, if the Flats were any shorter I don't know we would have beat Lucifer. Only caught up to him about three fourths of the way down, and then it wasn't easy to get by. He has heart, that horse does. Don't ever think otherwise. He's all heart inside that wide chest. But Saladin had the legs on him, and we pulled clear with about fifty, maybe sixty yards yet to the finish. Time we passed the judges Saladin was almost a full body length in front.

"I tell you something else too, something I learned out there today. Lucifer is the heavier built and gets off the mark quick, like I said. But by the end of the race he was near used up. Kinda like you on a Saturday night. Dragging. But old Saladin here, he was just getting into the fun of the thing. He felt like, fast as he was, he could hold that pace for a long way yet. He wasn't hardly breathing hard, and Lucifer was paddling with his forefeet and starting to lunge into his stride. This mule here, he's a distance runner for sure. Got to remember that in the future. Saladin will run his best in the long haul."

"In the future? We'll have a hell of a time getting any money down on him again, James. Any animal that whips Lucifer will be hard to make a match."

James grinned. "I wasn't thinking of running him back at Flat Hopes again. I know better'n that. But as I recall, white boy, you de on'y pale-looking sumbitch that knows how fast this mule can go."

"You don't think all those boys are gonna talk about what happened down there today?"

"Hell, yes, they will. But not to no white man. Do you really think that blue-eyed nigger Charlie Day is gonna go back to his bossman and tell him, Mr. Penn, I sneaked off with your stud horse today and ran him in a race but he lost to a yella mule? Do you really think he's gonna say that to Mr. Penn, Dex? Or any of those other boys say the same where a white man can hear? No indeed. By fall of dark tonight, there won't be a black boy in this parish that doesn't know about my Saladin beating Mr. Penn's Lucifer horse. But there won't be any white man know a thing about it. Not unless you tell them.''

Dex rubbed the side of his nose. And grinned. ''In that case . . .''

''In that case, white boy, here's your half of the winnings. Whoo-ee! Ain't this just something now.''

• 35 •

"It's about time you got back," Dex complained.

"I stopped in New Orleans for a few days on my way home. Had to come through there and thought I might as well enjoy the city for a change. Besides, what is it to you?" Lewis said.

"What is it to me? It's eight days past the end of the month, and I'm the one who's had to listen to all the worrying and complaining from the hands. No one has been paid, remember? Or did that little detail slip your mind while you were downriver enjoying yourself?"

Lewis waved a hand dismissively. "Tomorrow. I'll pay tomorrow. You can tell them that if you like."

"What's wrong with this afternoon?"

"Tomorrow." Lewis gave his older brother a long look, one that Dex found unreadable. And that was most unlike Lewis. Normally Dex could figure him out at a glance. Not this time.

"Aren't you going to ask me if I had a nice time?" Lewis said.

"Sure, brother, I'll play your game. Did you have a nice time over in Galveston?"

"Indeed I did, thank you. And I had an even nicer time in New Orleans."

"I'm happy for you, I'm sure," Dexter said in a dry tone that he hoped would piss Lewis off. It did not.

"The Jamaicans were lovely. Very lively. You know?"

"I hear there's a lot of the French pox going around among the sporting women in Jamaica these days."

"You're making that up."

Dex shrugged. "It's what I heard. I don't claim to know from personal experience. Do you?"

Lewis ignored the question. "I'll tell you about my stop in New Orleans in three weeks. On the Saturday evening. I'm hosting a gala that night. I would particularly like for you to attend. Can you manage to do that, Dexie?"

"I doubt that I have anything to wear. Sorry."

"Have the tailor make something up. Something special. I want you to look your best."

"On twenty dollars a month? I don't want to pour out my substance on nonessentials, Lewie dear. Better to save what little I have for licorice and liquor and life's little pleasures."

"Have your tailor send the bill to me. I won't count it against your allowance."

"My, how generous you've become. You really must have had a fine time on your trip."

"Yes, I told you that. You'll see."

Dex found Lewis's prattle odd but not particularly interesting. "Speaking of my twenty dollars . . ."

"Tomorrow," Lewis said. "When I pay the niggers."

"Fine. Whatever."

"By the way, I've hired a new overseer."

"Poppa liked Jonas well enough."

"Poppa pampered his niggers. Besides, he had the advantage of owning his labor. I have to take care of things the modern way. It isn't the same now as when Poppa was in charge."

"He managed these past years just as well as he did before."

"He was soft on the niggers."

"He was fair," Dex countered. "Nothing wrong with that."

"Regardless of what you think, Mister Stennet will be here in a week or two. He will take charge of things like discipline and accounting."

"Now there's a combination for you. Discipline and accounting."

"Mister Stennet is a man of experience."

"I notice you didn't say 'gentleman' of experience."

Lewis smiled, although with no trace of mirth. "Mister Stennet is no gentleman, I promise you."

"He sounds like a man I can hardly wait to meet."

"Things will be different under Mister Stennet's care."

"And what are you paying for the benefit of all this experience and counsel, brother dear?"

"A hundred a month."

Dex rolled his eyes. "That's everything you'd hoped to save by cutting the hands' wages."

"Dexter, you're even softer than Poppa was. You have no idea how much more I can make this land produce."

"You're referring to money, I presume, not cotton. I don't see how anyone could make more cotton than Poppa did."

"Both. I intend to increase both yields," Lewis said.

"I wish you'd listen to reason about the hands. They're already unhappy about being paid late. Hell, they've had to sign notes at the mercantile to get food for their families. If you go through with—"

"What did you say just now? Our niggers have been signing due notes?"

"Yeah. A lot of them have, or so I hear. I told you, they've been coming to me regular for the past week complaining and worrying about this."

"Over at the Crossing?" Lewis asked.

"Sure. At Ben Deene's store for sure. I don't know about anyplace else."

"Thank you for telling me that, Dexie."

"You'll be sure and pay out tomorrow, Lewis?"

"I said I would, didn't I?"

"I can tell them that?"

"Tomorrow night. After work. They can come by the house and draw whatever is coming to them."

"I'll make sure they all hear that news today. Believe me, it will make things go better around here once that worry is off everybody's backs."

Lewis gave his brother another enigmatic smile, then disappeared in the direction of the study. Dexter went out to have the red horse saddled. He wanted to make sure every crew on the place knew they would collect their pay come the morrow.

• 36 •

"Aunt Lottie, it's the middle of the afternoon and my room hasn't been made up yet." Dex glanced at the clock over the mantle. It was barely past three, so it wasn't like he was running out of time, of course. At breakfast this morning Lewis had said he would be back around five and would give Dexter his allowance before going out to pay the hands. That wasn't so important—not as long as Dex still had money left over from his mule winnings—but Dexter wanted to be there when the crews were paid. Lewis was up to something. Dex didn't know what, but he knew his brother well enough to know that something was in the wind. Something more than Lewis was letting on.

All of that would happen later, though. At the moment Dex was feeling peeved because his boots had not been blacked, yesterday's smallclothes were still lying in an untidy heap on the floor of his bedroom, and the bed remained unmade. That was not the way things were normally run at Blackgum Bend, and he did not particularly like it.

Aunt Lottie grumbled and scolded under her breath for a moment, then said, "It's Clara. I told her to make up

Master Yancey's room. I expect she didn't know I meant for her to do both o' them today, Mr. Dexter. Don't you worry y'self. I'll find her an' get her at that right away quick.''

"Where's Annetta that she wouldn't be making up Lewis's room for him, Aunt Lottie?"

The black woman rolled her eyes heavenward. "That nigger girl Netty, she done run off, Mr. Dexter.''

"Run off? What do you mean?"

"I mean she quit. She don't work here no more, that's what I mean. Is 'at all right? She don' be forced to stay here if she don' want, do she?"

"No, she certainly has the right to quit any time she wants. Of course, she does. It just . . . surprises me, that's all.''

"She upset because Master Yancey kick her out of . . . well, it ain't for me to say what he kick that girl out of. Not none of my business, you understand. But when Master Yancey he come back from his trip, he don' want that Netty girl no more. He di'n' bring her presents like he usually done. The whole time he gone she goin' around this house braggin' to Clara and me an' everybody else how Master Yancey gonna bring her a fine gown, all silk an' satin an' lace. Jewelry too, she say. He gonna shop in the city an' bring her pretties to wear 'cause he find her so pretty. You know?''

Dex grunted. Lewis could be generous like that sometimes. When he wanted to be.

"Then Master Yancey come back an' not bring that girl nothing. Tell her not to come aroun' . . .'' Aunt Lottie paused and seemed uncertain whether she should continue or not.

"I know Netty was spending the nights in Lewis's rooms if that's what you're trying not to say, Aunt Lottie.''

"Yes, sir. Well, that's what she used to done, but not no more. Not since Master Yancey got home from his trip. He told her not to come round no more after that.''

"Well, it isn't any of my business either, and to tell

you the truth, Aunt Lottie, I don't care which of the girls Lewis has spend the nights with him. I'm not interested in that. But I do want my room made up properly and on time. Will you see to that in the future, please?''

"Yessuh, Mr. Dexter. I find that Clara girl right now an' get her up to your rooms, sir. Sir?''

"Mmm?''

"We be short-handed now that Netty leave. Can I find me another girl to be helping out in the house? I got someone in mind, but I don' want to tell her until you say.''

"I think you'd best ask my brother about that, Aunt Lottie. If I give permission he might think I'm over-stepping myself and say no just to show everyone that he can. Better you wait until Lewis gets home and ask him.''

"Yes, sir, Mr. Dexter, sir, thank you.''

How very odd, Dex reflected as he wandered into the study in search of something to read while he was waiting for his room to be made right and his boots to be readied.

Perhaps this overseer—what had Lewis said the man's name was? Dex couldn't remember—perhaps this fellow would be fetching along a new "employee" in Lewis's favor. Someone he'd found in Galveston or N'Orleans.

Not that Dexter cared. It just seemed unusual, that was all.

· 37 ·

"What a nice surprise," Dex said as he stepped out onto the verandah and discovered that they had a guest. "Will you be staying for supper, sir?"

"I expect to have that pleasure, yes." Sheriff Burton Ryan, ever eager to ingratiate himself with a registered voter, smiled and pumped Dexter's hand as if they were the dearest of longtime friends.

In fact Dex could hardly abide the man, considering him to be a drunk, a boor, and an incompetent. And he was fat and ugly too. "It's always a pleasure to see you, Sheriff," Dex said with a smile.

"My pleasure, believe me."

Dex could accept that as truth. The sheriff's appetites were legendary. Dex hoped Aunt Lottie had baked an extra large ham. Or killed a half-dozen extra chickens. Maybe both.

"What brings you out our way, Sheriff?"

"Your brother asked me to come back with him this afternoon."

"Ah, yes. Well, I'm certainly glad he did. Very glad."

Ryan, Dex noted, was dressed for official sheriffing business, so to speak. That is, he was wearing his badge—

the biggest Dex had ever seen—pinned prominently onto the lapel of a coat that should have been cleaned, or better yet discarded, a dozen years ago, back when Burt Ryan weighed a good thirty or forty pounds less than he did now.

The man also was carrying a large revolver displayed in a pouch on the front of his belt so that one could not possibly fail to notice it. That was unusual. Guns normally were evident in the parish only for hunting purposes or for New Year's revelries. Sheriff Ryan almost never bothered to carry his.

Dex was about to ask where his brother had gotten to when Lewis came out of the house to join them. He was carrying their father's old cash box and a sheet of paper.

"Ah, yes. I expected you would be the first in line," Lewis said in a cheery tone.

He stopped and made quite a show out of the simple act of opening the cash box, selecting a twenty-dollar double eagle, and handing it to his older brother.

Dexter could tell from Lewis's expression that he was enjoying this most thoroughly, having a witness there to see him dole out a pittance of an allowance to his own brother. If there was anything that Lewis might possibly enjoy more than having this power, it was the idea that others were observing it in action. And who better to see Dexter's humiliation than Burt Ryan, who could be sure to describe this tableau for his many cronies and drinking partners.

Dex understood Lewis's motives quite well. He did hope, though, that his brother had no idea how very little Dexter gave a damn what Lewis Yancey or Burt Ryan or any of the rest of them around here thought, said, or did.

None of it was anywhere near as important to Dexter as it was to Lewis, so Lewis's petty victory carried no sting in it for Dex.

"There you go, Dexter. Until next month."

"Thank you, brother dear," Dex said lightly.

"Now, Sheriff, would you join me, please? I want to pay off our people."

"Expecting trouble are you, Mr. Yancey?"

Mr. Yancey was it now? Dex had never heard anything like that from the sheriff or any of his crowd. Not until now. But then had things gone as they were supposed to, *he* would be Mr. Yancey these days, and Lewis would have remained Young Lewis to the genteel white folk in the parish.

"Not really," Lewis was saying, "but with niggers you never know."

"That's true," Ryan agreed. "You can't ever trust a nigger."

No, of course not, Dex thought. You could fuck their women, expect them to cook your food, clean up your messes, even wet-nurse your babies. But you could never, ever trust them, no, sir.

The really silly thing there, Dex reflected, was that both Lewis and Sheriff Ryan were quite perfectly serious in their assessment. Neither one of them would ever see the irony, or the stupidity, of their views.

"Come along then. Let's get this over with," Lewis said.

With the parish sheriff and Dex in tow, Lewis left the wide porch and walked out past the barn to where Blackgum Bend's field hands and crew foremen had gathered to receive their long-overdue pay.

· 38 ·

"All right, all right, let's get this over with. Quiet down, all of you. Come over here." Lewis was standing on the bed of a farm wagon. Sheriff Ryan stood close by his side. Dexter chose to remain at ground level, the better not to be noticed making faces if Lewis made an ass of himself.

"I have a list here of who is owed money," Lewis announced, showing his sheet of paper to the hands, all of whom were much too far away to be able to read it. If any of them could read, which itself was doubtful.

"As you already know, wages were adjusted last month to twelve dollars per hand, six for women and half-hands." A half-hand, technically speaking, was a child under the age of twelve. That was the legalistic view of things. In practice, children were expected to work in the fields beside their families, but were not carried on the ledgers even as half-hands. Half-hand pay was distributed only in cases of direst need, and then only by the more generous-natured planters. Charles Yancey had carried several half-hands on his book. Dexter doubted that Lewis would long continue their father's practice.

"Rent also had to be raised by just a very little," Lewis

was nattering. The crowd, Dex saw, was restless and unhappy. But quiet. Very quiet.

"Most of you have been very free with your spending
too. Very foolish, that. You have to learn to control yourselves. Just because you want something doesn't mean
you can go out and buy it, particularly on credit like
you've been doing."

Dex was puzzled by this line of yammering. Why the
hell would Lewis care what the nigras spent? Or how?

Then the clouds began to part—figuratively speaking,
that is—as Lewis smugly continued.

"Many of you issued IOUs at the shops down at the
Crossing. I want to remind you that those slips are legal
and binding debt obligations, every one of them. This afternoon I bought up your IOUs. I hold them under lock
and key, and the amounts owed are now owed not to the
store where you issued them, but to me as holder of, um,
said notes." Lewis seemed a trifle confused himself as to
how he should proceed, so it probably was reasonable
enough for the uneducated hands to be wondering what
in hell he was talking about. Judging from their expressions, Dex concluded that, yeah, they were pretty thoroughly confused at this point.

"Sheriff, would you please offer a few words of explanation here?" Lewis invited.

Which, Dex saw, explained Burt Ryan's presence for
the evening.

"All right now, you niggers listen to me and listen real
close," the sheriff said in a loud, clear voice that brought
grimaces and worry lines onto the dark faces before him.

"You owe money to this good man here. That's between him and you. What I am here to tell you right here
and now is that there isn't one of you gonna run off and
leave a legal debt unpaid. You hear me? Any man,
woman, or pickaninny amongst you tries to leave this
plantation without paying off what he owes to Mr. Yancey
here, I'll run his black ass down and put him in my jail.
And the son of a bitch will work hard labor for the county
until his IOU is paid off.

"Is there anybody here that doesn't understand what I'm tellin' you? Any one of you run off owing money, you've broke the law and me and my deputies will come down on you. Hard."

Ryan stood there for a few moments longer, sweeping the faces before him with a menacing glare.

Hell, Dex thought, a threat like that would be enough to put the fear into a white man. How much worse for an uneducated black who suddenly found himself right back in the same chains of slavery that he thought he'd escaped already.

Not that anyone would call it slavery. But it was. It surely was.

Between them Lewis and the sheriff had come up with a way to return to the tried and true.

Dex pitied the poor sons of bitches who worked the fields of Blackgum Bend.

"Now I do have money here," Lewis was saying, probably trying to get through the rest of this before the shock wore off his audience and they started to get pissed off.

Lewis consulted his paper. "I have cash money over and above your rent and IOUs for, um, let me see here, for seven of you." He opened his cash box and rested it on one hip while he continued to peer at the paper. "Those seven are. . . ."

Dex didn't bother to stay. He couldn't bear listening to any more of this bullshit.

Lewis was intent on making more crops and taking out more cash from the ground than their father had?

The fool, Dex thought. He had no idea that he was instead industriously ruining everything their father and grandfather had so lovingly built on this land.

◆ 39 ◆

For about half a second there Dex froze in place, his heart in his throat and cold fear clamping tight around his chest. For just about that long he thought their sins, his own and Lewis's too, were catching up with them and that Beelzebub riding a pale ghost horse had come to wreak havoc on the household.

Then he recognized the animal, and knew it wasn't a pale ghost horse but a pale yellow mule. And the rider wasn't Beelzebub but James.

Close enough, Dex thought. He took a moment to carefully examine the glass of mellow white whiskey in his hand, shrugged, and tossed off what remained. It would be only polite to start with a fresh tipple when James arrived.

Dex watched as Saladin passed by the house and on into the pecan grove. Minutes later he heard the crunch of footsteps on gravel and James emerged from the shadows to join him on the darkened porch.

Dex poured a tot of whiskey into his glass and handled the jar to James, who first looked back to see that the house windows were dark, then took a seat in the rocking chair beside Dex's.

"Have a drink. Hell, have several. I've got a head start on you."

James examined the jar. "I hope this wasn't full when you started drinking this evening."

"Aw, who remembers."

"Nobody sensible, that's sure." James took a long swallow, smiled, and had another. "I know where this came from. It's the good stuff."

"My poppa had taste. Didn't always have much luck in his choice of sons, but the man did have good taste when it came to likker. Have another."

James had another. He smelled of the jar, and decided on a third swallow to top off the other two. "You know, of course, that it's probably illegal for you to give whiskey to a slave."

"Which you aren't. You got outa here just in time to avoid that."

"Lucky me," James said. He had another drink.

"Don't empty that without offering me another pull."

"You have a glass of it in your hand. Drink that."

"Oh, yes. So I do." Dex accepted the advice in the spirit that was intended. He drank of the half glass he was holding, and reached for the jar to pour some more.

"I suppose you know what's happening out in the Quarters about now," James said.

"Is that what you came over to tell me?"

"Uh-huh, it is."

"You sure I oughta know?"

"Ought to? Probably. Want to? Probably not."

"That bad, is it?"

"Not as bad as it should be."

"What d'you mean?"

"If it was up to me," James said, "I'd go upstairs and beat the hell out of your baby brother, then burn the house down around him."

"You're a mean son of a bitch when you drink, d'you know that, James?"

"Yeah, well, it isn't up to me. And I probably wouldn't

do that anyhow. But I got to tell you that *Master* Lewis is not what you'd call popular right now.''

''So, since I assume the plan is for something short of beating and burning, what are they gonna do, James?''

''They say they'll walk off.''

''Sheriff Ryan will get up a bunch of drunks with shotguns and ax handles and declare open season on black butts if they do. Do they know that?''

''I've told them.''

''Did they listen?''

''No.''

''Just gets worse and worse, doesn't it,'' Dex mused. He sighed and drank some more of the whiskey. For some reason it tasted weak and watery to him, with neither the excellence of flavor nor the relief of impact to recommend it now.

''I was thinking maybe you could talk to them. They still respect you, Dexter.''

''Am I supposed to be flattered by that?''

''Dex, I don't give a shit right now if you're flattered or pissed. What I care about is those people. They're going to land themselves in jail if somebody doesn't do something to stop them. I don't want that to happen. And don't bullshit me. You don't want it to happen to them either. They're my people, but they're your people too. You care what happens to them. Don't pretend that you don't.''

''I care? So fucking what. I can't do anything to help them, James. I'm not the one with any say around here.''

''They'd listen to you, Dex.''

''And just what do you want me to tell them? Accept going back to slavery? Put a smile on your black face and show your white teeth and make like everything's wonderful? Go on and work and take the shit Lewis is piling on top of you? Stay a field nigger the rest of your miserable life and teach your children that that's all they'll ever be too? Is that what I'm supposed to go tell them, James?''

''You could tell them . . . Jesus, Dex, I don't know

what you ought to tell them. What choices do they have now? They can be slaves in the field or convicts on a chain gang as free men. There's a fine pair to pick from.'' James shuddered and emptied what had been left in the whiskey jar.

Dex finished what he had in his glass too. "You and me, James. We're a hell of a team, aren't we? We're full of something, all right. I just wish it was good advice. But we seem to've run out of that.''

"Look, will you just . . . come down to the Quarters? Talk to them? It doesn't hardly matter what you say when you get there, Dex. Just so the people know there's a Yancey that still cares if they're alive or dead. You know? Won't you do that for them? Please?''

Dex sighed. "I don't have any hope to give them, James.''

James gave his oldest and closest friend a sad, bitter smile. "These people haven't had hope nor expected any from the day they were born, Dex. They're just field niggers. You know? It isn't hope they ask for. Just a crumb they can hang onto, just knowing that somebody in this house here knows they're alive and wants them to stay that way.''

"All right, dammit. I'll come. Just don't . . . expect anything of me. Okay?''

"I expected you'd come. For right now, Dex, that's enough.''

"It will damn sure have to be. Now help me down those stairs, will you? Lousy things won't hold still. I dunno why.''

◆ 40 ◆

Sausage, eggs fried deep in the sausage grease, biscuits so light they had to be held down with great scoops of sausage gravy—it didn't get much better than that, Dex was thinking as he piled his plate full. Clara offered one salver after another, then refilled his coffee cup and withdrew to the side of the room. Dexter was halfway through his breakfast when Lewis came in to join him.

Lewis, Dex decided, looked about like Dex himself must have that night he'd talked to the hands. That had been, what? A couple weeks earlier? Something like that. Dex gathered that last night must have been Lewis's turn for a touch of drink and—or so one would hope—debauchery too. One seemed a bit of a waste without the other, after all.

"You look bright-eyed an' bushy-tailed," Dex said cheerily.

Lewis gave him a baleful look and eased gently down into his chair at the head of the long table.

In point of fact Lewis looked quite perfectly awful. His hair was sketchily combed and had a greasy, unwashed look about it. He was unshaven and red-eyed and even paler than usual.

"Have fun last night, brother?" Dex prodded happily.

"Yes, I did as a matter of fact." Lewis groped awkwardly on the table for his napkin, but only managed to drop it onto the floor. Clara rushed over to retrieve it, shake it out, and spread it onto her employer's lap.

"Still having fun?" Dex asked.

Lewis glared at him, then shook his head—and winced thereafter—when Clara presented the platters of sausage and eggs. Dex knew good and well what the sight of greasy food could do on a morning like Lewis was having.

Dexter grinned and took a second helping of biscuits and gravy for himself. Why not. It was all right there, so why not save Clara the trouble of fetching it all again.

Lewis settled for a few biscuits crumbled into a bowl and dowsed liberally with coffee, cream, and sugar. Coffee soup, their father used to call it. He'd long recommended its use when the stomach was queasy, particularly when one's stomach got that way in this particular manner.

Funny thing, Dex realized now. Through all those years he had seen his father walk gingerly and ask for coffee soup on many a morning. But never once in all that time had Dexter actually observed his father in a state of inebriation. He'd never thought about that before, but it was true. He wondered now if his father took deliberate care to keep his sons from seeing him in his cups. Or if it simply happened to work out that way.

It was deliberate, Dex decided quickly, albeit more on the strength of emotion than direct evidence.

"Good sausage," Dex suggested. "You should try some."

Lewis looked a trifle green, and Dex grabbed for his napkin to hide the smile that tickled the corners of his mouth.

"Laugh all you like, damn you," Lewis grumbled, "but I'm having the last laughs these days."

"Really, Lewis? How's that?"

"You told me the niggers would walk out on me. Remember?"

Dex nodded.

"There's not a one of them that's left the plantation. Did you know that, Dexter?"

He nodded again. Sure, he knew that. But then he also knew why no one had walked away from the fields. Yet.

"They'll do what they're damn well told," Lewis crowed.

"You called it, all right."

"You're damned right I did. I did the right thing. And we're going to prosper. I guarantee it."

"We, Lewis? Why should I care how much money you put into the bank? All I get is twenty dollars a month, regardless. Isn't that right?"

Lewis pawed weakly at the air over his head. Dex assumed, but was not entirely sure, it was supposed to be a gesture of dismissal.

"Lots of money, Dexter. Piles of the stuff. More than Poppa ever produced off this ground."

"Uh-huh. Sure." He supposed Lewis would go right on believing that. Up until time to pick and gin, that is. Dex suspected that his brother was going to be amazed by how little cotton Blackgum Bend produced this season.

Amazed enough, perhaps, to change his ways and go back to treating the hands decently. At least that was what Dex was hoping for.

"Poppa knew what he was doing when he willed the place to me," Lewis bragged. "He knew what was best."

"I'm sure he did," Dexter said in his most agreeable tone.

"Don't you get sarcastic with me, big brother."

"Wouldn't think of it," Dexter said cheerfully. "Not a bit of it."

"You're up to something, aren't you?"

"Me? Not at all. I've merely accepted the way things are, and I'm learning to adjust to doing things your way. I never gave Poppa any trouble, Lewis, and I don't expect to give you any either." He smiled brightly. "Just trying to get along, you see. Nothing more."

"If I believed that, Dexter, I might consider giving you an increase in your spending money."

"I'm sure you will do whatever you think best for this plantation and all the people who depend on it."

"That's right. That's exactly what I will do."

Dex smiled again. "Then we haven't anything to disagree about, do we?"

Lewis mulled that over, obviously wondering if Dexter was somehow gulling him about this, but unable to find anything to complain about in his brother's statements. "I . . . no, I s'pose we don't at that."

"Good. You know I never like to fight. Not if I can find a way around it."

"Yeah, well . . ."

Dex took a last, huge bite of biscuit and gravy and pushed his plate away. "If you'll excuse me now, Lewis, I need to ride in to the Crossing today. I'm to have a final fitting for my new suit of clothes. Got to cut a suitable figure at your soiree come Saturday, you know."

"That's right. Saturday. You are planning on attending, aren't you?"

"Wouldn't miss it for the world, brother."

"Good. Excellent." Lewis, in spite of other distractions, managed to give Dexter a smug and haughty look down the length of his not particularly patrician nose.

Dex grinned at his brother and gently tugged his forelock, then strode away. He really did have a fitting with the tailor later on. Although on reflection, he thought it something of a shame that he hadn't come up with a suitable lie instead. It seemed a pity to waste truthfulness on Lewis these days.

• 41 •

"Good morning, y' dirty old man. Found any young communicants to diddle lately?''

"That's *Father* Dirty Old Man to you, Mr. Yancey. And in answer to your question, no, the old ones will just have to do.''

Both men laughed. Father Peter Swain was several years younger than Dex and was blessed—or considering his calling, perhaps instead was cursed—with the sort of round and cherubic baby face that would keep him looking like a boy in his teens well into his middle years.

He was also totally devoted to his God and his parish. Dexter generally found priests to be pious only in public, riotous in private. Father Peter was such an exception that Dex not only liked him, he respected him too. That was, he thought, a first.

"Is there something I can do for you, Dexter?''

"No, thanks. I'm just going past. On my way to the cemetery.''

"Would you like me to come with you?''

"No. Please don't.''

"Of course. It will be all right, though, I hope, if I include you in my prayers,'' Father Peter offered.

"That's nice of you, thanks."

"But of course, my son. After all, it's what I am here for." The young priest smiled, and Dex returned a broad grin.

"Thanks for telling me that. I'd been wondering what it is you do with all your time."

That too was something of a joke between them. Father Peter was as energetic as he was enthusiastic about his work. He was perpetually on the move, visiting, comforting, advising—whether or not advice was sought— teaching, imploring, and above all, praying. The man was rarely still, and when he was he could generally be found on his knees.

"I'd best be off now," he said. "I have some visits to make and errands to run. Don't forget to pray when you get there."

"Yes, Father," Dex said, his voice carrying a hint of contrition that Father Peter obviously heard, for the priest cocked his head and hesitated as if to speak, then changed his mind and went hurrying off toward the church.

Dex did indeed feel more than a little bit sorry. Not that he had lied. Certainly not. But he told far from the full truth when he said he was on his way to the cemetery.

He waited a few moments to let Father Peter reach the church and disappear inside. Then Dex walked around to the back of the small rectory and tapped lightly on the kitchen door there.

"Oh. Good morning, Sister. I didn't expect to see you here today."

Sister Eleanor sniffed loudly and gave Dex a critical examination. It was plain that she found him wanting. "Who did you expect to see if not me?" the sister demanded.

"I, uh, I wondered if Mary Ellen had any messages to send to her mother. I'll be passing by their place on my way home later."

"Miss Murdock is quite capable of communicating with her mother if or when she pleases, Mr. Yancey. She doesn't need the likes of you sniffing around. You only want to lift the poor child's skirts. No, don't give me that look. I know your kind, Mr. Yancey. Indeed I do. I was a young girl myself once, you know. You can't fool me."

"No, Sister, I'm sure I can't." Dex glanced past the glowering sister's shoulder. Mary Ellen was in the kitchen. She held a finger to her lips to tell Dex not to speak, then held the finger extended upright. One minute. She winked and silently gathered her skirts up so she could slip away without Sister Eleanor noticing that she'd been there.

"I'm sorry if I've distressed you," Dex apologized.

"It isn't I you should say that to," the sister cautioned.

"Yes, Sister."

"Go on now. Miss Murdock has no need of you and neither do I."

"Yes, Sister. Good day to you now." Dex touched the brim of his hat, bowed, and backed away from the door. He walked out behind the rectory to the generations-old cemetery.

· 42 ·

There was no reason why burials needed to be above ground here. Well, actually there was one reason and it was reason enough. Fashion. In New Orleans cemeteries were all built above ground. Crypts, tombs, and mausoleums were the rule there, not by vogue but of necessity. New Orleans was built virtually at—some said a little bit below—sea level, and any coffins placed into the earth were very apt to be floated up to the surface again come a little wet weather. There were some who found this annoying, so cemeteries there were all above ground.

Here, the only reason to bury above ground was in order to ape the New Orleans fashion.

Naturally, therefore, about a third of the burials at Our Lady of Hope Parish were above ground.

Dexter made his way quickly through the array of tombs, tombstones, and granite statuary to an imposing gray stone mausoleum with the name Calderone carved above the lintel. The mausoleum was larger than most houses, complete Grecian-style columns highlighting a front porch and ornate stonework on either side of a deep-set pair of massive oak and wrought-iron doors.

The Calderone family's final resting place was a grand one indeed, and Dexter admired it greatly.

He also found reason to be glad that a combination of age, diseases, and the westering movement had taken the last of the Calderone clan—if any yet remained—far from Louisiana. The mausoleum stood in a state of elegant neglect, unvisited in recent years. Except by Dexter. He came here with some regularity.

Glancing around to make sure no one else was nearby, an event that had never once occurred, but which he always fretted about, he trotted lightly up the few steps leading into the final resting place of the Calderones and stopped at the huge, dark doors.

Another look about and behind reassured him that he was alone here. He took hold of a padlock the size of a small melon and twisted.

The ancient, rusted-out lock swung open, and was quickly removed from the iron hasp. A few seconds more and Dexter was inside. He pulled the door closed behind him and felt himself surrounded by silence and a faint, very slightly musty odor.

The only light inside the mausoleum came from a pair of stone grillwork ventilators set into the front and back walls high under the eaves. The air inside was cool and dry and not unpleasant.

Ranked on either side of a center aisle Dex could dimly see square slabs of stone, each carved with names and dates, to show the resting place of one or another Calderone. The dates were presented in an orderly flow beginning with Giuliana Calderone, who died in 1783, and progressing through Duncan Arnold Calderone, died of wounds sustained in battle, July 19, 1863.

Duncan was the last, and in spite of the fact that he himself had been only a child when Duncan rode off to war, Dex remembered this last Calderone. Or thought he did. It might have been imagination, but Dex felt sure that Duncan had been tall and dark and laughing.

That would have been early in the conflict, of course, before the damn Yankees came so soon to occupy Louisiana and take the state and its people out of the mainstream of the fight, an event which had been bitter for Louisianans to accept at the time, but which gave them exemption from the horrors of destruction that swept through most of the South later on.

Now Duncan was buried here along with all his Southern pride and hope and glory.

Or wasn't. A good many families never were able to retrieve the earthly remains of their loved ones, and a good many markers were placed in loving memory of boys whose bodies lay in other but no less hallowed soil.

Dex had often wondered if Duncan Calderone's body really was here or still rested somewhere else, in Vicksburg perhaps or Gettysburg. Either of those could account for the wounds he died from shortly afterward.

Dex walked over and looked at the carving. Not that he really needed to see. He remembered it word for word and date for date from his many visits to this quiet and lonely old place.

He wondered anew if Duncan indeed was here. And if he was, was he inserted into the mausoleum cavity head first or feet first?

That was a question that had always niggled and teased, but one which Dex had never quite gotten up nerve enough to ask of anyone who might know. Which was he facing when he looked at these blank stone squares, moldering feet or decaying skulls?

It was a puzzlement to him.

But not for very long.

Behind him Dex heard the grate of iron dragging across stone and the creak of a long-unoiled hinge.

He turned.

And smiled.

Mary Ellen Murdock slipped inside the mausoleum to join him and ran lightly into Dexter's arms.

· 43 ·

Mary Ellen Murdock was not the name she'd been born with. No one knew what that might have been. She'd been found as a toddler by a family named Murdock—or so they'd claimed—and left at the age of three or thereabouts at Our Lady of Hope, a nuisance and a burden to the loving Murdocks.

She was raised by committee, the ward of a succession of priests and nuns and housekeepers. When she was old enough she became a member of the household staff, working in the kitchen for the most part, constantly encouraged to accept a calling and become a nun.

From her point of view, the church had been good to her. But it was not her aspiration. The yearnings Mary Ellen felt had nothing to do with cloisters or prayer. Nor, for that matter, with anything a priest could give her either. Well, at least no priest who took his own vows with any degree of sincerity.

Mary Ellen's yearnings focused in a soft and tender area that lay not deep within her heart, but instead was tucked warm and snug between her thighs.

Dex had heard the often-abused term "nymphomaniac'' on more than one occasion, the word usually being misunderstood and/or misapplied.

In Mary Ellen's case, though, it just might fit.

The girl was just plain horny.

Dex had first discovered this when an urgent need sent him running for the nearest outhouse, that being the one behind the church rectory. He hadn't taken time to knock before entering, and the latch hadn't caught. What was caught inside was Mary Ellen. She was sitting with her skirt around her waist, her drawers around her ankles, and two fingers of her left hand inserted as far as she could get them into her own vagina.

Dex hadn't known until that day that girls liked to do it to themselves when nothing better was available, just like boys.

At the time he had been, he thought, sixteen or so. Mary Ellen would have been eighteen. And not shy.

"Come in," she'd offered. "You can finish doing me if you want."

"I have to piss awful bad."

"Good. I'll watch. It will get me in the mood."

"It looks to me like you're already in the mood."

"Don't you want to fuck?"

"What I want is to piss."

"Then can we fuck?"

"Sure. Now please get out of my way or I'll piss in your lap. I swear I will." He was already unbuttoning his fly as he spoke.

Mary Ellen did indeed watch. And began to smile and sigh when she saw what young master Yancey brought out of his britches.

That had been a fair number of years back, and Mary Ellen was as horny now as she'd been then. Just as eager, just as ready. Dex had no idea who else in the parish she was screwing—he suspected Father Peter was a great disappointment to her, although not all the past priests had been—but whenever he felt in the mood he needed only to drop by the rectory. Whenever Mary Ellen saw him, she knew what he was offering and never failed to slip away so she could meet him in the Calderone mausoleum.

Today he was most definitely in the mood. And he didn't have to ask about Mary Ellen. He could, and did, take her for granted.

One of the nice things about Mary Ellen was that foreplay was not needed. A stiff dick and a few minutes of time were all the girl required.

She slipped inside the mausoleum now and immediately began shedding clothes, dropping them willy-nilly on the floor as she hurried to the back of the structure, to the pallet Dex had made there ages back and which Mary Ellen maintained with an occasional change of blanket and renewal of the Spanish moss stuffing that filled the striped blue and white mattress ticking.

Mary Ellen Murdock was not beautiful by any stretch of the imagination. She was thin to the point of emaciation, had bony hips and virtually no tits. Her nipples were dark, wrinkled little raisins pasted onto a chest as flat as that of a ten-year-old boy, and she had a chin she could have used to open cans with.

It was the bane of her existence that men looked at her without lust. Without lust? Without any semblance of interest whatsoever.

She was plain, homely, drab, and ordinary.

She was also a bundle of raw energy when she had a cock inside her.

Without bothering with preliminaries like kissing or touching, Mary Ellen helped Dex shed his clothing—her own was already off before she reached him—and grabbed his pecker as if reaching to pull a sausage down from a hook.

She hauled him down onto the pallet, positioning herself deftly in the way of his progress so that by the time he got there she was already lying beneath him with her legs spread wide and her pussy wetly receptive.

Mary Ellen grabbed Dexter's hips and tugged, plunging him deep into the heat of her body.

Dex knew what was coming next. Other than him, that

is. He braced himself and hung on. That was all he needed
to do. Mary Ellen was quite capable of handling the rest.

The girl cried out as Dexter's stiff flesh filled her. She
yelped and moaned and thrashed madly up and down,
back and forth, clawing with hands that raked his back,
clenching her legs tight around his waist and clamping
him firmly in place, pounding and pummeling, her belly
slapping hard against his and the sharp ridges of her pelvic
bones gouging and thumping as she churned with all the
vigor of a steam-driven paddle wheel running wild.

Sweat generated by all the frantic humping began to
coat her skinny body, changing the noises of belly against
belly so that now there was a distinctly wet sound to the
belly-slapping.

Mary Ellen began to mew and keen, the thin sounds
starting deep in her throat and escaping through tight-
clenched teeth.

Dex felt his responses gather and grow.

Not this time, dammit. Not so *soon*.

That was the problem with Mary Ellen. She was
greedy, dammit. She couldn't slow down for even ten
seconds. She wanted to pump and writhe and churn without ceasing.

Always Dex tried to hold back. To extend the sensa-
tions and make them last a while before he spewed out
all his seed and strength like water bursting out of a new
well.

Always he tried. Always Mary Ellen won. Always she
brought him soaring hard and fast to the edge and then
dumped him over it.

Dex gritted his teeth. Counted by threes in an attempt
to distract himself and cause a small delay. Two minutes
would be wonderful. One would be practically a miracle.

Nine, twelve, fifteen, eighteen, twenty-one . . .

"Ahhhh!"

"Yes. Yes. Yes."

Dex's body stiffened. He felt the hot sap rise and gush
forth.

Mary Ellen only clung to him all the tighter, her

scrawny frame displaying almost unreal levels of energy as she continued to gyrate and thrust, not so much as slowing down to acknowledge Dexter's pleasure.

And her own was virtually continuous. That was one of the things about Mary Ellen that never failed to amaze Dex.

She started having orgasms within ten seconds of his initial entry, each and every time they were together, and she kept it up for as long as she could move.

When the girl finally stopped it was from sheer exhaustion, and she would lie there sweat-slicked, pale, and limp until Dex would think this time she'd gone too far, this time she'd fucked herself near to death.

He thought that every time.

For about ten minutes. Then it was her habit to shudder and return slowly to life, gasping and coughing and weak. That phase always lasted another few minutes, until she was able to rise and wobble away, dressing bit by bit on her way to the doors, and then to disappear without a word of good-bye.

Dex felt the wondrous gather and release, then for a time felt little but annoyance as Mary Ellen continued to beat the dead horse. And then, as always too, he felt the tingling return of desire as her continued pumping and pounding brought the blind snake once more back to life until he was again hard and ready.

Ah, Mary Ellen. Small and shy and demure. Right!

Dex held himself rigid above her frantically plunging body and allowed the girl to have her way with him.

It was the gentlemanly thing to do.

• 44 •

The sound of a distant steam whistle floated across the fields. Dex cocked his head. Grunted. It was their signal, all right. Nothing for him to worry about, though. Lewis was inside, in the study, and he would take care of sending someone down to the landing. Dex returned to his reading.

A few moments later Lewis stepped out onto the porch. "There you are."

"Yes, and here I've been. Is anything wrong?"

"Certainly not. Far from it, in fact. I've sent for the carriage already. I would like you to ride down to the landing with me."

"This sounds like an occasion," Dex said, laying a slip of pasteboard between the pages of his book as a marker and laying the book aside.

"It is. So come along, won't you?"

"Be glad to. Just let me get my hat."

"Fine. Fine."

By the time the carriage was prepared and the drive to the landing completed, the *Gossamer Lady* was already lying close by the quay, a gang of Negroes ashore with the lines being made fast to the bollards.

In addition to Lewis and Dexter in the carriage, a heavy wagon trailed behind with the barnyard hands riding in it ready to provide muscle for whatever cargo was being delivered.

Lewis was as excited as Dex could remember seeing him in . . . well, since he'd come home from Galveston and N'Orleans. That was exactly how long it had been since he'd seen Lewis this enthusiastic about anything.

"There now, there," Lewis said, standing and waving to someone on board the tall and ornately dressed stern-wheeler. Nathaniel, the boy handling the reins of the carriage, must not have seen Lewis standing erect like that, for he chose that moment to wheel the carriage aside and bring it to a halt. The unexpected motion threw Lewis off balance, and would have sent him tumbling to the ground had Dex not grabbed his coattail to steady him.

"Damn you, Nathaniel."

"Yes'm, Masta Yancey, suh, sorry, suh, sorry."

The words were said so quickly, and with such a mournfully exaggerated expression of sorrow, that Dexter doubted their sincerity. Perhaps Nathaniel had indeed been aware that the boss was not seated.

Not that Dex intended to question the boy. And Lewis failed to recognize anything suspicious.

"Hurry up, boy. Get the step down. Quickly now."

"Yes, suh, Masta Yancey, suh." Nathaniel set the parking brake with meticulous care, climbed slowly down from the high driving box, and retrieved the bright-painted box that served as a step into the carriage. He set it in place and swung the door open so Lewis could dismount in comfort.

By that time the *Lady*'s gangplank had been lowered and secured, and a pair of passengers were disembarking. Aft of the passageway a group of burly stevedores were unloading crates and trunks and what surely looked like a clavichord.

The couple obviously intended to stay a while, but Dex was fairly sure he did not know them. Distant relatives? He didn't think so.

But he certainly was willing to make their acquaintance. Or that of the lady, at least.

The man Dexter took in at a glance and as quickly dismissed. He was just another gent, well enough dressed, a trifle on the beefy side, with bushy whiskers and a red nose and slightly graying hair. Older than Dex and Lewis by years. Dex was certain he had never seen this fellow before.

The woman who accompanied him, however, Dex would like to see much, much more of.

She was elegantly dressed in a flounced and ruffled gown of pale yellow, and carried a parasol to match. It was neither the gown nor the accoutrements that held Dexter's attention, though, but the female creature that both highlighted.

The woman was . . . beautiful. Breathtakingly so. She had dark hair that was coifed to a fare-thee-well, high cheekbones, full lips that were an unnaturally brilliant shade of red—that boded well, Dex could not help thinking, for the sort of woman who went about in public wearing lip rouge could often be inveigled into wearing nothing at all in private—and what was surely the longest, most slender, most tender and delicate neck Dex ever did lay eyes upon.

Her gown was cut delightfully low, exposing the rounded upper slopes of breasts that appeared modest in size but quite perfect in proportion to a waist that a gentleman—if he were no gentleman—could span with naught but with his own two hands.

The crinolines and skirts of her gown prevented Dex from forming judgment as to the lady's hips and lower limbs. But the upper parts of her were so exceptionally agreeable that he doubted he would overmuch care should her lower portions prove to be elephantine.

That did, however, seem a course of investigation that would be worthy of his very best efforts. Whoever this exquisite creature was, Dex would truly like to know her better. Even, uh, intimately. As it were.

He cleared his throat, shot his cuffs, and thought it a

damn shame that he hadn't dressed better for this most unexpected occasion.

Still, Saturday night approached. He would be at his very best for the gala. He surely would have another opportunity to present himself at that time. And . . . ah! Of course.

That had to explain it. Whoever these people were, Lewis must have become acquainted with them during his recent travels. They might even be the guests of honor at this ball Lewis was so enthused about.

Another thought struck Dexter, and he began to smile just a little.

Lewis had sent poor Netty packing. Was this beauty the reason? Had the new master of Blackgum Bend come to a sudden arrangement concerning the lady's future?

Mmm, could be, Dex thought. It seemed entirely possible that the gentleman was her father. Come to announce a betrothal?

Dex rather hoped so. He had no desire to marry himself, of course. Nor, for that matter, did he possess the means, even had he had the desire.

But it would be pleasant to have such a beauty in the family.

And in all the years they'd shared, Dex had yet to meet a girlfriend of his dear, dear brother who could not be wooed and won by Lewis's older and rather more dashing twin.

Not that Lewis knew this, of course. Nor need he.

Still, the thought was a pleasing one. Dexter checked quickly to reassure himself that he was fully tucked, buttoned, and brushed, then alighted from the carriage with all the considerable poise and grace he could muster.

· 45 ·

"Dexter, I want you to meet Mr. Stennet, our new overseer. Mr. Stennet, my 'big' brother, Dex."

Stennet nodded curtly and did not extend his hand to shake. Well, neither did Dex. There was something in the man's eyes that Dex did not like. They were small and beady, he thought. Or, okay, they weren't. But they should have been.

Actually the man looked quite ordinary. A trifle large. A trifle coarse. But there was nothing outstanding about him really. Yet Dex found himself repulsed by the fellow for no good reason, except, perhaps, the fact that he was here and taking charge of their father's plantation and Dex just damn well didn't like it. Perhaps that was all there was to it.

As for the woman who accompanied him . . .

Dex swept his hat off and made a leg. "And the lady would be . . . ?"

He was still half expecting to be introduced to Lewis's future bride. Or to Stennet's daughter. Or even his wife. That too was possible, wasn't it?

One possibility Dex had not considered was the response he got. Both Stennet and Lewis broke into laughter.

"Lady?" Stennet sputtered. "Lady, is it? Jesus!"

It took Dex a moment to recognize the reason for their humor. Then it dawned on him.

The young woman who was traveling with Blackgum Bend's new overseer was a sloe-eyed beauty. That hadn't seemed particularly significant. Many women had dark eyes. Beautiful eyes, they could be. As were these. But now that he was looking more closely, Dex could see that the girl's nose was very slightly broad at the base, her lips just a bit thick, the golden tone of her flawless skin carrying the merest hint of the tar brush?

"I don't . . . that is to say, I didn't . . ."

Stennet laughed all the louder. "Looks like an octoroon, don't she? Or less, eh? Fact is, son, she's a quadroon at best. Pure nigger any way you look at it. But handsome, ain't she?"

"She, um, yes. Of course." What the hell else could he say. Dex clamped his hat back onto his head.

"One thing you keep in mind, boy," Stennet declared. "The girl is mine. All mine. Don't you even think about throwing that skirt over her face. She's private property. You sniff around what's mine, boy, I'll break you in two."

Dex gave Stennet a hard look, and his brother another. The hired help, and so this Stennet was, had no business speaking like that to a Yancey. Not to any Yancey, never mind which of the two of them was running the plantation.

Yet Lewis said nothing to correct the overseer.

"Her name, if you wanta know, is Jessie. That's short for Jezebel. God knows what she used to be called, but she calls herself Jezebel now. It fits. Or used to. Now she belongs to me. Don't you forget it."

"Yes of course, lest you . . . how did you put it? You would break me in two?" Dex smiled when he said that.

"That's right, boy, an' don't you forget it."

"Oh, I shan't forget that, Mr. Stennet. No indeed, I

believe I should find that very difficult to let slip from my mind.''

"Dex!'' Lewis said, a note of warning in his low voice. But then, of course, he knew his brother far better than Stennet was ever likely to.

Dexter smiled brightly. ''Not to worry, brother dear. No cause for worry whatsoever.''

"I hope not.''

Stennet seemed already to have dismissed the subject. He climbed into the carriage, Lewis close behind him. Dex paused for a moment; then he too entered the carriage leaving Stennet's property for Nathaniel to load, which the young black was quick to do.

Dexter found himself having some difficulty trying to keep from staring at Jessie. In an attempt to avoid being rude, and to eliminate the likelihood of bloodshed before the new overseer had time to unpack, Dex turned his attention away from the dark-eyed beauty and tried small talk instead.

"I assume you will be with us for some time, Mr. Stennet.'' It was an assumption only, not a desire, but he did not say that part aloud. ''May I inquire as to your name?''

"Mister Stennet,'' Stennet said.

"But your first name?''

"That is my first name. Mister. My father had a sense of humor.'' The overseer scowled. ''You will find that I do not.'' Stennet turned and called up to Nathaniel, ''Make sure you drive past the fields, boy. I want to see how my new niggers work.''

Boy. He called Nathaniel that as a matter of course. It occurred to Dex that Mr. Mister Stennet had called him the same.

Fine fellow, that Stennet. Dex was just *ever* so glad Lewis had hired him.

Behind them the Blackgum Bend people were busy loading Stennet's possessions into the farm wagon, while the *Gossamer Lady*'s paddles were loudly churning water into a white froth. The boat began slowly to pull away from the landing.

· 46 ·

Dex posed, turned, turned back the other way again as he checked himself in the mirror. He tilted his head this way and then that. Grasped his lapels and lifted his chin. Turned again. All the while eyeing himself with a critical view.

Well, critical in theory. In truth there wasn't really much room for criticism. He looked damn-all fine if he did say so. The tailor had done a marvelous job. But then he'd had such excellent material to work with.

His new coat was a plum-colored cutaway with wide satin cuffs and matching lapel. The new shirt was ruffled. High-waisted trousers and vest were a soft, pale gray. His cravat picked up flecks of color to match the plum, and was surmounted by a large stickpin that was judiciously, if barely, small enough to avoid being thought fake, yet large enough to be mightily impressive. It was, of course, as artificial as Lewis's best wishes.

Dexter declared himself ready for the ball, made one final check to see that his handkerchief was impeccably crisp and clean, and made his way grandly down the stairs.

The house was already ablaze with light and abuzz with

conversations. Guests had been arriving for the past several hours, and if any more came they would have to start stuffing them into closets just to have somewhere to put them all.

Lewis's gala, Dex had to concede, promised to become the success of the season.

Every genteel family in a thirty-mile radius seemed to be there. Dex saw the Barchesters, and revised that to include a forty-mile radius. Practically everyone he had ever known, everyone of quality anyway, was either present already or soon would be.

Blackgum Bend boasted no ballroom as such, but the entire south side of the big house had been converted to use as one. All the furniture had been removed from the parlor and the wide sliding doors leading into the drawing room spread open, creating one long area cleared of all obstruction. A string quartet held forth on one side of what was normally the drawing room, and a few chairs had been placed nearby for those who chose to listen but not dance.

A buffet established in the rearranged dining room was proving popular, and out on the side porch an area had been established where the gentlemen could find whiskey, cigars, and rocking chairs.

Elegant ladies swirled in and through the crowd like so many tropical birds in brilliant plumage.

Serving girls, their kinky hair hidden beneath spanking-new white mobcaps and their figures swathed in aprons and white shifts, moved discreetly about offering sweetmeats and tiny pastries and innocent lemon punch.

The beaming host of all this grandeur had parked himself at one end of the makeshift "ballroom" where he held court. Merriman Thibidoux and Lucy Anne appeared to hang on every word. Dex was not especially surprised. Not considering the conversation that had passed between them the last time he saw Lucy Anne. And, for that matter, the last conversation he'd had with her father. The old fart.

Lucy Anne noticed his arrival. Their eyes met, and Dex

bowed slightly in her direction. He hoped she knew better than to take that seriously, the bitch. He gave her a smile as brilliant as all the candles in the chandelier combined. And then some.

Lucy Anne returned the smile, and turned to rise on tiptoes and whisper something into Lewis's ear. Not that she had so very far to lift herself, Lewis being so much shorter than Dex was.

Dex turned away and surveyed the possibilities that lay within the rooms.

He felt a brief moment of dissatisfaction when he realized that virtually all the eligible females in the parish were already here and there was not a single one of them who held much interest for him.

He had slept with . . . he counted . . . five of them to date. Well, not exactly slept with. Enjoyed the favors of was a more appropriate way to put it. And at that the ladies' favors were mostly limited. The only one he'd actually fucked was Emily Wilmerton, and that only because it was widely known that Emily had abandoned virginity early on. She'd been an accomplished little minx long before Dex ever got to her, and was counted a feather in no young gentleman's cap. A rite of passage, perhaps, but not exactly a conquest.

Apart from Emily, though, it had all been manipulations and enjoyments involving something other than full coitus.

Not that Dex was complaining. It was all good sport, and he would be happy to romp with any one of them again. Except perhaps for Lucy Anne. He was rather pissed off with her and her father.

The one woman he kept thinking about, though, was quite naturally not in attendance. Mr. Mister Stennet was there, lurking about like a lizard in a corner, or so Dex considered it. But it would have been unthinkable for the man to've brought his dusky mistress to a gathering of this nature.

Damned shame that was too, Dex thought as he reached for a glass of punch and a sweet pastry. Jezebel's looks would have shamed every female in the place.

Which, of course, would have been more than reason enough to make sure she was not seen by the gentry. Something like that simply wouldn't do.

A man couldn't help but think about that one, though. Mr. Mister Stennet must surely be a very happy man. He was—

"Is that for me, Dexter? Thank you." Lucy Anne gave him a dimpled smile and deftly plucked the punch glass out of his fingers. She took a hummingbird-sized sip of the punch, snagged the pastry out of his other hand, and smoothly deposited both glass and confection onto the tray of a passing servant. "Would you spare me a few moments, Dexter dear?"

There were people nearby, and at an affair like this no nuance of vocal tone or facial expression would go unnoticed.

Dex smiled. Bowed. Offered his elbow for Lucy Anne to take.

"Can we speak outside, please?" she continued. "With some privacy?"

"Of course." He bowed again.

Her wishes were not exactly his commands. But what the hell. If she wanted to say something—like for instance if she would care to apologize for her father's intolerably rude behavior—that would be all right.

He led the way out of the "ballroom" and into the cool quiet of the night air.

◆ 47 ◆

"No, not here. Isn't there anywhere that we can't be seen, please?"

"There's no one to hear."

"I don't want anyone to see us either. Please."

Dex shrugged and continued on, out past the flower garden and into the deep shadows of the pecan grove to the bench there.

"Wouldn't the barn be better?" she asked.

"You never know what eyes might be watching in the barn. Some of the hands sleep in there."

"Oh. No. That wouldn't do, would it."

"I didn't think so." Dex used his handkerchief to carefully wipe the seat of the bench, then spread the cloth for Lucy Anne to perch on. He rather hoped she'd get splinters in her pretty butt, but she didn't.

"I told Lewis I wanted to have a word with you in private, Dexter."

"Oh?"

"I didn't tell him what I wanted to speak to you about."

"That's fair," Dex said. "You haven't told me either."

"Be patient. I'm getting to that."

"Yes, of course."

"Before I say anything else, dear . . . would you do something for me, please?"

Throttling her came to mind as a pleasant possibility, but all he said was, "If I can, certainly."

"Oh, you can. I know you can." She gave him an impish smile and a giggle and slid across the bench to press herself tight against his side. Her mouth found his, and he could taste a hint of lemon on her breath and feel the soft probing of her tongue.

Dex kissed her. He didn't particularly want to. But he found himself doing it anyway. Lucy Anne was particularly talented with her mouth. Including when it came to kissing, but not at all limited to that.

"Thank you," she whispered when finally the kiss ended. She did not, however, withdraw from him. She laid her head on his chest and sighed. "I have missed you ever so much, Dexter dear."

"Have you really?"

"Yes. Have you missed me?"

"Not especially."

Lucy Anne lifted her chin to look at him for several long, silent seconds. "I've hurt you. I am so very sorry about that, Dexter. Truly I am."

"Of course you are." He didn't mean it. Did not for a moment believe she was sorry. But he almost wished that it was true.

"There is something you have to know, dear. And something that I would very much like for you to do."

"Is that so?"

"Yes, dear, it is so."

"And this thing you want me to do for you?"

"First the thing that I must tell you." She reached up to touch his face and kissed him again, this time lightly and perhaps apologetically. "I am not a virgin any longer, my dear."

Dex blinked. That one did take him quite aback. "You say . . . ?"

"It's true. As long as I could remember, dear, it was

you who I wanted, you that I expected would have me first. And only. I only wanted to be with you, Dexter. You know that, don't you?''

He grunted. He hadn't wanted to marry the girl anyway. But dammit, he'd expected the refusal to be his. After all, that was why he'd kept on saying no whenever Lucy Anne wanted him to pop her cherry. And that had been going on for, what, the past several years anyway. He'd been staunch and decent and thoughtful. Now, dammit, she'd gone and spread her legs for somebody else.

"And what I want you to do, my own true love, is to take me. Tonight. Right here and now. Please? You know how I've wanted you. And now there's no harm to be done. I'm not a virgin now. If you take me you'll take nothing away from me. And you will . . . you'll give me a memory, Dexter. The most wonderful memory I could ever hope to have. Would you do that, Dexter? Would you take me now? Please?''

There was only one proper way to respond to that, of course. He'd been insulted by Lucy Anne and he'd been insulted by her damned father, and now the girl wanted him to get a hard-on and poke her already used cunt just on her say-so?

What the hell kind of idiot did she take him for anyhow?

Lucy Anne pushed the top of her gown to waist level, exposing her tits. She raised up off the bench and pulled her skirt high. She wore crinolines, but no pantaloons or other impediments to his entry.

"I'm already so wet, honey, just from thinking about you. Fuck me now, dear. Please."

He should stand right up, turn his back, and march stiffly away. That was what he ought to do, by gum.

Well, he was standing up good and stiff, all right. But not in the way he knew he should.

Lucy Anne reached for the buttons of his trousers. Her mouth was hot against his and her tongue probing past his cheeks while deftly and from long practice, she peeled his britches loose.

Well, shit, Dex grumbled. Silently and to himself only.

• 48 •

Dex felt all wet and sticky inside his trousers. It was uncomfortable. Not that he was complaining, mind. But it was annoying nonetheless. He smiled and nodded and helped himself to a small pastry. Peach. Tasted pretty good too. He thought about the lemon punch that was being passed around indoors, and decided that was not exactly what he wanted right now. A whiskey julep would be more like it. He bowed to Lucy Anne, who seemed oblivious to him now anyway, and excused himself.

Lucy Anne amazed him. He knew damn good and well that she was leaking sticky stuff down the insides of both her legs. Hell, he'd put it there himself and knew she had to feel the trickle and tickle of it, but to look at her you would certainly think that butter wouldn't melt in the girl's mouth.

Huh. It wasn't only butter she could melt with that mouth. He knew that from some personal experience too. Not tonight, though. No need for that sort of caution now.

Someone else had already gotten to her. She hadn't specified exactly who, of course. He would not have expected her to. And didn't particularly care except in an idle sort of way.

Dex would have enjoyed popping Lucy Anne, certainly'd had more than opportunity enough and offers
enough in the past, but it was just as well that it hadn't
been him. They likely were both better off in the long
run, neither of them obligated to the other. Yeah, just as
well. He yawned and began drifting toward the side door
that led out onto the porch where the whiskey and cigars
could be enjoyed.

Down at the far end of the crowded rooms the music
came to a sudden stop, and the dancers stopped as well.
The loud drone of many conversations ceased, and all
eyes turned in the direction of Lewis, who now was standing on something—Dex couldn't see what—to elevate
himself above the general head level of his party guests.

"My dear friends," Lewis said. "If you would indulge
me with your attention, please, there is an announcement
that I would like to make."

"Hear, hear," someone rasped from off to the right.
Whoever it was sounded like he was more than a little bit
into his cups already, and the night had a long time yet
to go.

"Thank you, thank you," Lewis said. He paused,
cleared his throat, reached down for someone to hand him
a cup of punch, and drank from it. Finally he said, "The
reason I have brought you all together for this most wonderful evening, dear friends and neighbors, is that it is my
very great honor to announce that Miss Lucy Anne Thibidoux has, with her father's gracious approval, accepted
my proposal of marriage. Banns will be posted at Our
Lady of Hope, and we shall be wed immediately following this forthcoming fall harvest."

Lewis continued speaking, but whatever he said was
lost in a rush of clapping and yelping and shouted congratulations.

Dex could make out the top of Lucy Anne's head as
she stood now close by Lewis's side.

Dexter smiled. It was all working out just fine, wasn't
it. Lucy Anne had herself a Yancey to marry and Merriman Thibidoux had his river landing. Lewis had a blush-

ing bride to show off in society now, and a white bedmate
to produce the requisite sons and heirs.

Well, it wouldn't be so bad for Dex either now that he
thought about it.

Could be damn well convenient actually. Lucy Anne
and both Yanceys under one roof? After all, not half an
hour gone the girl had demonstrated the depth of her love
and loyalty to Lewis Yancey, hadn't she?

And now she was betrothed. How very nice for her.

Dexter sighed. He probably wouldn't have done anything differently out there in the pecan grove even if he'd
known. But now it was nice to be able to remind himself
that he really hadn't had any inkling.

As for the next time . . . well, that would just have to
take care of itself, wouldn't it.

Dex pushed his way through the throng while down at
the far end of the room Lewis held forth on some topic
or other. The call of a good julep was strong, Dex decided. And much more interesting than what was going
on indoors.

◆ 49 ◆

"Congratulations, baby brother."

Lewis gave him a hooded look. Or as close to one as he could manage out of eyes that looked like they'd soaked overnight in a glass of blood. The servants had had to carry Lewis to bed sometime during the small hours of the morning.

Now it was the middle of the afternoon.

They were having breakfast.

Dexter hadn't exactly had an evening that would have been approved by the Women's Christian Temperance Union.

He was, however, handling the pain of his hangover better than poor Lewis. And he'd put himself to bed without assistance. It had taken all his by-then-rather-limited powers of concentration to do it, but he'd gotten it done. That was what counted. He'd gotten it done.

Lewis hadn't.

But then Dexter'd had somewhat more experience in that area too, supporting the popular theory that practice makes for perfection.

"Clara, fetch my brother some bacon, would you?" Dex said. "And some of those eggs."

"You hate me, don't you."

"Are you saying that because I congratulate you on your engagement? Or because I suggest bacon and eggs for breakfast?" Dex asked, dabbing at his mouth with a napkin and pretending that his acidly roiling stomach was quite under control, thank you.

"You know what I mean," Lewis snarled.

"Actually I don't. Enlighten me."

"D'you think I didn't know? You wanted her for yourself. You always did. Everyone in the parish knew that. But she's mine now, big brother. Miss Lucy Anne Thibidoux belongs to *me*. Only me. And everyone in the whole parish knows that now too. How does that make you feel?"

"I thought I already suggested that, Lewis. I said 'congratulations' to you, and I meant it. I'm happy for you. I'm happy for both of you." He turned his head. "I'd like some of that toasted bread if you please, Clara."

"Don't change the subject."

"About being happy for you?"

"The bread, dammit, the bread."

Dexter's eyes widened. "You don't want me to have bread with my bacon? Whyever not?"

"I'm not interested in talking about bread, dammit," Lewis roared.

"Good, because neither am I." Dex accepted a thick slice of the crusty bread and slathered it thick with freshly churned sweet butter and a mound of strawberry preserves. His stomach was beginning to feel much, much better now.

"I've thought about this," Lewis said. "After the wedding, Dexter, I shall want you to move out of the house."

"Really? Why?"

"You know why."

"I do not."

"I don't trust you, Dexter."

"I don't expect you to, Lewis, but surely you know you can have confidence in your wife."

"Well, yes. Of course. Naturally I can trust Lucy

Anne.'' Dex thought his brother had a slightly haunted look about him when he considered the prospect of trusting a randy young wife. Lewis was obligated to express full and complete confidence. Publicly, that is. Whatever a young and suspicious bridegroom might privately feel, on the other hand . . .

Dex shrugged and took a bite of his toast and jam, then followed it with a deep swig of strong coffee. ''So there you have it. Trust your wife if not your own brother. Besides, dear Lewie, I don't particularly want to leave. Wherever would I go?''

''Anywhere, damn it all. Baton Rouge. N'Orleans. It doesn't matter.''

''It would matter to me.''

''You've always liked the cities.''

''That was before you put me on an allowance of twenty dollars a month, Lewis. I misdoubt that I could maintain myself comfortably on that pittance. I couldn't live in the Crossings on twenty a month. How much more would I need in New Orleans?''

''We can arrange something . . . suitable,'' Lewis suggested.

''Are you trying to buy me off, Lewie?'' Dex asked with a chuckle.

''I wouldn't have put it quite that way.''

''But the fact remains, eh?''

''How much d'you want?''

''Nothing, Lewis. Not a penny. No, excuse me, let me amend that. I shall take whatever I can get, of course. But I intend to remain here at Blackgum Bend. This is my home as much as it is yours.''

''Not now, it isn't. And I don't want you under this roof after Lucy Anne arrives.''

''I won't go.''

''Like that, is it?''

''Exactly like that,'' Dexter agreed.

''We shall see,'' Lewis said darkly. ''We'll just see about that.''

Dex considered giving his beloved brother a verbal shot

across the bows. Then reconsidered the impulse. The best and heaviest ammunition in his locker would have been a taunt about Lucy Anne and her amorous inclinations. Who did what to whom, that sort of thing. But that was not only unworthy, it would be stupid. And once stated, such hurtful, harmful words can never be called back.

He settled for asking Clara for more grits.

· 50 ·

Breakfast two days later was somewhat more ordinary, starting with the fact that it was served in the morning. It was only a quarter to eight when Dexter's and Lewis's meals were interrupted by the arrival in the house of the new overseer.

Lewis waved to one of the chairs that separated him from Dexter's end of the table. "Join us?"

Stennet grimaced, as if to imply that it was decadently barbarian to be eating so late in the day. In fairness to the man Dex did note that Stennet, in shirtsleeves and muddy boots, looked like he'd already spent considerable time in the Yancey fields. The back of his shirt was dark with sweat, and streaks of dust caked the folds of flesh in his neck.

On the other hand, Dex thought as he reached for another biscuit, perhaps the man didn't care to bathe. That too would explain his disheveled appearance.

"Would you take some coffee then?" Lewis persisted.

"Water. I'd favor a glass of cool water."

Lewis nodded to Clara, who hurried out of the dining room. Water was not a beverage often consumed there.

Lewis took up his own suggestion about the coffee,

then blotted his lips with a snowy-white napkin before inviting Stennet to speak. "I take it you've been out this morning?"

"Aye, and all day Sunday and yesterday too. I have to tell you, Mr. Yancey that I am impressed. Surprised too."

"How is that?"

"Your fields. They are in remarkably good condition."

"And this surprises you, you say? Do you assume that I am incapable of supervising—"

"No, sir, nothing like that," Stennet was quick to inject. "I know you're a busy man but a capable one. Especially after seeing the way your crops are coming. It's just . . . may I speak freely, sir?"

"Please do."

"Quite often when I come to a new place I find that the niggers are lax. They're lazy under the best of circumstances, but often when I accept employment, it is because there has been trouble with the blacks."

"You know the situation here. I was truthful with you about that, I believe," Lewis said.

"Yes, sir, you were. And when I heard your hands' wages were being cut, well, frankly, sir, I expected some of them to sulk and cause trouble. It's the normal sort of thing. Either they don't work at all, or go out into the rows and pretend to work, or—the worse thing and more common than you might think—they go through the rows and deliberately chop the young cotton plants instead of the weeds. They get mad and turn mean. They're like that often."

"Not here," Lewis insisted.

"No, not here," Stennet agreed.

"Do you hear that, Dexter?" Lewis asked, staring down the table toward his brother.

"Oh, indeed I do," Dex acknowledged.

"You tried to talk me out of my plan, but you don't know these niggers like I do. You coddle them. Always have. Mr. Stennet understands that a firm hand is needed. So do I. I was firm with them, and they're whipping right into shape."

"Whipping, Lewis?"

"It's a figure of speech, Dexter. Don't get excited."

"Like I was saying," Stennet intruded, perhaps in an effort to head off any conflict between the brothers, "your hands have been doing their work pretty much like always. They're lazy, of course. You have to expect that. But there's been none of the sabotage that I've seen elsewhere. They're chopping only the weeds and doing a clean job of it at that. That is why I say I'm surprised, Mr. Yancey. I expected trouble. There isn't any."

"I am considerably less surprised than you, Mr. Stennet," Lewis said.

"I'll be doing the things I told you before, sir," Stennet said, "but there won't be need for anything . . . special. If you know what I mean."

Lewis nodded. Obviously he knew what the man was talking about. Dexter did not.

"What changes do you contemplate, Mr. Stennet?" Dex asked.

The overseer looked first to Lewis, then to Dexter. Obviously he did not know if he should answer that or not.

"I'm not trying to interfere, I assure you," Dex said with a smile. "Just curious, that's all."

"Yes, sir. Well, then. The usual. I'll be making sure the crews are out in the fields as long as possible. Keeping a close eye on them to make sure they don't start any mischief. But to tell you the truth, in light of what they did when there wasn't anybody but niggers out there as foremen, seeing as how they acted all right then, I really don't think they'll give me any trouble now."

"No, our people are good workers. Poppa wouldn't have any that weren't," Dex said. "May I ask something else, Mr. Stennet?"

"Sure, go ahead."

"You look like you are out working every bit as long and as hard as the hands have to. Just how early do you start your day, sir?"

Stennet's chest swelled a bit with pride as he responded, "I'm up a full hour before dawn every day of my life, Mr. Yancey." He laughed heartily. "And I do mean 'up' if you will, sir. Have to have my morning blow job, never fail. Then a stout breakfast and out the door before daybreak. I expect my niggers to do the same." He snickered. "Don't demand their wenches do them first, of course. Would discourage that if anything. It ain't healthful for a man to get his rocks off and then do hard labor right after, you know. But I want them out there standing alongside the field and drawing their tools by the time the eastern sky starts coming pale. Want them in the rows by the time there's full daylight. A full day's work for a full day's pay, that's what I always say, Mr. Yancey. What I always get too. Believe it."

"Goodness. And you follow such a strict regimen yourself as well?" Dex asked.

"Every day except Sunday, sir. Sundays I like to take a walk through the fields of the mornings, but that's all." He laughed again. "Sundays my home piece knows not to bother putting clothes on. Be a waste of time, if you know what I mean."

Dex smiled and nodded. He decided not to wink. That might have been a bit much, after all. "Surely you don't spend all day out in the fields with your hands, though," he suggested.

"The hell I don't, sir. It's the only way to make sure everything is done right and that's to see to the doing of every little thing. I leave the house before daylight and I'm not back again until it's too dark for me or the niggers to get anything done." Stennet accepted the tumbler of water that Clara gave him, and paused for a moment to give the young girl a critical examination.

Clara withdrew to the side of the room, and Stennet turned to Lewis and said, "Get a little more tit on her and I might want to borrow the use of her sometimes."

Lewis chuckled. Clara, for her part, looked quickly away from the two white men. She blushed, her already dark cheeks becoming even darker. Dex could do nothing to help the girl. But he wished he could. Still, a gentleman did *not* apologize about any white man's behavior. It simply wasn't done.

"Jezebel isn't enough for you? Or d'you want something easier to handle than her?" Dex couldn't help but comment.

"Jessie does what I want when I want," Stennet boasted. "And if I want a little strange now and then, change my luck so t' speak, that's my privilege. And none of your damned business."

"Calm down, the both of you," Lewis put in. "You will have to understand, Mr. Stennet, that my brother has a sometimes odd sense of humor. But he's harmless." Lewis looked at his brother and added, "Now."

Dex lifted his coffee cup in a silent toast. Then he set it very carefully back onto the saucer and quietly left the dining room. He wasn't hungry anymore.

· 51 ·

"D'you want something to eat, Mister Dextuh, sir?"

"No, thanks, Aunt Lottie. I'm not hungry yet. Maybe later."

"You jus' let me know, sir. I take care o'you."

"You always do, Aunt Lottie," Dex said with a smile. "Isn't Lewis having his lunch now, though?"

"Masta Lewis . . . excuse me, sir . . . Masta Yancey, he gone off to visit with them Thibidouxs this afternoon. He say he won't be back till late so's not to hold supper for him neither."

Dex wondered idly if Lewis and Lucy Anne would take a drive down by the river this afternoon. To the old fishing shack perhaps. But then no, that was unlikely. Lucy Anne had cause to think of it as a trysting place, but so far as Dexter knew Lewis did not. Lewis was somewhat more fastidious than Dex was about such things. More than Lucy Anne was too, for that matter.

The unbidden thoughts of Lucy Anne Thibidoux and the fishing shack gave rise to thoughts about Lucy Anne Thibidoux naked. And Lucy Anne Thibidoux's nipples. And in particular about Lucy Anne Thibidoux's mouth.

Lordy, but that girl could suck cock. Mr. Stennet

might brag about his Jezebel blowing him before the dawn each morning, but the man might not be so quick to speak if he'd ever tried Lucy Anne. Dex felt reasonably sure that Lucy Anne could suck a pint of juice out of a dried-up corncob if she decided to apply herself to the task.

Everyone has to have a talent, after all. That was Lucy Anne's.

Dex reached down to rearrange his trousers. There was a bulge in his lap that was thumping and bumping and trying to push its way past his buttons. It seemed something of a pity that old Lucy Anne was busy this afternoon, else Dex might ride over and have a visit with his soon-to-be sister-in-law.

Lucy Anne being already taken, Dex's thoughts turned next to Jezebel. Or Jessie, as Stennet preferred.

Damn, but she was one fine figure of the female persuasion. And never mind her color or her blood. She was just one almighty handsome filly, and that was that.

Hot as a pistol in bed too, he would have bet. Some women a man can take one look at them and know. Jezebel was like that. One look and a man went to getting hard.

The thought of her naked and hot every morning before dawn, those beautiful lips parted. Wet. Soft. That pink, delicate tongue . . .

Dex scowled. Damn it anyway to've gotten into this line of thinking. He wriggled and squirmed a little, the book in his lap forgotten now.

He considered riding into town. He could stop by the church and see if Mary Ellen was available.

It was a long way to town, though.

And what the hell. He didn't owe Mr. Mister Stennet anything.

Didn't much like the son of a bitch either.

Dex laid his book aside and stood.

It wasn't so awfully far to the old carriage house, the one that used to be Blackgum Bend's guest quarters.

A five-minute stroll or less.

The old structure was what Lewis had given Stennet for the overseer's use.

It wouldn't hurt for Dex to go by there. Just to make sure the plantation property was being adequately taken care of.

⋅ 52 ⋅

He only intended to go down to the old place on the other side of the household garden, but even so, Dex took a few minutes to tidy up. He slicked his hair down, checked the knot of his tie, brushed his coat, and retrieved his best hat from the rack in the vestibule before starting off into the early afternoon sunshine.

He ambled along with a cane in hand—an affectation perhaps, but one that he enjoyed—and waved to the barn hands and to old Jubert's young wife, Milly, who was working in the garden. The wax beans and pole beans were coming ready for the picking, he noted.

On the far side of the garden he was accosted by a grinning little boy of ten who ran up to him and tugged gently on Dex's sleeve.

"What is it, Albie? I didn't think to bring any candy with me today if that's what you want."

"No, sir, Mr. Dexter, sir. I can buy my own candy. If you say it's all right, 'at is."

"If I say what is all right, Albie?"

"That new bossman Mr. Stennet, he say he pay me a dime a day if I fetch stuff for him, carry his lunch out to him, stuff like that there, Mr. Dexter. Is that . . . I mean,

I know I don't belong to nobody, not nobody. But I kinda like bein' your hand, Mr. Dexter, yours an' Master Lewis's. So I thought I ought for to ast you if it all right for me to work for Mr. Stennet too.''

"A dime a day? I wouldn't want you to miss out on that, Albie.''

"So it all right for me to work for Mr. Stennet?''

"If you want to, sure. You aren't already on the payroll for anything, and even if you were, I think it would be fine for you to be making a little extra. Sure, you go ahead and do whatever he tells you.'' Dex ruffled the child's hair and received a huge, pleased grin in exchange for the permission.

Dex remembered when ten cents had seemed a whole world of money to him too. How much more must it seem so to a pickaninny like Albie.

"Thank you, Mr. Dexter, sir. Thanks a lot.'' Albie ran ahead, dashed up the staircase leading to the living quarters over the old carriage house, and went inside without knocking. Dex followed him up the stairs, and on his way up was met by Albie, already hurrying off toward the fields with a towel-draped bucket that no doubt contained Stennet's dinner.

"You take care now, Albie.''

"Yessir, Mr. Dexter, sir.'' The boy grinned at him and raced away.

Lord, Dexter thought, the energy of youth. To say nothing of its innocence.

Now, however, did not seem a good time to be thinking in terms of innocence. He tapped lightly on the carriage house door, and removed his hat when he heard light footsteps coming in response.

Dex hadn't even seen the girl and already he was getting a hard-on again just from thinking about the one good look he'd gotten of her before.

• 53 •

"M . . . ah, that is . . . g'day, Jessie." He caught himself in time, if barely, but he'd almost committed a horrible breach of propriety. He had very nearly greeted her as "Miss Jessie," and that would not do. She was gorgeous, it was true, but she was still black—a quadroon or darker, wasn't it?—and it would be unthinkable to speak to her as if she were a lady.

Jezebel heard the aborted sound, saw him standing in the doorway with his hat in hand, and a thin smile tickled the corners of her lovely mouth. She knew. He hadn't actually said it, but she knew.

"Yes, Mr. Yancey?" Her voice was as soft as her lips appeared to be. Low and soft and as delicate as angels' wings.

Dex didn't even try to answer immediately. He was enjoying just standing there.

He thought he'd remembered that she was beautiful? He hadn't remembered the half of it.

The other day back at the river landing he'd seen Jezebel dressed to travel in her finest gown and fanciest hair.

Now she was dressed for housework, which is to say that she was scarcely dressed at all.

Dex would have had to admit that the difference on display today was all for the better.

Today Jezebel's hair was unpinned. Gleaming like black satin, it flowed long and loose and free to the small of her waist.

And the small of her waist was impossibly, agreeably tiny.

Dex had no idea what she'd been engaged in in the back room before his arrival—cleaning her new home perhaps or preparing to bathe—but obviously she'd been wearing rather little to do it in. In order to answer his knock at the door just now she'd grabbed an oversized bathrobe, presumably Stennet's, and thrown it hastily on.

The robe was much too big for her, and she hadn't taken time to tie it closed. She stood now clutching the folds of cloth together at her waist. This left a deep vee of honey-gold flesh that ran from her throat—he'd almost forgotten how long and slim and perfect her neck really was—down virtually to her navel.

Her breasts, small and tidy and delightfully firm, were almost fully exposed, covered only on their outer halves to barely conceal her nipples.

Below the waist—he remembered now that the wide, full cut of her gown the other day had made him wonder just how she might be built from the waist downward—below the waist she was as perfect as above. A gap in the poorly closed robe gave him tantalizing glimpses of legs that were long and slender and flawless, ankles that were tiny, and feet that were as bare as Dex found himself wishing the rest of her to be.

He took his time about examining all there was to see. Then he smiled at her. "I came to see if you are settling in comfortably."

"I am, thank you." He noticed sweat lightly beading Jezebel's upper lip. It was not all that warm a day. He surmised he must have interrupted some sort of activity then. Scrubbing, mopping, there was always much to be done when moving into a new place.

Not that he was sorry he'd broken into her afternoon. Hardly. "May I come in?"

"Mr. Stennet wouldn't like that, Mr. Yancey."

"Mr. Stennet doesn't have to know quite everything that happens at Blackgum Bend."

"Mr. Stennet has a way of finding out the things he wants to know, Mr. Yancey."

"Why are we talking about your, um, employer anyway?"

The girl smiled and shrugged. The slight movement of her shoulders caused her hair to glimmer and flow like ripples cavorting across a still pond. "Is there something else you would like to talk about?" she asked.

"Many things," he said. "I, uh, thought you might like to go for a drive around the property. I know of a lovely, isolated little place on the riverbank. It's quiet. And very private. You might like it."

"I wouldn't want to cause you trouble, sir."

"There wouldn't be trouble, Jezebel. No one need know."

"But I would know, wouldn't I?"

"Oh, I would certainly hope you would find the . . . drive . . . a memorable one."

Jezebel laughed. He loved the rich, throaty sound of her laughter. He was not so fond, however, of the knowledge that she took his invitation so lightly. "I think not, sir."

When she spoke, when her lips moved, Dex could not stop himself from thinking about what Stennet had said. Those lips wrapped around a stiff cock the first thing each and every morning. That lovely throat flowing full with a man's thick and sticky juices are every sunrise.

Looking at her, knowing what he did about her, Dex wanted her. He could feel a swelling at the nape of his neck, and his breath quickened and became shallow.

He could not remember wanting any woman this badly. Not for ages.

He very nearly reached out, very nearly grabbed and took her. By force. The impulse was there.

Jezebel must have seen it too. Surely it was a male reaction she would recognize for surely it was one she had seen many and many a time in her life before now.

She stepped back away from him and one hand flew to her throat to clutch the robe shut there while the other held the folds of cloth together at her waist. "Please," she whispered. "Don't hurt me."

Dex blinked. God, had she thought he was going to rape her?

And . . . *had* he been close to that?

Dex hated the sort of man who would force himself onto the defenseless, the sort of crude and ugly soul who would assume liberties and make demands that were beyond all reason or decency.

Had he been about to degrade himself and become like that?

God, he hoped not.

Involuntarily he cried out, ashamed and embarrassed, and stumbled half a step backward from the open doorway. "I didn't . . . that is . . ."

Jezebel shook her head. "It's all right. But go now. Please, Mr. Yancey. Please leave now."

She was beautiful. And she had the right to tell him no if she damn well wanted to. Dex felt his cheeks flush with a rush of heat that this time had nothing to do with arousal. He jammed his hat back on and stammered out a hoarse. "Sorry, Jessie. I'm sorry."

He turned and fled down the stairway to ground level, and practically ran all the way back to the mansion.

• 54 •

"I want a word with you."

Dex stopped. Gave Stennet an unfriendly glare. It was rude for an employee to speak so bluntly to a member of the gentry, and Stennet knew it. The rudeness was deliberate and challenging, and if the son of a bitch wanted trouble, Dex knew where he could find all he wished of it.

"You're lucky," Stennet said as he came nearer.

"Is that so?"

"Did you think I wouldn't find out?"

"Frankly, sir, the depth of your ignorance is a subject I do not care to plumb. As to this particular comment, I have no idea what you are talking about."

"My woman. You made a visit to my woman yesterday."

"Did I?" Dex shrugged. "Perhaps I was looking for you."

"You knew I spend my whole day out with the niggers and the crops. I already told you that."

"It might amaze you, Mr. Stennet, how very little attention I am inclined to grant your pronouncements."

"You called on my woman. You want her, don't you?"

Dex did not deign to answer.

"Damn right you do, but that one is private property. She turned you down. Wouldn't let you inside. Good thing for both of you that you didn't see the back side of that door or I'd've beat the crap out of her first and then you. You remember what I told you, don't you? You think I didn't mean it?"

"One's capabilities do not always match one's desires," Dex suggested.

"I told you, boy, you go to messing around my woman and I'll take you apart. And don't think you can sneak inside my place. Doesn't matter if I'm around or not. I'll always know. Count on that."

"Very good of you to give me a second warning, I'm sure," Dex said in a dry, sarcastic voice.

"It's the last one you'll get. Count on that too."

Dex considered the responses that were possible. Then turned and walked silently away. Stennet would no doubt count this a victory. Let him. The exercise of patience was among the attributes of a gentleman.

◆ 55 ◆

"Pass that jar, will you, white boy?"

"Lazy darkie. You can't reach for it yourself?"

"It isn't that I'm too lazy," James reasoned. "It's that I'm too drunk. I'm like to fall off the porch if I lean over that far."

"Hell, in that case let me help you." Dex picked up the jar—damn thing had somehow become almost empty, he noted—and handed it to James. They were sitting on the edge of Aunt Maybelle's front porch, Dex leaning against one of the support posts and James seated with his legs dangling. "Your mama can still cook," Dex offered. "It's a wonder you don't get fat."

"Keep eating like you did tonight and you will for sure," James said.

"Don't hog that jar."

James returned it, and Dex had a long swallow of the mellow white whiskey. "Lordy, but that stuff is good. Put hair on a man's chest and lead in his pencil."

"Speaking of which," James said, "you been getting any lately?"

Dex looked at him. "What is it to you if I have?"

"Isn't so much what you're getting that I was thinking about, but what you aren't getting."

"How's that?"

James reached for the jar, and Dex handed it over. James tipped his head back and finished the quart they'd started with. He eyed the empty jar and sighed. "I was gonna save you some, but . . . you know how that goes."

"Greedy nigger."

James grinned. "Smart, though. Ended up with the last of it, didn't I?"

"Your point is well taken. You're a *smart* greedy nigger. Now what was this you were saying about me not getting any pussy?"

"I never said you weren't getting any. I was talking about some that you aren't getting, but the statement was particular, not a generality."

"I stand corrected on that point too. Thank you. But if you're talking about my dear and beloved soon-to-be sister-in-law . . ."

"Miss Thibidoux? No, white boy, I know you're tapping that right regular. Every time ol' Lewis takes off on one of his buying trips and sometimes when he's home." James grinned and shook his head. "That Lucy Anne, she must be one horny white girl."

"She is. Lewis thinks that's fine. He might not be so happy about it a few years from now when he finds out she wants more than he can provide without outside assistance."

"He walkin' around with a smile on his face lately, is he?" James asked.

"The few times I've seen him, he is," Dex said. In the several months since their engagement was announced, Lewis had spent most of his time traveling. To Baton Rouge to arrange for a contractor to come to Blackgum Bend and remodel the mansion into something suitable for the joining of the Yancey and Thibidoux fortunes. To New Orleans in search of furnishings, or Vicksburg to shop for carpets, or even St. Louis to shop for God knows what.

Dex had no idea how much Lewis was spending on his preparations for the upcoming fall wedding. But he hoped it was a lot.

In the meantime, it was clear to Dex now why Lewis had wanted an overseer on hand. His brother would not have been willing to entrust the operation of the plantation to Dexter, and he obviously had been looking ahead to these frequent and sometimes extensive absences.

Dex hadn't in the least minded Lewis's travels. If anything, he found them to be rather convenient. And the more money Lewis squandered, the better.

"So what is this sudden interest in my sex life?" Dex asked. "And come to think of it, how the hell would you know about me and Lucy Anne? You don't even work at the Bend any more."

"Man, don't you know by now that you white folk don't have such a thing as a secret? From each other maybe, but not from the servants. 'Bout everything you do we know about."

"Some things happen behind closed doors," Dex protested.

James only grinned. "And who d'you think it is cleans up and changes the sheets afterward? You'd be surprised what us darkies know." The grin expanded. "And tell about."

"Could be I'm happier not knowing," Dex conceded.

"Back to what I was sayin' before, I was trying to pay you a compliment."

"You were?"

"Well, sort of."

"I don't mind compliments. What's this one?"

"It's how you aren't so awful bad for a white man."

"Gosh, James, thank you for telling me that. I feel ever so much better knowing you think that way about me."

"Ain't what I think that I'm talking about. It's Jessie that says it."

"Jessie?"

"You know. Jessie. Jezebel. The one colored girl I've

ever known you to go panting after with your tongue hanging down to your knees.''

"She's fine," Dex agreed. He frowned. "You know, I hadn't really thought about it before. But I do get a hard-on when I look at that one. I don't, generally. Not with the nigra girls. I don't know why that is exactly. It sure isn't that I don't find some of them mighty pretty. It's just . . . I don't know.''

"You haven't figured that out?''

"Haven't ever thought about it, I don't guess.''

"Hell, we know. Us coloreds know. That's why everybody likes you, Dexter.''

"Likes me why?''

" 'Cause you don't want to take advantage. You don't make people do things, don't lord it over folks. You don't mess with the darkie girls because you think they'd be scared to tell you no an' would be lifting their skirts just because you're white and they got to.''

"If that's so, then why would I be so attracted to Jezebel? Aside from the fact that the girl is gorgeous, I mean.''

" 'Cause Jessie isn't just beautiful, she's strong. She'd tell you no. Hell, Dex, she did tell you no. And you walked away. Oh, you thought about it. First time in your life, I bet, but you thought about it. She could see that. Then you walked away. She liked that about you. Respect it. And she's heard plenty more about you since then. From the other people over there. You know?''

"How the hell would you know all this?'' Dex asked.

James threw his head back and roared. "You don't know that, white boy?''

Dex shook his head.

"Why d'you think Jessie was running sweat and breathing hard when you stopped in that day?''

"She was . . . I dunno. Working in the bedroom maybe.''

"She was in the bedroom right enough, but she wasn't working. I was the one doing all the work.''

"You?"

The grin returned. "You think you're the only one recognizes quality when he sees it? I wanted that girl the first time I laid eyes on her, just the same as you did. Difference is, I'm black. You aren't. Jessie only makes love to black men. Which brings me back to that compliment I been trying to tell you. She says if she was ever to make love to a white man she'd pick you. She likes you well enough that she's damn near tempted to break her vow and make love to you."

"Excuse me . . . and I mean no offense, you understand . . . but how is it that she claims she never spreads her legs for white men? She's sleeping with that pig Stennet every night. He claims she blows him first thing every morning."

"That isn't the same," James said.

"Excuse me?"

"What Jessie does with Stennet, that's just fucking. In her mind that doesn't count. She's always been pretty, always had that special something that makes men want her. She's been fucked by white men since she was ten years old. But that's only what happens to her body. None of that touches her inside, down in there where it counts. She never gives herself to those men. Just her body. That bastard Stennet and all the ones before him, they don't get the part of her that she gives to me. And it was a real compliment when she says she'd be tempted to give herself to you."

"I'll be damned," Dex muttered. "You don't think she'd, uh . . ."

"Damn, I hope not. You and me, Dex, we've shared a lot of things in our lives but never a woman. I don't know as how either one of us would handle that was it to happen."

"You're prob'ly right." Dex smiled. "She sure is one fine chunk of womanflesh, though, isn't she?"

"You don't know the half of how fine she is, Dexter. The looking-at part is good, but the doing part of Jessie . . .

her real name is Hannah, if you want to know . . . that part is even better.''

"You're a lucky man to be tapping that.''

"Don't I know it.''

"You wouldn't be thinking about getting serious about Jessie, would you? I mean, Hannah?''

James grimaced. "Sure. Fifteen dollars a month would carry us a helluva distance, wouldn't it.''

"At least you don't have rent and food coming out of it. And you're drawing fifteen dollars, not twelve like over at the Bend.''

"A man of my color has no prospects around here, Dex.''

"You sound like you're thinking about leaving.''

James paused for a moment before he spoke again. "I won't be going while you need me. Not till fall anyhow.''

Dex nodded. That Jessie girl—Hannah—she was something, all right. "You wouldn't have any more of the good stuff put away somewhere, would you?''

"No, an' it's a good thing I don't or you wouldn't be sober enough to find your way home tonight.''

"I don't have to be sober to get home, dammit. What d'you think horses are for anyhow?''

"In that case, white boy, I'll go see if there's another jar in Mama's pantry.'' James got to his feet and walked rather unsteadily into his mother's cabin.

· 56 ·

"I'll be going down to N'Orleans again," Lewis said at supper one night. "Do you want anything?"

"Yes. A bigger allowance."

"After the wedding. When you move out. I told you not to worry. I'll take care of you."

Dex made a face. There was no point in arguing. Lewis no longer listened anyway. "How long will you be gone this time?" Dex asked.

"I don't know. A week, ten days. Does it matter?"

"Let me have my twenty dollars before you go, will you?"

Lewis hesitated, then gave Dex a smug, self-satisfied smile. "Why not." He dipped into his pocket and produced a double eagle that he contemptuously flipped into Dexter's lap.

Dex refused to take the bait. "Thanks."

"It's the least I can do."

"Yeah, that's what I thought too."

"Pardon me?"

"Never mind."

Lewis spread the most recent available copy of the *New*

Orleans Picayune open in his lap while Dex stood and
started for the door.

"Burning a hole in your pocket already, is it?" Lewis
asked without bothering to look up.

"If you say so," Dex returned without bothering to
look back.

He left the house and went out to the barn. "Marquis."
He leaned down to touch the sleeping servant lightly on
the shoulder. "Wake up, Marquis. I want the mare saddled."

"Yessuh, Mr. Dexter. Right away." The young stable
hand scrambled to his feet and hurried away to fetch the
fine-boned little bay mare from her stall. Five minutes
later Dex guided the mare down the lane onto the public
road and reined her to his left.

"James. Psst!" Dex hissed softly. "Are you awake in
there, James?"

He waited. After a minute or two the door swung open
on creaking hinges and a barefoot James stepped out onto
the porch. "What the hell are you doing here at this time
of night, Dex?"

"I need somebody to get drunk with."

"I know better. What is it? Really?"

"I want to know how much cash you have left over
from what we won over at Flat Hopes that time."

"You serious?"

Dex nodded.

James rubbed his eyes, then shrugged. "A little over a
hundred, I think. You have to know exactly how much?"

"No, that's close enough. I've got about eighty dollars
laid by, including the allowance money Lewis just gave
me."

"You're a big spender," James said.

"It isn't easy to hang onto the stuff, is it?"

"Harder for you than for me, I'd say."

"Anyway, we're needing it. Lewis is going down to
New Orleans again. He's leaving tomorrow, he said. We

need to start making some preparations, and while he's gone would be a good time to do it."

"All right. What d'you wanta do first?"

"First thing, bring all the cash you can lay your hands on and meet me Sunday morning. You and Saladin."

James grinned. "We going where I think we going?" Dex bobbed his head. "That's right, we are."

"Hour or so after sunup be soon enough for you?"

"That will be fine."

James shook his head. "I had some plans for Sunday. While that white son of a bitch is out making his rounds through the fields. I expect that will just have to wait, though, won't it."

"I could take your place if you like."

"Mighty nice of you to offer, Dexter. I'll tell Jessie you're willing to make the sacrifice. But the fact is, we be needing you down there too, don't forget."

"Oh. That's right. It was just a thought."

"Sure, I believe you."

"Go back to bed, James. You look awful."

"It's these damn fools run around in the middle of the night waking honest folks that cause it."

"There's honest folks around here?"

"My mama."

"But I didn't wake your mama. Please make a note of that, will you?"

"You did so," Aunt Maybelle's voice called from inside the cabin. "Go on now an' let us get back t' sleep or I'll take a switch to yo' backside, boy. I done it befo' an' I can do it again."

"Yes, ma'am," Dex said quickly. "Sorry."

"You ain't neither."

"No, ma'am, but I'm real polite." Dex winked at James and wheeled the mare away for the ride home to Blackgum Bend.

• 57 •

On Sunday morning Dex met James at the oak grove just west of the Crossing. He laughed when he saw James had cut ear holes in the brim of a decrepit old straw hat and tied it onto the yellow mule like a sunbonnet. The effect was . . . silly. At best.

"You don't think you're gliding the lily overmuch with that getup?" Dex asked.

"Hell, no. It's not but a bunch of half-drunk white men we're out to fool today. You white boys are easy."

"Actually I kinda like the hat. Gives him a saucy look, sort of." Dex uncapped a rather large flask that he pulled out of a saddlebag, tipped it back, and swallowed.

"Starting early, aren't you?" James suggested.

"Try it."

"No, thanks."

"Go on. Just a sip."

James rather reluctantly accepted the flask and smelled of it before taking a swallow. He grinned. "A little weak, isn't it?"

"I did water it down a mite." The flask contained no whiskey or brandy at all, just pure, sweet well water.

"You ready for this?" James asked.

"Soon as you hand over your money I will be. I, uh, put my allowance in here too."

"How much've we got there altogether?"

"How much are you putting in?"

James told him. "I added in what I have left from my pay. Mama said it was all right after I told her what it was for."

"That makes over two hundred total then. Two-twenty and a bit."

"Think that should be enough?"

"If we both do our parts right it should be."

"Saladin will do his," James predicted.

"He better, or we're all in a bunch of trouble. You, me, and just about every hand on the plantation."

"He will. I guarantee it."

"That sure as hell makes me feel better," Dex said with a smile.

James reached down and stroked the tall mule's withers, then used his fingers to comb through the thin and ratty tufts of mane that graced Saladin's otherwise handsome neck.

"Time we be getting on," Dex said.

"Aftuh you, Bawss," James said in an exaggeratedly mush-mouthed drawl.

"Keep that up, black boy. It'll make us a lot o' money today."

"Yezzuh, Bawss, yezzuh." James threw his head back and laughed. And why not. It was a beautiful late summer day. There were white clouds in the sky, birds wheeling in the air, and bountiful prospects for them to look forward to. If, that is, each of them, Saladin included, did his part for the next few hours.

· 58 ·

It was called the Paradise Valley Hunt and Turf Club, but the location was far from paradise and the only kind of hunting that had been done in the area, at least during Dex's lifetime, was for quail, with dogs and shotguns, and had nothing to do with foxes or horses. Furthermore, it was not even a real club. There were no written rules or formal memberships, it being understood that if a man was a gentleman he was naturally welcomed. And if he was the sort of obtuse newcomer—a carpetbagging damn Yankee, say—who had to ask about joining, he would not have been allowed in anyway.

Still, several generations of gentlemen who frequented and appreciated the Club had gone to the bother of laying out and properly fencing a mile oval racetrack and several banks of bleachers. Starting posts were provided, and a stewards' tower where judges could view the finish line in comfort—and beyond the reach of any guests who might tend to disagree with the calls of close finishes. A roofed but open-sided pavilion gave shelter to the tables where whiskey, brandy, or wines were dispensed by colored servants wearing red vests and white shirts.

Race meetings were held on the third Sunday of each month, rain or shine.

Touts and bookmakers were not allowed, but no proper gent would have thought about riding his own entry in these monthly affairs, and professional jockeys were allowed if not actively encouraged. The horsemen generally trained and put up their own servants, chosen from among the smallest and lightest of those available.

James and Saladin would be giving up a good twenty-five or thirty pounds when the starting gun fired. That was a large handicap. But then Saladin had already beaten George Penn's Lucifer, and Lucifer was the fastest horse in this end of Louisiana. Dex had confidence in the mule, never mind the silly straw hat. Or the weight. Dex believed Saladin could outrun damn near any horse in the country in anything but a sprint. And races at the Paradise Valley Hunt and Turf Club ran twice around the track. Two miles of hard pounding on a course that, the name aside, was bare clay that was harrowed and lovingly dragged on each and every third Saturday of the month. The only turf in sight was outside the fences.

There was no doubt in Dex's mind that Saladin would win it at a walk.

To encourage the betting and improve on the odds, Dex and James played very much the same game they had back at Hope Flats months earlier, the difference being that this time it was Dexter and not James who feigned alcohol-induced courage and impulsively, and loudly, challenged any and all comers.

"On that little mare of yours?" someone taunted him just as loudly.

"Damn right with that li'l mare," Dex slurred back at him. "Thi' is my day. I feel it. Y'know? I feel damn lucky t'day. Gonna win t'day. I know it for certain sure."

That drew a round of laughter. And an even bigger one when an apprehensive and wide-eyed black servant surreptitiously tugged at Dex's sleeve and stammered, "Masta Dextuh, suh, please don't be mad, suh, but dat mare, suh, she been bred. She lose dat foal fer sho' d'you run her in de race, masta, suh."

Dex waved the concerns aside with an airy; "Hell, in that case I'll run my nigger's mule. I tol' you gents, this here is my day t' shine. It don't matter what I run, I'll win it anyhow. Put your damn money up an' see if'n I don't."

The gentlemen laughed loud and long, and several were kind enough to try and dissuade Dex from his entry.

"No, dammit, I mean it. Can't run my mare, dammit, I'll run the mule. It don't matter."

"You're willing to back your mule with money are you, Yancey?"

"I am, Tyler. 'Deed I am."

Tyler Ebberle turned to Father Branbury of St. Francis Parish, who by custom was their oddsmaker and arbiter, and asked, "What are the odds, Pere?"

"Ten to one," the priest responded quickly.

The old fart, Dex noted, wasn't nearly as impulsive as Amos at Hope Flats. Damn it! Thirty to one would have been quite a lot nicer than ten to one. Three times better in fact.

"How much you going to lay?" Tyler asked.

"I got . . . I got . . . shit, I dunno what I got." Dex turned his pockets inside out, spilled coins in all directions, had considerable difficulty gathering them all, and then was only able to owlishly blink at the jumble of cash in his hand. "I dunno. How much I got here, Tyler?"

Ebberle was kind enough to count the money for him, then announced for all to hear, "Mr. Yancey of Blackgum Bend is offering to wager two hundred twenty-one dollars and fourteen cents on that mule tied over there. 'Gainst all comers is it, Yancey?"

"Damn right. All comers," Dex confirmed.

"The odds, gentlemen, are ten to one," Tyler added very loudly. "I want fifty of that myself. How about the rest of you?"

There was a positive clamor to get the attention of Father Branbury after that.

None of the gentlemen was required to produce cash for the priest to hold, however. Unlike at Hope Flats, it was assumed that a gentleman would cover his gambling losses without delay and without fail. A man might fail to pay a storekeeper, a tailor, or any sort of merchant with impunity. He might even neglect a court judgment without an eyebrow being raised. But failure to immediately pay off a gaming debt would have meant complete and instant dishonor. It would not have occurred to Dex to make a bet here on this course for gentlemen only if he could not back it with cash already in hand. He knew full well that no one else here today would do so either. If he won— when they won—Dexter and James would ride away with more than two thousand dollars in the little mare's saddle pockets.

Once the betting was complete, Dex passed the time sipping at his flask. And beginning to wish he'd thought to bring another along containing something of more interest than springwater.

Eventually post time approached, and Dex wobbled over to the fence lining the front straight along with all the other gentlemen in attendance. Off to their left the starter, the honor going this year to Alfred Coyle, waved the horses, riders—and one mule—into a line and gave them a moment to settle.

Then Dex could see Coyle extend an arm skyward. He saw a puff of smoke to announce the start, and as one the horses and riders leaped into furious motion.

The horses did that. And their riders.

Even before the sound of the starting gunshot reached Dex's ears, however, he saw the one mule in the line— James had gotten rid of the hat before coming to the line, thank goodness—rear onto its hind legs in a blind panic and wildly paw the air with its forefeet.

James—Dex could scarcely believe it—James lost his seat and slid back onto Saladin's skinny butt.

All around Dex there was a roaring of laughter.

He hardly noticed. What he was thinking, abject humiliation aside, was that neither he nor James had ever thought to find out how the mighty Saladin reacted to the sound of a gunshot.

Starts were made by way of a shout back at Hope Flats, and there was likely not a mule alive who was not thoroughly familiar with the sounds of shouting, their nature being what it was.

But a gunshot... Obviously that sound was new to Saladin.

The horses were running flat out now, their jockeys crouched low over their necks.

All the runners, that is, save for Saladin, who was only now finding the earth with all his feet again while James clung half on and half off his back and was trying to regain his seat.

The race, dammit, was over before it hardly began, Dex noted with a sinking feeling in his stomach.

· 59 ·

Dex's ears burned to the sound of the laughter as down to the left of the delighted crowd Saladin and James finally set off down the racetrack. The horses were already past Dex's position on the rail, a good two hundred yards or more ahead of the yellow mule.

Saladin began coming with long, lazy strides. Hell, Dex couldn't blame James for not bothering to press the mule. With butts, tails, and dust all there was to look forward to, there was no sense in even continuing. If it'd been him, Dex thought, he would have pulled off the track and gone quietly home.

Well, quietly once he got away from the hooting, jeering crowd of Louisiana gentlemen, that is. He did wish they'd shut the hell up.

In the meantime, though, James and the mule swept along in the wake of the race that was being conducted out in front of them.

Poor James, Dex saw, was playing out his end of it to the hilt, leaning low over Saladin's neck, riding on short stirrups, gliding smooth and easy as if they were out for a Sunday romp. Which, Dex conceded, they were. Now. Damn shame too. He'd been so sure about this. Why, oh, why hadn't he ever thought about the races being started with a gun here? That was stupid. And his own damn fault. He had only himself to blame. But such a pity. He frowned and looked away.

Dex thought about going and buying a drink. Except he wasn't sure if he would have enough cash left over for a whiskey. He didn't know if his stake had been covered to the last penny or not. Likely, considering the match he and James had gone to such great lengths to arrange. Dammit.

"Jesus!" someone nearby blurted out. Dex noted that the laughter had died down and now the gents were staring out across the track. Dex turned back to see what they were looking at.

There was the pack, starting to string out now as they reached the three-quarter pole. Poor Saladin still trailed, far back from all the others.

Well, not terribly far, really. Not but by forty yards or so, Dex judged.

He blinked. Forty yards? The mule had been five times that far behind just a minute ago. Surely he couldn't be . . .

By the time the horses came around the last turn onto the home stretch, Saladin had caught the trailers and was moving up on the rest of the bunch. George Penn's Lucifer was running near the front, but not trying to challenge the early leaders as his jockey, a professional rider out of Natchez, held his speed down to preserve the horse's stamina.

Saladin, incredibly, was not twenty yards back of Lucifer as the pack thundered by the viewing stands and into the first turn for the second lap around the track.

Men who'd been sitting on the bleacher benches came to their feet and crowded against the rail as the pack moved onto the back stretch, and they all could see a tall, yellow animal striding fluidly along with the rest.

Lucifer's rider made his move as they came into the third turn, and James took Saladin out beside him, deliberately taking the wider and longer outside route, but staying out of any possibility of encountering trouble along the rail.

Lucifer drove to the fore as they rounded the final turn onto the home stretch toward the finish line.

And there Saladin was, his long, leggy gait so smooth it would have appeared slow had he not been running close to other animals.

Dex could hear cheering now as the gentlemen realized what they were witnessing and, money be damned, began to whoop and shout their encouragement for a magnificent performance.

"Come on, you big-eared rat-tailed son of a bitch!"

Dex had no idea whose voice that one was, but he echoed the sentiment if not the words.

But then so was almost everyone else there.

As easily as if he were a champion out to show the mortals how it should be done, Saladin flowed around the laboring, badly winded Lucifer and pulled further and further ahead with each new reach of his forefeet.

By the time they reached the finish Saladin was a good two and a half lengths in the front, and Lucifer trailed wearily in behind, with Silas Vent's red stallion Magic Boy running third and seeming to close in those last few rods against a dispirited Lucifer.

"By God, man. By God, that was wonderful."

Dex blinked. It was Tyler Ebberle. He thumped Dexter on the back and was grinning so hugely, Dex would have thought the man had placed his money on Saladin.

"I never saw anything like before in my whole life long," Ebberle declared. He was the first who said that within Dex's hearing. He was far from being the last to say it that day.

And in truth, Dex had to agree with every one of them.

He'd seen it. He could scarcely believe it himself.

Late in the afternoon Father Branbury looked Dex up and accepted the offer of a whiskey—Dex could afford to buy whatever he pleased to drink now—when he handed Dex's winnings over.

"Thanks, Padre."

"Oh, you've already thanked me, son. Made myself a tidy profit on this race, I did."

"How's that, Father?"

"Why, I bet on the mule, son."

"If you thought the mule would win, Father, whyever did you set the odds at ten to one?"

"Lord help you, Dexter, I didn't think the poor creature had a prayer of victory when I chose those odds. That was straightforward and honest, I assure you. It was afterward that I decided to make my own bet." He looked around to make sure they were not being overheard, then leaned a little closer. "One of the nigras came to me to ask for twenty dollars on the mule. That told me two things, son. One was that all the nigra servants and workers round here today must have been pooling their money in order to come up with that sum. The other thing I knew then was that they had knowledge that I didn't. So I took their advice and yours and laid a small sum on your mule. But would you tell me, son? However did the nigras know?"

Dex grinned. He might as well tell it. After all, they wouldn't be able to find long odds against Saladin anywhere in Louisiana, not ever again after the story of this race was told and retold and told again.

"We ran him first at Hope Flats, Father. You've heard of the meets there?"

"Aye. Been to one or two myself if the truth be known."

"We ran him there earlier this summer, and he beat Lucifer then too."

"I didn't know Lucifer ever ran there," the priest mused.

"George doesn't know it either. So please don't tell him, eh?"

"Not a word, son. As quiet as the confessional, I assure you. But thank you for telling me."

"Thank you for those odds, Padre."

"You'll not get them a second time, you know."

Dex patted the bulging pouch that held Saladin's winnings. "I may be a greedy man, Father, but I'm not stupid.

Next time I'll disguise him.'' He laughed. ''As a cow perhaps. What d'you think?''

''Ah, now I consider myself forewarned. If you bring a saddled cow here next time I'll make the odds ten to one again, but I'll peg them against you.''

Dex touched the brim of his hat in a good-bye to the priest and made his way through the crowd, accepting congratulations and delighted comments from everyone he passed, back to the shaded area where Saladin and James were waiting.

◆ 60 ◆

They perched on the edge of Aunt Maybelle's front porch eyeing the pile of gold and silver—mostly gold, very little silver—that lay in a heap between them.

"God, that's an awful lot of money," James said.

"More than I expected to come home with," Dex admitted.

"Should be plenty for what you want."

"I can get along fine with half that much for my trip."

"What about the rest of it?" James asked.

"I been thinking about that on the way back. For right now I want you to put it away someplace."

"We don't have any safe place to keep this much money. And I can't be here all the time."

"Your mama is always here," Dex said. "besides, who's going to think she would have that kind of cash stuffed in her mattress? Far as anybody over at the Turf Club knows, the betting and the winnings were all mine. None of them would come here thinking to find a fortune."

"That's true enough."

"Tie it up in a bag an' put it in the flour jar or some such as that," Dex suggested. "It will be safe as in a bank. Then later on . . . we might want to dip into it some, of course—we're entitled. But what I was thinking is that we should take part of it and use that to pay off the IOU markers my damn brother is using to turn the hands into serfs.''

"You wouldn't mind doing that?''

"Course I wouldn't mind it. They been loyal Yancey workers every one of them. They don't deserve the kind of treatment Lewis is giving them. Wouldn't have been treated this way if it'd been left up to me, but that's neither here nor there. Now they're deep in debt an' the sheriff won't let them walk free again until those debts are cleared. So what the hell.'' Dex began to grin, warming all the more to the idea as he told James about it. "Let's you and me take this free money and use it to help our people.''

" 'Our' people, Dexter?''

"As much mine as yours, by God,'' he declared.

"All right. I'll have Mama put it by. Be all right if she knows what's in the bag?''

"What, you think I wouldn't trust your mother? Of course she can know.''

"How come you want to wait for later on before the hands buy back their notes, though? How come we don't just do it at the end of this month?''

"Because I don't want to do anything that might tip Lewis to the notion that things aren't all going to go his way. I want him going on just like he has been, lord and master of his little fiefdom here. We won't show any hand at all until it's too late. Then, well, then things will just have to change.''

"I hope so,'' James said. "Lord, I do hope so.'' He idly picked up shiny golden coins by the handful and let them sift through his fingers. "Sure do admire the sound that makes. You know?''

"Damn right I know,'' Dex said with a grin.

"So when are you leaving?''

Dex shrugged. "No point waiting around now that I've

got the wherewithal. I'll take, say, twelve hundred of this and catch a boat north tomorrow.''

"You need me to go along?"

"Not this time. I won't be traveling as a Southern gent, don't forget. Not once I get past Vicksburg, I won't.''

"You going all the way to Pittsburgh, you say?" James sounded more than a little envious. He himself had traveled as far as New Orleans on more than one occasion, but Pittsburgh—that was practically a foreign country.

Dex nodded. ''Vicksburg first, but just long enough to change boats. I've gone there before to gamble and the like, so no one will think anything about that. Especially now that it's known I have some money in my pockets. I won't stay there any time, though. Just change to a different boat, one with a crew that doesn't know me. I'll book passage under a different name from there. Go to Pittsburgh. Then come back down the Ohio.''

"The Ohio. Monongahela. Allegheny. Damn, Dex. You're gonna see all the things we only read about before now.''

"If this idea works out, James, I'm gonna have to get the hell out of Louisiana. Fast. You know that, don't you?''

"I thought about it. Where you gonna go when that time comes?''

Dex stared off toward the early evening sky. Inside the cabin he could hear Aunt Maybelle rattling pans as she prepared their supper. The air was soft and fragrant, and a slight breeze ruffled the wispy gray strands of moss that dangled from the overhanging trees. A lump came into his throat. This land was home. He was going to miss it. More than he'd bothered to give thought to until this moment.

"Dexter?''

He snapped out of the sadness of that brief reverie. "Sorry. Woolgathering. I guess I hadn't really thought much about where to go. Just that I'll have to.''

"You know where I'd go if it was me?" James offered.

Dex raised an eyebrow and waited.

"West," James said firmly. "Big country in the west, they say. No leftover slavery bullshit. They say a man can be as tall and free as he's man enough to makc of himself in the West. They say a black man can find good work there. Draw pay the same as any other, never mind what his skin looks like. Carry a gun even. No lynchings."

"I heard there're lynchings sometimes."

"Not for the crime of being a Negro," James said. "Man can get hisself lynched there for being a thief or a robber or a dumb son of a bitch. But not for being a black man."

"That's what they say, is it?"

James nodded. "It's what they say."

"Wild out that way," Dex said. "I've heard that too."

"Sounds interesting to me, white boy."

"If you was to head west when you get your scrawny white ass run out of Loosiana," James said with a smile, "I might be talked into going with you."

"I wasn't going to put it exactly that way," Dexter said.

"What, about being run out?"

"No. Scrawny. That's the part I was objecting to."

James leaned back and cocked his head, pretending to stare at Dex's butt as he sat on the edge of the porch there. "Sorry," he said after a moment. "But I got no choice about this. It's scrawny, all right."

Dex laughed. "Come up. Let's count twelve hundred of this out for my bankroll. Then you take the rest inside and give it to your mama to hide."

"You're staying to supper, aren't you?"

"Unless you think you're man enough to drive me outa here."

"I could do just that if I took a mind to. Only reason I don't is that Mama would get mad at me. You know how she loves to show off how much better her cooking is than that old Lottie's."

"Your mama won't be happy until the both of us are hog fat," Dex said.

"It would be a kindness to her if we was to get that way, it's true."

"Well, I expect I'm hungry enough right now to please her. Hurry up and count my money off. I don't know what she has on the stove in there, but it's smelling awfully good."

·61·

Pittsburgh was not as exotic a destination as James might believe, but Dex found it more than different enough for his tastes.

Pittsburgh not only looked different than a southern city, it even smelled different. In the South one smelled heat and wood smoke and flower blossoms. Here the air was pungent with the scent of coal fires, mud, and half a thousand aromas that Dex could not begin to identify.

Pittsburgh was most definitely *not* a part of the South.

For the past several days even the foliage was foreign to Dex, hardwoods for the most part instead of the soft-woods Dex was accustomed to, maple rather than gum, laurel instead of azalea.

But at least there were trees. That was one of the things he always found slightly disquieting about poor Vicks-burg, and one of the reasons he seldom traveled there, grand a city though it was. Vicksburg had been devastated during the war. By now the buildings were mostly rebuilt, and there were few enough obvious signs of past destruc-tion. Except for the trees.

Aside from the effects of cannonballs falling by the

thousands, perhaps by the scores of thousands to hear the older residents tell it, the city under siege had lost nearly anything combustible to the need for firewood and shoring timbers for the tunnels in which even the citizenry had had to live during the last days of terror.

Now, even these years later, the only trees to be found in the gracious city were small. There was scarcely a stately oak or a mature pine anywhere in the whole of Vicksburg.

Pittsburgh, on the other hand, was surrounded by wooded hillsides. And by entire forests of chimneys. The city lay in a pall of smoke, most of it resulting from eager, active, burgeoning commerce.

Dex stood on the deck of the *William T. Sherman* and watched the city materialize out of the mists of a cool drizzle.

He had chosen the *Sherman* back in Vicksburg for several good and sufficient reasons. One was that he quite naturally had never taken this steamer before. The other was that it was a guaranteed, absolute certainty that no one aboard this boat would know him or be known by him. After all, what self-respecting Southerner would set foot onto a paddle wheeler named for the devil incarnate.

The crew—some of the laborers were white men, which Dex found more than a little shocking—made short work of tying the boat fast and dropping the gangway. The captain himself was on hand to bid his passengers good-bye.

A steward carried Dex's lightweight and very nearly empty trunk ashore, then accepted a two-cent copper with surly disdain—but he did take the coin, Dex noted—and abandoned both trunk and passenger on the quay.

"You there. I need the hire of a carriage."

The man pointed but didn't speak. Dex left his trunk where it was and went in that direction in search of a hack. When he returned ten minutes later the quay was empty. Empty, at least, of the one particular object Dex had expected to find there.

"My trunk, dammit. It's gone."

"Didn't pay nobody to watch over it, eh?" the hackney driver observed.

"Of course not. Why should I?"

"Ay, mister. Yer trunk is gone an' yer asking me why you shoulda paid for its safety? Kinda thick, ain't you?"

"Wait here. I'll ask if anyone saw . . . what are you laughing at?" In point of fact the driver hadn't laughed. Snorted a little perhaps, but it was not a full-blown laugh. Now he laughed.

"Are you telling me no one will've seen anything?" Dex asked.

"You're slow, mister, but you do learn eventual-like."

Dexter sighed. Took a slow, baleful look around—which accomplished nothing, not even to make him feel any the better for it—and climbed into the hack unimpeded by any necessity to drag luggage along with him.

He supposed he should have been grateful for the convenience of it all. Somehow he was not.

Dex struck a pose. Turned half around to his left. Reversed position to present the other profile. Tilted the new hat first one way and then another until he was satisfied with the set of it.

The person he saw in the hotel room mirror was a virtual stranger to him. And no Southern gentleman by any stretch of the imagination.

Instead of Dex's customary pearl gray planter's hat, charcoal coat, and tightly fitted dove-gray trousers, he now found himself peering at his idea of a perfect Yankee trader. Black silk hat with a flat, medium-height crown and narrow brim. Black frock coat and trousers. Stiff celluloid collar and black bow tie. Silver-colored brocade vest. Shoes and spats rather than boots. It all looked quite strange to him.

But it also should give the precise impression he wished to convey.

He had a gold stem-wound watch with a gold chain and gold-and-ivory fob. A pair of light, slim, beautifully crafted little .32 rimfire revolvers tucked out of sight in shoulder holsters—he foresaw no need for them, but they were so damned pretty with their floral engraving and ivory grips that he hadn't been able to resist them—and a walking stick with a brass duck's-head grip and thick, sturdy barrel. The cane was quite as beautifully made as the revolvers, and could be put to much the same purpose if required. Hidden inside the shaft of the seemingly ordinary walking stick was a slim and whippy sword blade, sharpened on both edges for most of its length and fashioned from steel of extraordinarily fine quality.

As with the pistols, Dex hadn't set out with the purchase of a sword cane in mind. A cane was all he wanted, and that essentially as a prop to put on display. But when he saw this lovely article he couldn't resist it, fond as he was of both epee and foil. Besides, it felt good in his hand, almost an extension of his arm when with a twist of the handle and the slither of steel on brass the blade leaped free of confinement. That was the truth of it. He'd just plain liked the sword and had treated himself to it.

Now, he thought, he was more than ready to travel south again. Well, tomorrow, he would be.

This evening his cards would be done, and the stationery he'd ordered. The printer had promised everything by six at the latest. So this evening Dex could pick up those last remaining necessities. Then tomorrow he would board the *Wallace Greene*—he'd already booked a cabin—and be off. To Cincinnati this time.

Dex stood on the quay waiting for the call for passengers. Stevedores were already engaged in loading the *Wallace Greene*. Dex took particular note of the fact that his brand-new trunk was carried aboard. It held his normal clothing plus all the articles he'd had to replace when the original trunk was stolen. Damn it anyway. He was still annoyed by that.

That, however, had occurred to an entirely different person than he was now. Nearly the only aspect of himself that he hadn't changed over the past few days was his voice, and he thought he could hide the soft, liquid sounds of his Deep South accent by putting a hard edge on his words. Speaking in a short, clipped tone.

A few yards away a Yankee businessman was taking leave from his family. The man, dressed not very much unlike Dexter now was, was a small, rather dapper sort with a closely trimmed mustache, a fraternal insignia of some sort on his watch fob, and a flock of children—all boys, Dex noted—surrounding him with hugs and kisses and frantic good-byes.

The businessman's wife stood close by to shepherd the boys. She was thirty or so, dark-haired and handsome, if a trifle thick in the body for Dex's taste. When the boys were done with their good-byes, the wife stepped forward. She said something in a low voice and touched her husband's elbow, but made no display of public affection. Dex read nothing from her expression, but when the gentleman turned to board the steamer, Dex noted the sparkle of unshed tears in the lady's eyes as she gathered her sons close around her skirts and waved her husband good-bye.

Dex ambled along behind the gentleman, and tried out his Yankee accent once both were aboard and standing at the rail.

"Fine-looking family," Dex suggested as woman and boys waved and the *Wallace Greene* drifted gently away once her lines were loosed.

"Thank you, sir." There was an accent of some sort in the man's voice, but Dex could not place it. Certainly it was neither French nor Spanish. He would have recognized either of those. This was something harder, more guttural. German? Or Bohemian? Something like that, he suspected. "Und you are?"

Dex smiled and offered his hand. "Horace Vaughn, sir. Commodities broker. At your service, sir."

The Yankee shook hands and announced himself as "Conrad Roderus. Merchant."

"Pleasure, sir."

"Ach, yes. Pleasure."

They shook hands again, but had exhausted what conversation seemed necessary. Dex bowed slightly—he wondered if it was all right, if Yankees did that too just like civilized gentlemen did—and wandered off down the deck in search of a drink.

Cincinnati was almost a replica of Pittsburgh, at least so far as Dex could tell. It too was frantically busy with the bustle of commerce, smoky and smelly from the fires of industry both heavy and light. Yankees, Dex thought. Damn, they were a busy bunch. Always clamoring for profit, ever in pursuit of something that was just out of their reach.

Well, perhaps he could put something into their grasp now.

The captain very nearly missed his landing, the slow but insistent current of the Ohio catching the *Wallace Greene* and pulling the stern away from the wharf. The crew had to shoot a light line ashore and then haul heavier lines across so the stern-wheeler could be warped tight to the dock.

The passenger gangway was quickly deployed, but they were having some trouble getting the cargo platform lowered. Dex gathered it would be some time before his trunk could be brought ashore with the rest of the cargo. No matter, though. That would give him time to line up a porter and transportation. He did not intend to lose his trunk to dockside thieves here as he had back in Pittsburgh.

He was thinking about that and idly observing the departure of the other passengers when he saw his merchant friend from Pittsburgh disembark in Cincinnati. Dex saw. And began to laugh.

The fellow—Conrad something, was it?—was being greeted by a loving family with hugs and kisses and great joy for the daddy who'd perhaps been long away.

There was a sturdily handsome blond wife of thirty-something—the one in Pittsburgh had dark hair if Dex remembered correctly—and a flock of small boys of roughly the same sizes, ages, and shapes as the first, up-river batch.

No, there was a difference, Dex saw now. This bunch had a girl child among them. He was sure all the Pittsburgh children were boys. His good friend Conrad had the pleasure of a daughter in Cincinnati apparently.

Dex left the boat and passed close by Conrad and his family. The merchant—he had business in both river cities perhaps?—looked at Dex over the shoulder of the smallest of the boy children, nodded very slightly. And winked.

A happy fellow this Conrad, Dex thought. And no wonder. His children loved him. So presumably, did his wife. Whichever one of them one wished to comment upon.

Dex laughed along with the German businessman's happiness, and went into Cincinnati in a decidedly good humor himself.

All he had to do now was to locate the proprietors of the Danielson Cargo Co., Inc., so Mr. Horace Vaughn of Vaughn, Knight and Blanchard, Commodities Brokers, could arrange a contract.

Then downriver again, to Louisville this time, for the final steps in this phase of his plan.

The really odd thing, Dex was discovering, was that by now he was beginning to quite thoroughly enjoy himself.

He would have expected instead to feel ashamed.

But the truth . . . well, the truth was that he was damn well having fun now that he'd begun.

It was all coming quite easily to him. Vicksburg, Pittsburgh, Cincinnati, next Louisville, and then back to Vicksburg, where with a change of clothes and a change of name, Horace Vaughn would for the time being disappear and Dexter Yancey could return to Blackgum Bend.

Poor Lewis. He still didn't know what he'd wrought when first he'd defrauded and then pissed off his very slightly older brother.

But he would learn. Oh, yes, Lewis would most certainly learn.

Dexter's smile was getting bigger and bigger as first one thing and then another fell into place.

"Did you hear that, Dexter?"

"Who could possibly hear anything over the sound of all this racket?" Dex responded to Lewis's question. They were in the study, Lewis at the big desk and Dexter seated with newly arrived issues of the New Orleans newspapers. Upstairs, workmen were renovating a full third of the second floor into a suite of rooms for Lewis and Lucy Anne. The house had been filled with the sounds and mess of construction for weeks, the noise going practically from dawn to dusk and the clutter seemingly, at least to Dex, endless.

Lewis inclined his head in the direction of Stennet, who had moments earlier joined them. "Tell him what you just reported to me."

In a loud voice, slow and carefully enunciated as if to a child or a half-wit, the overseer told Dexter, "It will be a bumper crop this year. Best yield ever. We will start picking in three weeks at the most. Best crop ever, I'm certain."

Dex wasn't sure just how it was that Stennet felt qualified to make such a claim, considering the fact that the man had never set foot onto Blackgum Bend until well after this crop was in the ground and growing and he could have no knowledge of past performance. Obviously that little detail did not bother Lewis.

"See," Lewis exclaimed happily. "I told you I'd make this old ground produce, and I am."

Lewis hadn't had a damn thing to do with it, Dex mused. Their father was in charge when the crop was planted, and Stennet had supervised its later care and growth. And of course neither Lewis nor Stennet would ever have laid hand to a hoe personally. Yet Lewis honestly believed he was the one who was responsible now for the yield. Amazing, Dex considered. Absolutely amazing. But he kept that to himself.

Dexter glowered at Stennet, ignored his brother, and went back to the newspapers.

"Have you thought about where you will go after the wedding?"

"To bed. To sleep off a good drunk more'n likely."

"I'm serious about that, Dexter. I want you to move out. It wouldn't be comfortable for any of us, not you or me and certainly not for Lucy Anne, if you were to remain here at Blackgum Bend," Lewis said at lunch one day. "I know you were sweet on her. You intended to marry her. Now you're jealous. No, don't give me that look. Deny it all you like but you are jealous of my successes, and we both know that."

"If you say so." The accusation hardly seemed worth arguing about. Especially since Lewis had already announced another trip—somewhere, Dex hadn't been paying attention; to buy something, Dex hadn't bothered to inquire about what—and Lucy Anne had already sent word to Dexter that she would be available to him during Lewis's absence.

Lucky Lewis, Dex thought. He'd be getting such a demure and blushing bride in Miss Thibidoux.

"Is that all you have to say to me?" Lewis demanded.

"Certainly not. I would also ask you, brother dear, to please pass the candied yams." Apart from momentary hunger, though, Dex did have something of a problem to consider. He was going to have to find a new place to meet Lucy Anne for future rendezvous. The fishing shack was no longer a good idea, and he needed to come up with something that would be both comfortable and private. Especially private.

For half a second there he visualized Lucy Anne Thibidoux fully naked, her skin lightly sweat-sheened in the heat, spread out on the pallet in the Calderone family mausoleum. He wondered . . .

"What are you smiling like that for?" Lewis snapped.

Dex blinked. Looked at his brother and smiled a little more. "Nothing. Nothing important. Clara, would you come fetch me those yams, please? Apparently my brother can't be bothered."

The whine of saws and the sounds of pounding hammers filled the air.

"Are you sure nobody will notice this?" James asked.

"Hell, everybody on the river will notice. The point is, nobody will care." Dex grinned. "Trust me."

James shrugged and turned his attention toward the river where a crew of at least thirty hands, every one of the Blackgum Bend people who could spare the time, swarmed over the new, raw-timber jetty that was being extended off the pilings of the old fishing shack.

"Y' know Dex, this is *some* scheme you dreamed up. You sure are a sly devil. Slippery as a diamondback, I'd say. 'Times you got the bite of one too."

Diamondback, huh? Dex liked the sound of that. "It *is* coming along pretty good, isn't it," he observed.

"Sure. One more weekend and we'll have it done."

"Do you think we'll have enough timber?" Dex asked.

"Some of the boys are cutting more pine today. They'll wait till past dark, then haul it in. Everything we need should be here by next weekend. We'll finish up with this part of it then."

"And the bags? Will we have enough bags?"

"I bought all the burlap we could want. The women

are working on them evenings an' weekends too. We'll be ready.''

"Coming right down to it, aren't we?"

James nodded. "Right on time. Have you sent your letter to those fellas in Louisville?"

"Yes, and another to the shipping company in Cincinnati just as a reminder. It's all in place," Dex said. "Are you sure we don't need lanterns? We could afford to buy some.''

"Nope. No lanterns. We talked it over, me and the hands. It's gonna be harder working at night without lights. But it's safer. Better without."

"If they think they can do it."

"No *think* to it, Dex. They are damn sure gonna do it. They know what the stakes are. They'll get the job done or bust their black asses trying.''

"If they say they can do it, then I'll take them at their word.''

"I'll tell them you said so. It will please them."

"I'm gonna miss them something terrible, you know that?''

"I'll tell them that too."

Dex peered out toward the Mississippi, flowing with such grand and quiet power out beyond the sweating workmen who waded waist deep in the mighty river's waters.

Lordy, he really was going to miss this.

"Tomorrow," Stennet announced. "We start picking tomorrow.''

"And the yield?" Lewis asked.

"Should be even better than I told you."

"Good. I've already contracted with the gin. They're giving me a premium price for guaranteed delivery."

Guaranteed delivery? Dex stifled an impulse to roll his eyes. Their father had always cautioned against taking anything for granted, especially when it came to farming. A freak hailstorm, a tornado, any crazy damn thing could happen at the last second to dash a man's hopes and bring him to his knees. Charles Yancey would never have committed himself to a contract guarantee short of already having his crop picked and sitting in the barn. And even then he would likely have hedged the deal just to guard against the possibility of the barn burning down and taking his cotton with it.

Lewis, though, liked to push things to the limit.

But then Dex was counting on exactly that trait, so he could hardly complain about it now. He sat in his chair, a volume of Greek lyric poetry open in his lap, and pretended not to have overheard.

⬧ 63 ⬧

"Are you going out tomcatting around again tonight?" Lewis asked.

"What d'you care?"

"I don't care what you do with your time *or* your pecker, but I do care about the reputation of this family."

"Just how much trouble do you think I can get into on twenty dollars a month?" Dex asked.

"If you think I didn't hear about you winning all that money at the racetrack, think again. I know you have plenty in your pockets."

"If you heard about that, Lewis, then you also heard I took a trip up to Vicksburg right after. I'm broke again." Both statements were true. More or less. And if they fell considerably short of being the whole truth, well, that wasn't Dexter's fault.

"Having to come down off your high horse won't hurt you. It might even be good for you."

"Your concern overwhelms me."

"Try to be back before breakfast, will you?"

"I'll see you in the morning, Lewis. G'night." Dex reached for his hat and went out front to where Napoleon was waiting with the bay mare saddled and ready.

Dex rode out along the lane, looked back to assure himself it was dark enough by now that no one at the house could possibly see which direction he took, and reined not toward town but away across the Blackgum Bend fields.

By the time he reached the field where the hands had been picking cotton bolls throughout the workday, the darkness was so complete that Dex had difficulty seeing. He had to rely on the mare's far superior night vision in order to stay on the wagon path.

He only knew he'd reached the right place by sound. He could hear a soft murmuring and an occasional low laugh.

"James?"

"Right here." The sound came from immediately beside Dex's right thigh, so close and unexpected that he jumped. His movement translated to the horse, and she jumped sideways too. For a moment Dex was busy trying to keep his seat and bring the mare back under control.

"Sorry 'bout that," James said.

"How are you doing?" Dex asked.

He could hear the satisfaction in James's response. "Just about all the people turned out. A few stayed back to sleep early. They'll get awake 'bout midnight and come on out. Then this first crew can go home and get a few hours' sleep before tomorrow's work."

"This is mighty hard on them," Dex said.

"They knew it would be when they agreed to do it. Don't you worry about that. They'll do what's gotta be done."

"I checked the almanac this afternoon. The moon will be up in another couple hours. It should go easier then."

"They're managing, Dex."

"You aren't having any trouble keeping everything in order, I hope."

He heard the sound of James's chuckle come to him through the night. Either Dexter's eyes were adjusting to the dark now, or the starlight overheard was stronger than it had been. For whatever reason, he was able to see just a little now. He could make out James's form standing at the edge of the cotton field. Out in the field itself, in the midst of the straggly, waist-high plants, he could see shadowy figures moving about, bending and turning, and here and there the pale gleam of a straw hat or kerchief bobbing high and low.

"Your friend Mr. Stennet makes it easy for us," James said. "At the end of the day he marks the end of that day's picking by putting a stake in the ground. I don't know what he thinks he's keeping track of, but he carries a pencil with him and marks numbers on the flat of the stake. Something to do with the number of bags filled that day or whatever, I dunno. Anyway, he takes the crews off at dusk. Soon as he's out of sight they turn right around and come back. Then we move his stake over however many rows we want and go to picking again.

"Of course we won't be able to pick quite as clean at night as they do during they day, but even so I think we'll be able to night-glean about half the crop," James said.

Dex laughed. "Half? D'you think so?"

"Close to it. We'll have to be careful whenever we get near the end of a field. We can't be too obvious about this. I mean, if they stop at night with only two rows left, we wouldn't want to clean them overnight and have your Mister Stennet come back to a whole new field the next day. But yeah, I think we can come real close to taking half."

James chuckled again. "The hands are helping during the day too."

"They aren't trying to steal the bolls under his nose, I hope."

"No, I warned them not to do that. It would only cause trouble if anybody was caught. Might tip Stennet and Lewis off that something was up too, and that'd be worse than somebody being caught. What they're doing is making a big show of how awful hard they're working. Busy hands, lots of singing, all the usual. But they bend and reach two or three times for every boll they actually pick and drop into the bag. Stennet can stand right there and see how busy they are. We don't want to give him anything to complain about. He doesn't notice how extra long it takes for a hand to fill his bag.''

"Perfect," Dex said. He dismounted and handed his reins to James. "Take care of her for me, will you please? I can't see well enough to be sure of where to put her so her hoofprints and droppings won't be noticeable come daylight tomorrow."

"You're going to stay with us?"

Dex grinned. "James, I've grown up with cotton all my life, but do you know what? I've never once gone out and picked any of it myself. Well, this is my chance. And without getting all hot and sweaty while I do it."

"Those soft white hands of yours aren't gonna like what cotton can do to them."

"I brought gloves."

"You don't pick cotton with gloves on, stupid."

"Us white guys always do."

James laughed and led the mare away. Dex helped himself to a long, canvas bag, and dragged it out between the rows to join the hands who'd been hard at work all day and now were voluntarily continuing deep into the night. That was, he figured, the least he could do.

· 64 ·

"I've never seen you wear gloves at the table," Lewis said. "Whatever have you done to yourself?" He laughed. "Surely last night's whore wasn't *that* wild."

Dexter treated his brother to a scowl. "Something spooked my horse while I was leading her. She reared back and tore the rope right through my hands."

"Rope burns?" Lewis asked.

Dex nodded.

"I hate rope burns. They hurt like hell."

These weren't rope burns. But they did indeed hurt like hell, Dex had to concede. He'd had no idea picking cotton could be so almighty damaging to one's hands. One wouldn't think that it should be. After all, cotton was soft and fluffy. The hard, brittle shells of the mature pods, however were anything but soft or cottony. The field workers developed thick calluses that gave them some measure of protection from the cuts and punctures. Dex had no such protection, and this morning he was paying the price for that. Tonight—if he tried to pick again tonight—he would wear gloves and never mind if that slowed his efforts . . . not that he was so fast that he had to worry about that anyway. Likely no one would be able to tell the difference between his accelerated efforts and his slow ones.

They heard a light tapping at the dining room door. Stennet was there. It wasn't like him to be polite, Dex noted. The man usually barged right in when he wanted to discuss something and to hell with the common courtesies.

"Can I have a word with you for a minute, Mr. Yancey?"

That too seemed out of the ordinary, Dex thought. Lewis apparently did not notice anything. "Speak up, man, do."

"Perhaps in private?" Stennet suggested.

"Nonsense. We're at lunch. Have your say and be done with it."

"Yes, well, um . . ." Stennet glanced toward Dexter. Obviously he did not want Dex to hear. Then when he did continue, Dex understood the reason. The overseer did not want to confess to any weakness or failures in front of this man whom he detested.

At least Dex hoped that Stennet detested him. Dex would hate for his own feelings to go unreturned in that regard.

"The thing is, Mr. Yancey, well . . ."

"Go on now before my squab gets cold," Lewis prodded.

"It's the yield, sir."

"Yes, what of it?"

"I can't . . . I can't understand this, sir. But . . . it seems very small."

"What d'you mean small? Just last week you were promising me a record yield. Now you're telling me the crop is small? What the hell is this, man?"

"It's . . . I really don't know what to tell you. I watch every move the niggers make. You know that, Mr. Yancey. I know my job, and I've been watching this crop all summer long. All the plants look heavy. The bolls seem just fine. And the niggers are working as hard as anyone could drive them. I mean, really, I couldn't get more out of them if I was using whips. I swear it. They pick hard and fast from sunup to sun-gone and the plants look just fine, but when I go to tote up the filled bags at the end of the day, Mr. Yancey, the figures aren't anything like what I've expected them to be."

"How far off do you think those figures were that you gave me, Stennet?" Lewis demanded.

The overseer looked distinctly uncomfortable. He rocked up onto tiptoes and down again. Turned his hat around and around in big, blunt-fingered hands. Looked unhappily toward Dexter and licked lips that appeared suddenly dry.

In a hushed whisper he choked out the single word "Half."

Lewis came partway off his chair, a look of horror on his face. "Half? Half, you're telling me? How the hell could you have been that far off your estimate? What am I paying you for if you can't make cotton, dammit?"

"I . . . I swear to you, Mr. Yancey, I truly cannot understand this. And believe me, I've watched those niggers like a barn cat covering a rat hole. I've even taken to shaking the crews down before they go in from the fields at dark. To make sure they aren't trying to steal or hide anything. But all they carry away with them each time is stink and sweat. I can't . . . I don't understand it, Mr. Yancey. But I'm thinking now the yield isn't going to come anywhere near what I thought it would." Stennet looked quite thoroughly miserable. Dex thought it couldn't happen to a more deserving fellow.

"You have to do something, Stennet. You have to."

"Sir?"

"I contracted for delivery on the basis of the yields you told me, Stennet. Guaranteed delivery, remember? I told you that before I asked you to make your estimate."

"Yes, sir, you did tell me that, and I . . ."

"You gave me figures that were off by half, is that what you're saying now, damn you?"

"It is, sir, but I . . ."

"You've ruined me, you son of a bitch," Lewis yelled.

Dex suspected every workman inside the house and half of the hands outside could hear Lewis screaming at his heretofore pet overseer.

"How could you have been so fucking stupid?" Lewis shrieked.

"Mr. Yancey, I . . . I know you are upset. You have every right to be angry. But this . . . this is not called for. You can't speak to me like that. Not in front of your brother and the niggers."

"I will speak to you any way I damn well want to speak to you. D'you understand me, Stennet? If that cotton yield isn't somewhere close to what you promised me, I'll be forced to pay penalties to the gin. I'll . . . I don't know what I will have to do. Buy cotton from other growers at whatever prices they say in order to meet my contract. I could be taken to court. Humiliated. My God, man, at the very least I'll be humiliated. Everyone in Louisiana will know. I'll be a fucking laughingstock. Worse. I don't know. And it's your fault, man. It's your damned fault."

"I do not think we should discuss this any further, Mr. Yancey. You aren't being reasonable about this. You aren't. . . ."

"I don't fucking *intend* to be reasonable, Stennet. Not about this I don't, and you can try to get that through your thick head. I want you to go back over every row you've picked. Those lazy black-ass sons of bitches are leaving cotton on the plants. They're leaving it on the ground. Whatever. Now go back through those rows and glean the rest of my crop. Do you hear me? I want that estimate met."

"I've been very careful to see that the plants are picked clean, Mr. Yancey. I can assure you there hasn't been any wastage in the fields. Practically none. You know no one can get every last boll, but . . ."

"*Get* every last boll, Stennet," Lewis roared. "Keep your niggers out however long it takes. Go over every row five times if that's what you have to do. But bring in every last bag you told me you could. Do you hear me, mister? Every last bag or the penalties are coming straight out of your pocket, not mine.''

Stennet gave Lewis a withering look, the sort he'd always reserved for Dexter in the past. "You don't have a contract with the gin alone, Mr. Yancey. You have a contract with me too. And it don't say anything about penalties or me having to pay for your blunders. If you think otherwise, sir, we'll have a court an' judge work out who's right."

Lewis was so mad he could scarcely sputter. Stennet didn't seem a lick happier than Lewis was. Of them all, Dex thought, probably he was the only one who was having a nice time at the moment.

He kept his expression impassive and reached for the ham platter. Aunt Lottie might not be the cook that Aunt Maybelle was, but she wasn't so awful bad either.

· 65 ·

This all-night nonsense was getting to Dexter. He could hardly imagine how it must be for the hands who had to work all day in the heat and then most of the night too. Unlike them, Dex could sleep most of the day away, and even so he was exhausted.

Still, they were just about done now. The fields were thoroughly picked over. More so than Stennet ever imagined.

Dex and James waited at the fishing shack for the last two wagons to arrive. They'd worked out a system in which the picking was done through most of the night hours, then mules and wagons were brought around to each picking crew to load the bags of new-picked cotton and carry it to the wooden riverbank near the old shack for storage.

The wagons were brought out just before daybreak in time to deposit their loads of liberated cotton—Dexter did not see it as stolen; rather he considered it as having been repossessed from Lewis; and anyway, as Lewis's twin he surely should be entitled to half, it was a matter of birth-right—so the bags could be unloaded and the wagons back out into the fields again in time for Stennet's morning arrival there.

Stennet, unsuspecting, was delighted to see his crews out so early and ready for work.

Of course he might not have been quite so happy had he known why they were early. Or why the cotton yield was so unexpectedly low.

"Right on time," James said with obvious satisfaction as the last wagon came into sight on the seldom-used path along the northern extreme of Blackgum Bend property.

"Have the boys unload this last bunch and make sure it's all covered. Not that anyone out on the river would likely think anything even if they did notice it, but there's no sense in taking the chance on that."

"You're sure the boat will be here?" James asked.

"That's the schedule. Thursday morning."

"The captain knows what to look for to mark the landing?"

"I wrote them with full instructions," Dex assured him.

"We'll have to have a work crew here to meet them and help load."

"If the overseer doesn't give our people some time off once the picking is done," Dex said, "we'll just have some of the boys claim they're sick. He won't smell a rat in that. He's been working them hard during the day. It won't surprise him if some start to lay back now that all the hard part is done with."

"Thursday," James said.

"Thursday," Dex agreed.

"Shee-it!" James exclaimed.

Dex grinned at him. "I agree completely."

⋄ 66 ⋄

Dexter, James, and the hands completed their larceny of fully half the Blackgum Bend cotton crop in broad daylight.

The stern-wheel steamer *Aaron Coy* tied up to the newly built landing shortly before noon on the Thursday, just as instructed, and a swarming, smiling work crew made short work of putting the cotton aboard.

Dexter, dressed in his Yankee businessman clothing, stood beside the boat's captain while down below the sweating blacks completed their task.

One of those sweaty men was James, who had given up gainful employment for this more interesting pursuit. James would be in charge of affairs here in Dex's absence upriver, the first among those affairs being the disassembly of the new wharf. As soon as the *Aaron Coy* was safely out of sight, the timbers would be pulled up and taken away. By nightfall there should, hopefully, be no evidence remaining to show where a river steamer would have been able to land anywhere nearer than Blackgum Bend to the south or Brede Farms to the north.

"Very unusual, sir," the *Aaron Coy*'s captain, a man

named Foster, said at one point as the bags of cotton were carried aboard.

"How is that, sir?" Dex could not address the captain by name for the simple reason that although introductions had been made immediately upon the boat's landfall, Dex hadn't quite caught everything the captain said and had no idea now if Foster was his first name or his last.

"Cotton is generally transported in bales, is it not?"

Dex nodded. "Quite right, sir, that is the norm."

"But you chose otherwise, I see."

"This is an experiment, Captain," Dex said without pause. "The operators of the gins throughout the cotton-growing regions seem to believe they have a monopoly on all the business in their neighborhoods, you see."

"Yes, I can understand that they would," Foster said.

"My thought is that I can offer the growers the same price for their cotton and then sell it at a profit by taking it in large volume to gins located in areas where the crops have been poor in a particular season. Pick my customers based on their needs, you see. If they have little business this year, they will welcome my cotton and pay me well for the opportunity to gin it. Come the next season I may be dealing with someone else entirely. In any event I shall buy where there is a glut of supply and sell where there is a heavy demand."

"But why should the growers . . . you did say you yourself are a broker and not a producer, did you not, Mr. Vaughn?"

"I did," Dex agreed.

"Then I ask you, sir, why the growers should agree to sell to you at the same price the gin would pay—which I believe you mentioned a moment ago—and not to the man with whom they've done business routinely in the past?"

Dex smiled. "Very simple. I allow the growers to make a larger profit even though there is no difference in price. How? Because I accept their cotton in burlap. It needn't be baled or transported at all. They reduce their handling and their labor costs. They profit from this. I profit from my selection of a gin to sell to. It works out nicely for everyone. Or so goes my theory. This season will prove me or break me, one or the other.''

"And if you cannot profit?''

"Then your company shall have no more trade from Horace Vaughn, I fear,'' Dex said.

"Well, I certainly wish you well with your venture, Mr. Vaughn.''

"Thank you, Captain.'' Dex bowed slightly. "Fetch me and my cotton swiftly and safely to Louisville, sir, and we shall find what sort of proof lies within the pudding.''

Foster saw that the cargo was all aboard. His deck crew was busy covering the cotton with tarps and lashing them down, while on shore the Blackgum Bend work gang seemed to be celebrating something. The gentleman excused himself and began to see to the business of getting under way again.

It was by then not yet the middle of the afternoon. With luck, Dex thought, before night all evidence of the larceny—or rightful recovery, as he preferred it—should be eradicated completely and no one the wiser.

· 67 ·

When Dex returned home two weeks later, he found Lewis in a deep funk and the plantation in a state of general turmoil. According to Napoleon, who responded to the boat whistle to meet Dex at the landing, the overseer had been fired and nearly every hand on the place had been told they would soon have to vacate their homes and leave Blackgum Bend.

Dexter was quite frankly shocked. His plan called for Lewis to be forced into a compromise. But the complete ruin of everything their father and grandfather had built here was *not* part of the program he'd envisioned. Not in any way, shape, or form.

Dex supervised the unloading of his luggage before he went inside. The trunk did, after all, contain a more than trifling amount of coin and currency. Then he hurried into the study, where Lewis was curled up with a bleak expression and a good whiskey.

"You, uh, aren't drunk, are you?"

Lewis looked at his brother without interest. "Nope. Tried that. It didn't do any good, and after a couple days it made me sick to my stomach. I got the runs. I didn't need that on top of everything else." He looked at the half-full glass beside him. "This is just in case I change my mind and want to try it again."

"Uh-huh. You, um, fired Stennet?"

"I did. Whole damn thing is his fault."

Dex knew better, but he made no effort to defend the overseer. He hadn't liked the son of a bitch.

"Not all of it," Lewis corrected himself without Dex having to say anything. "Enough."

"Is he still threatening to sue?"

"I don't know. Didn't ask. Wouldn't make much difference if he did or not. There's nothing left here for him to get even if he won."

"Lewis, we . . . excuse me, you . . . still have every acre of land that was here when Poppa died. Not an inch of that is gone. You just need to . . . make some adjustments."

"I suppose you have some in mind?"

"Actually, I do. Yes," Dex admitted.

"Well, keep them to yourself, big brother. As for me, I'm whipped. Wiped out. Can you believe it? One stinking season and I've lost everything I stole from you. If that isn't poetic justice, then what the fuck is, huh?" He had a swallow of the whiskey, considerably diminishing the level of liquid in the glass. Dex had the thought that if Lewis wasn't drunk he was not exactly sober either.

"You can pull out of this, Lewis. Blackgum Bend is intact. Next year's crop should be good. There's no reason to panic."

"No reason? D'you have any idea the amount of money I've spent this summer? I went through our cash reserves before the end of June. All . . . this . . ." Lewis made a sour face and waved vaguely toward the upstairs where, Dex noticed now, there were no longer the sounds of pounding and cutting. "It's all on credit. Every lick of it practically. And I don't have shit in the bank to pay those notes."

"What if I offered you a way out?" Dex suggested.

"You?" Lewis snorted, the sound bitter and as bleak as his expression. "What are you going to do, Dexie?

Loan me twenty dollars a month so I can pay the creditors on tick?''

"I've been upriver, Lewis.''

"Yeah? So?''

"So I came back with a good bit of money in my pockets, that's what.''

"What d'you want, Dexter? You want title to the plantation? You want back what we both know I stole from you while Poppa was dying? Is that what you want, Dexter?''

"No, Lewis. I know this is going to surprise you, but that isn't what I want if we should come to an . . . agreement here.''

"No?'' Lewis seemed to be taking a little genuine interest in the conversation now. He sat up a little straighter, leaned forward just a bit in his chair.

"No, I don't. I would want certain changes to be made, but I wouldn't ask for title to the property. Poppa left it to you. It was his to do with as he wanted, even if he was gulled into doing what he did, and I won't go against his wishes.''

Which sounded very nice, of course, but the truth was that Dex knew full well he would become the most unpopular white man in the parish—in the parish? hell, in the state; or beyond—once his conditions were put into effect.

His demands were the right thing to do. He was certain of that and unrepentant. He would stay the course and see that things were done the way he and James had talked them out months earlier. But Dex had no desire to remain in northern Louisiana afterward. Lewis could keep the plantation and welcome to it. Dex intended to turn his back on everything he'd ever known and go find . . . he had no idea in the world what it was he hoped to find. Or where.

"You're serious about this, aren't you?'' Lewis asked, half suspiciously.

"Dead serious,'' Dex said.

"Tell me what it is you want then. I . . . won't make

any promises until after I hear you out." Lewis barked out a short, bitter laugh. "Not that my promises are all that good anyway, you understand. Just ask our banker if you want an unbiased opinion on that subject."

"It isn't anything you can't do, Lewis, I assure you." Dex went to the sideboard and poured himself a generous tot of white whiskey—he was really going to miss the marvelously smooth and completely illegal moonshine that old Cornfed produced—then took a seat facing Lewis and began slowly and carefully to lay out the conditions under which he would bail Lewis and Blackgum Bend out of the financial morass that Dex himself had created.

· 68 ·

"You, sir, are a traitor to your own class. You are a disgrace." Franklin Reece sniffed haughtily and turned his back.

"Stupid white sonuvabitch," James whispered from behind Dex's back. "I told you you shouldn't of come here."

Dex shrugged but did not look around. "It seemed a good idea at the time. Hell, I haven't had any fun since I got home."

They were attending—if not particularly enjoying—a day at the racetrack. Dex had thought it would give him a chance to see how the winds were blowing. And maybe pick up a few dollars on Saladin.

Well, he was being shown quite perfectly well how the winds blew. Hot they were, and hostile. Reece was the only white man who'd been willing to speak to him at all, and the few blacks who said hello did so almost fearfully lest they be observed and thought to be a part of the movement Dexter Yancey had started.

That, of course, was the reason for the hostility. The plantation owners had had quite enough change in their way of life over the past few decades. They did not want some upstart like Yancey—they'd thought he was such a *nice* boy even if a bit of a wastrel, and *now* look—coming along and introducing ideas for change that their field hands might come to expect or, worse, to demand in the future.

Dexter's changes could undermine the entire labor structure that had evolved since those stupid damnyankee Northern sons of bitches did away with the perfectly reliable and comfortable system of slavery.

In a way they likely viewed this new change of Dex's as being even worst than the earlier one because this time it was being done by one of their own. At least with the Yankees, everyone understood that they were stupid and greedy and didn't really care anything about the niggers, what they really wanted was the imposition of tariffs that would force the South to sell to Northern mills instead of English ones. Slavery was only their excuse for belligerence, not their reason.

But this business at Blackgum Bend now, that was Dexter Yancey's own idea, and it was sure to spread. Soon or later, one way or another, all the field crews would be wanting the same for themselves. Now that one planter had started it, it would be difficult for everyone else to stop it. Now that Lewis Yancey had adopted the system, everyone else would likely be forced into it too someday, damn him. And damn that Dexter most of all.

"Cropping on shares," Dex had explained to Lewis that day in the study. "It's a system that's fairer to everyone. The hands are working for themselves, you see, so they'll work hard without having to be forced to it. You supply the seed and they supply the sweat, and at the end of the season you share the proceeds right down the middle. And another thing, Lewis. No more of this high-rent shit to keep them indebted to you. Each family gets a parcel to farm and a cabin to live in. That's part of your end of the bargain or there is no deal."

"What about what they owe already? What about them having something to live on until next year? How about that, huh?" Lewis had demanded.

"They'll manage somehow," Dex told him. "What the hell d'you care how?"

"You're right about that, I suppose. Piss on the black bastards. They can eat shit for all I care."

"There you go, Lewie. That's the attitude." What Lewis hadn't known at the time—still didn't, although hints and innuendos about Dexter's role in all this were sure to slip out eventually—was that Dex and James already had enough money set aside to pay off the existing debts and to carry the hands through until harvest next season. Lewis had provided that for them. Not wittingly perhaps, but he'd provided it nonetheless.

Now, though, at the Paradise Valley Hunt and Turf Club, Dexter was on the receiving end of his neighbors' disdain. He didn't like it. He understood it well enough. Had even thought he was prepared to cope with it. Hell, he'd even had thoughts about remaining here and riding out the storm, giving these people he'd known his entire life time to get over their anger. But . . . he wasn't so sure about that now.

Today, wherever he went, all he saw were the broad backs of the people he'd known and been close to for so long.

Except for Franklin Reece, no one complained or explained or accused. They didn't speak at all, simply seemed not to so much as notice Dexter's presence amongst them.

Dex leaned on the front stretch railing and sighed. He and James might as well take Saladin and go home, he was thinking. No one would accept a match with the mule, and even Father Branbury hadn't deigned to approach him.

It really had not been a good idea to come here today, Dex decided. He straightened and turned with the intention of leaving.

His way was blocked by Stennet, who looked even unfriendlier than all the others put together.

"You son of a bitch," Stennet snarled, and unleashed a punch that would likely have popped Dex's head off the top of his neck had it landed squarely. Instead Dex's unthinking response pulled him back out of the way far enough that Stennet's blow only grazed the point of his chin. And at that it was a hard enough blow to sting like hell.

"Damn you," Stennet roared, and reared back to try again.

"If you want a fight, man, fine," Dex said loudly. "I accept your challenge."

"You what?"

"Your challenge, man. I accept."

"Accept what?"

"A duel. You accosted me, did you not? You slapped my face. Fine. If it's a duel you want, then a duel you shall have. Naturally, as the challenged party, the choice of weapons will be mine. Announce your seconds, please."

Dex turned and surveyed the men who were standing nearby. They'd ignored him earlier, but no longer. Now every head in sight was turned in his direction, and he seemed to have very much the full attention of the race-going crowd.

"Mr. Ebberle. Would you be so kind as to stand as my second, sir?"

Tyler did not hesitate. With a slightly sardonic smile he bowed low and said, "My pleasure, Mr. Yancey."

Dex turned back to Stennet. "Well?" he demanded.

"But I . . . what's this shit, boy? All I want is to whip your ass. I promised before that I would. Now I intend t' do it."

"You shall have that opportunity, sir," Dex said, bowing. "Now announce your second and instruct him to confer with Mr. Ebberle if you please." Dex turned away and sauntered off in the direction of the refreshment pavilion. Not that he intended to take a drink beforehand, but he would not mind if he gave the impression that he did.

Tyler Ebberle hurried to join him. He did, after all, require instruction as to Dexter's wishes.

· 69 ·

"What's this shit?" Stennet bellowed.

"Swords, of course. Or to be more precise, the weapon is an epee. Very nice ones they are too." Dex briefly turned to Judge Wainwright. "Thank you for providing them, sir. They are very handsome."

"A hundred years old at least. You do know, of course, that dueling is illegal nowadays."

"Would you have me accept insult, sir?"

The retired judge harrumphed and coughed but said nothing. Dexter was not popular among these men now, but there was not a gentleman among them who would not approve of his decision to defend honor before all else.

"I still don't know what this crap is all about," Stennet declared.

"That is because you are no gentleman, of course. The fact is, you challenged me. I chose to accept despite your inferiority of station." Dex wasn't really sure Stennet would even recognize the insult. But everyone else certainly would.

"As the challenged party," Ebberle went on, "Mr. Yancey has the right to choose the weapons to be used.

As you can see, he has chosen swords. You now have the right of choice between these two. Pick one, Mr. Stennet. Mr. Yancey will be obliged to use the other.''

"But I just want to beat the crap outa him. Boots, fists, like that. Or knives. Guns. I don't care. I just want to beat shit out of him.''

"And so you may, sir. But with swords. Now, if you would please make your choice between them?''

Stennet glowered and fumed. His second turned out to be his new employer, Lawrence Dunbarton. Dunbarton pulled him aside and whispered explanations into Stennet's ear for some time before the challenger returned to the field of honor. Which in this case was a patch of grass between the front straight bleachers and the starting line.

"Are you ready, Mr. Dunbarton?'' Ebberle asked.

"We are. I shall select a blade for the gen . . . for, um, Mr. Stennet.''

"As you wish, sir.'' Ebberle held out the pair of exquisite old epees that the judge had had rushed over from his plantation close by. Dunbarton took his time examining each of the pair, testing the balance and the feel of each blade several times over before he finally made his selection and carried it to Stennet. Dex took the other. It felt fine in his hand. He swished it back and forth through the air, liking the feel of blade and grip.

The seconds had chosen August Porter to act as referee. Their first choice had been Father Branbury, but he'd declined, citing a conflict of interest in that Stennet was not a Catholic.

"Take your places, please,'' Porter instructed. "You will stand there, Mr. Stennet. You there, Mr. Yancey.'' He pointed.

"Prepare yourselves, if you please.''

Dex handed his sword to Tyler Ebberle, and was about to remove his coat and revolvers when with a roar Stennet leaped at him with his blade upraised.

It seemed an inopportune moment to discuss the niceties of the duel, Dex decided as he grabbed for the grip of the judge's antique epee and tried to assume a defensive posture in time to meet Stennet's charge.

• 70 •

It was not exactly a contest. But then that was the whole idea of claiming it a duel and deciding upon swords as his weapon. Dexter was if not a master of the sword, then at least awfully damned good with one. He'd been trained in the use of epee and foil since he was a boy. Moreover, he enjoyed them. He was not particularly fond of the saber, the use of which primarily involved two parties whacking and hacking at one another until one of them was bashed senseless. But the much lighter epee and foil required finesse and a certain amount of delicacy.

Stennet very probably had never held a sword of any sort in his rough hands until this moment, and dueling him with steel was more an exercise in humiliation than it was a combat.

Dex danced and darted, his blade flicking daintily in and out while Stennet stomped and shouted and wildly slashed thin air in places where he'd apparently expected Dex to stand and wait to be dismembered.

Stennet might have had a prayer—a slim one—had they been using cavalry sabers.

But this . . . Dex very deliberately nicked the lobe of Stennet's left ear. Then put a matching mark on the right.

He sliced neat chevrons onto both Stennet's biceps, and opened a gash, a rather deeper one than he'd intended, on the point of the man's chin.

It was not a fair fight. Wasn't intended to be. Dex was in a mood to vent his frustrations, and it was simply Stennet's misfortune to be on the receiving end.

Dex nicked and snicked and spanked the bigger, older man until Stennet's shirt was wet with his own gore and he was gasping for breath.

"Had enough yet?" Dex asked.

"Damn you."

Dex shrugged. And stung the back of Stennet's sword hand with the flat of his blade.

The handsome epee fell from Stennet's already sweat-slick grip and landed in the dirt.

Dex glided fluidly forward, and before Stennet had time to know what was coming, had the tip of his own blade nestled in the hollow of Stennet's throat.

"Yield, sir, or I'll finish you."

"I . . . I . . ."

"Yield and take back your insult."

"I . . . yield," Stennet gasped.

"So be it." Dex stepped back, reversed his grip on the hilt of the epee, and turned to extend it to Tyler.

He heard a gasp of shock from the crowd, and Tyler's eyes grew suddenly wide.

Dex spun.

Stennet had a pistol in hand, a small and lethal little two-shoot derringer that he must have had in his pocket. He was already aiming it at Dexter's back and was fumbling for the hammer when Dex turned.

Without conscious thought Dex hastily grabbed for a fresh grip on the epee and thrust.

The blade entered Stennet's throat a fraction of an inch below his Adam's apple, and the big man's eyes went wide in sudden fear as recognition of his error sank in.

Stennet tried to look down toward the little pistol in his hand, but he could not. The steel that impaled him prevent the movement.

Not that it mattered. Not any longer. Nerveless fingers lost their grip and the derringer tumbled to the ground.

Stennet stared bug-eyed at the man who'd just killed him. His mouth gaped as if he wanted to speak, but no sounds emerged.

Slowly, almost gently, Stennet sank to his knees.

Dex withdrew his blade, and Stennet toppled face-forward into the grass.

A few yards away Dex could hear a low murmur of Latin as Father Branbury began to pray.

"Jesus!" someone whispered.

• 71 •

"God knows you and I have never been all that close, Yancey, but you acted correctly today. I want you to know that," Tyler Ebberle said. "No one blames you for what happened. We all saw. Everybody knows you had no desire to kill that man. But the fact remains, you did do it. And you aren't exactly the most popular fellow in the country-side right now. May I offer you a word of advice?"

"Please."

"Leave this parish. If you're smart, leave Louisiana altogether. The law will be obliged to charge you and a jury—well, under normal circumstances I wouldn't think a jury would convict you. But now . . . you can't be sure of that. You'll be better off if you leave. Maybe you can come back someday. But for right now, I really think you should go. It will be better for you, and for that matter, better for all of us. It wouldn't be good for the community for all this to drag through the courts."

"It's good advice, Tyler."

"You'll do it?"

Dex nodded.

"In that case I will see that no warrant is issued before

tomorrow morning. The sheriff won't be able to reach your place until, let's say, until noon."

"That's more than fair of you, Tyler. Thanks."

Ebberle smiled. "If you need some cash to travel on, Yancey, I would be willing to make you an offer for that yellow mule."

Dex grinned. "You're all heart, aren't you, Tyler?"

"That's me. Nothing but."

Dex extended his hand, and was pleased that Ebberle took it without hesitation. "Good-bye, Tyler."

"Good luck to you, Dexter."

Later, on their way back to Blackgum Bend, Dex was barely able to dismount from his horse and make it into the weeds beside the road before he puked up everything he'd eaten for the past three days or longer. So it seemed to him in any event.

"Are you all right?" James asked.

"I will be. I guess."

"You never killed anyone before."

"Never expected to either," Dex affirmed.

"Not something you'd want to do again, I take it."

"You take it correctly, my friend."

"You'll leave tomorrow morning?"

"Nope. This evening. There's no sense waiting. Just in case Ebberle can't keep the hounds in check as long as he thinks he can."

"Or in case he was trying to set you up so you can be arrested tonight?" James suggested.

"An ugly thought like that wouldn't ever cross my mind," Dex declared.

"No, of course it wouldn't. Mine neither." James paused. "I'm coming with you, you know."

"What about your mama?"

"She knows I'd need to go soon anyway. Word about what you did is sure to get around. People will figure out that I probably helped you." James smiled. "Hell, I have to hold your hand or you just go and get in trouble. Everyone knows that. And if you aren't here for people to be mad at, who do you think they'll pick on next? You they just snub. You saw that today. Me they're more likely to take a whip to. Or worse. I don't especially want to end up as a tree decoration."

"West," Dex said.

"What's that?"

"We'll head west. Tell your mama that. Tell her we'll write to her."

"She can't read, you know."

"She can always find someone that can. And leave her some money. How much do we have?"

"Over and above what we set aside for everything else? Close to seven hundred," James said.

"Then leave her six hundred. We'll take whatever is left over after that."

"And just how is it that you and me are supposed to get along if we don't have but a few dollars between us?"

Dex grinned at him. "Don't worry, black boy. I'll think of something. After all, we were able to take Lewis for a hefty amount, weren't we? And I kinda enjoyed doing it too. We'll manage." He tipped his head back and laughed out loud, the excitement of the unknown starting to grow inside him as anticipation replaced the anguish he'd felt in the wake of Stennet's death.

Dexter remounted, and waited for James to climb back onto Saladin beside him. "Wait for me at your mama's place. I'll be by in a couple hours to fetch you. We'll head for Texas from there and . . . God knows where after that."

"I could meet you on the road. It'd be quicker."

Dex shook his head. "No way I could leave without giving your mama a hug and a kiss good-bye."

"All right then, *Diamondback*." James grinned. "Texas, huh? And I don't have to pick any more damn cotton?"

"The only thing you and me have to pick up from here on out is the hems of ladies' skirts. That's a promise."

Side by side they set out at a lope along the dusty Louisiana road. Dex had no idea where their travels would take them. But he was suddenly eager to find out. Texas first, and then . . . only God knew.

PENGUIN PUTNAM INC.
Online

Your Internet gateway to a virtual environment with
hundreds of entertaining and enlightening books from
Penguin Putnam Inc.

*While you're there, get the latest buzz on
the best authors and books around—*

Tom Clancy, Patricia Cornwell, W.E.B. Griffin,
Nora Roberts, William Gibson, Robin Cook,
Brian Jacques, Catherine Coulter, Stephen King,
Jacquelyn Mitchard, and many more!

**Penguin Putnam Online is located at
http://www.penguinputnam.com**

PENGUIN PUTNAM NEWS

Every month you'll get an inside look at our upcoming
books and new features on our site. This is an ongoing
effort to provide you with the most up-to-date
information about our books and authors.

**Subscribe to Penguin Putnam News at
http://www.penguinputnam.com/ClubPPI**